Reviewers love *New York Times* and *USA TODAY*
bestselling author

Susan Andersen

"A smart, arousing, spirited escapade
that is graced with a gentle mystery, a vulnerable,
resilient heroine, and a worthy, wounded hero
and served up with empathy and a humorous flair."
—*Library Journal* on *Burning Up*

"[A] fast-paced, charming romance
with plenty of heat and cool dialogue."
—*RT Book Reviews* on *Burning Up*

"A sexy, feel-good contemporary romance...
Palpable escalating sexual tension between the pair,
a dangerous criminal on the loose and a cast of
well-developed secondary characters make this a winner."
—*Publishers Weekly* on *Bending the Rules*

"Snappy and sexy... Upbeat and fun, with a touch of danger
and passion, this is a great summer read."
—*RT Book Reviews* on *Coming Undone*

"Lovers of romance, passion and laughs
should go all in for this one."
—*Publishers Weekly* on *Just for Kicks*

"Andersen again injects magic into a story that would be
clichéd in another's hands, delivering warm, vulnerable
characters in a touching yet suspenseful read."
—*Publishers Weekly* on *Skintight*, starred review

"A classic plot line receives a fresh, fun treatment...
Well-developed secondary characters add depth to this
zesty novel, placing it a level beyond most of its competition."
—*Publishers Weekly* on *Hot & Bothered*

P9-BVH-048

Ava's Taco Soup

1 lb ground turkey
1 onion, chopped
1 green bell pepper, chopped
1 large bag frozen mixed veggies (cook's choice)
2 cans diced tomatoes & green chilies (such as Ro Tel)
2 cans diced tomatoes
1 can black beans
1 can white beans
2 packages taco seasoning or 1/2 cup Costco taco seasoning
1 cup red wine
1 cup/can chicken or vegetable broth

Brown turkey, onions and peppers and toss in a large Crock-Pot. Add rest of the ingredients and simmer all day long. Leftovers can be frozen in ziplock baggies for on-the-go individual servings.

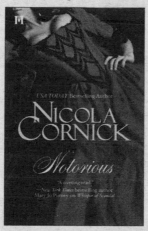

Susan Andersen

77574	JUST FOR KICKS	___ $7.99 U.S. ___ $9.99 CAN.
77498	BURNING UP	___ $7.99 U.S. ___ $9.99 CAN.
77419	HOT & BOTHERED	___ $7.99 U.S. ___ $8.99 CAN.
77393	BENDING THE RULES	___ $7.99 U.S. ___ $8.99 CAN.
77457	SKINTIGHT	___ $7.99 U.S. ___ $9.99 CAN.

(limited quantities available)

TOTAL AMOUNT $ _____
POSTAGE & HANDLING $ _____
($1.00 FOR 1 BOOK, 50¢ for each additional)
APPLICABLE TAXES* $ _____
TOTAL PAYABLE $ _____

(check or money order—please do not send cash)

To order, complete this form and send it, along with a check or money order for the total above, payable to HQN Books, to: **In the U.S.:** 3010 Walden Avenue, P.O. Box 9077, Buffalo, NY 14269-9077; **In Canada:** P.O. Box 636, Fort Erie, Ontario, L2A 5X3.

Name: _____
Address: _____ City: _____
State/Prov.: _____ Zip/Postal Code: _____
Account Number (if applicable): _____

075 CSAS

*New York residents remit applicable sales taxes.
*Canadian residents remit applicable GST and provincial taxes.

SEP - 2011

Susan Andersen

Playing Dirty

HQN™

Recycling programs
for this product may
not exist in your area.

ISBN-13: 978-0-373-77589-7

PLAYING DIRTY

This is dedicated to my little corner
of the immense Facebook community—
especially the ladies (and occasional gent)
of the SusanAndersenFanPage. You make me laugh,
make me think and—I gotta tell ya—make me
feel *much* more important than I actually am.
Your collective willingness to open up pieces of your lives
to my voracious curiosity just knocks my socks off.
You all rock.
—Susan

ACKNOWLEDGMENTS

I owe a huge debt of gratitude to Virginia Bogert of
Laughing Dog Productions for the fabulous information
and peeks into the world of a working documentary
producer. I so appreciate all the time you gave me,
your wonderful ideas and your patience
with my many questions.

I hope I did your information justice,
but if any inaccuracies arise, they are solely mine.

Playing
Dirty

PROLOGUE

Dear Diary,
I didn't know you could feel *such pain and still*
live.

Country Day School, Upper School building
Thirteen years ago

AVA SPENCER DANCED down the hallway toward the cafeteria, her hips slowly swiveling and her plump shoulders grooving to the Goo Goo Dolls' rendition of "Iris" playing in her head. She supposed she could've picked something faster, but hey. She was in the moment, feeling good.

Really, *really* good.

"Ava! Wait up!"

Glancing behind her, she saw her two best friends hustling around a group of stragglers who, like her, were running late for second lunch. The music in her head shut down as she waited for them to catch up, only to be promptly replaced by the everyday rhythms of school lunch hour: the squeak of shoes against linoleum, the slam of an occasional locker door, the laughter of little kids out on the Lower School playfield competing with the muted roar of the teens behind the lunchroom door just down the hall.

"What's up, girly girl?" Poppy demanded, striding up to her. The bangles on her wrist clinked as they slid down the arm she raised to brush back a curl that had strayed from the mass. "You're looking exceptionally happy."

"No fooling," Jane agreed. "It's not every day we see you boogie down the hallway."

"I am feeling *so* fine." If she felt any finer, in fact, they'd have to haul her down from the ceiling like a bouquet of helium balloons. She beamed at her friends. "I might even go so far as to say I'm feelin' beautiful."

And wasn't *that* amazing. She felt reasonably attractive most days, pretty on occasion, but beautiful? That was something so rare it was the next best thing to never. Given her constant struggle with weight, it wasn't an adjective anyone at home ever applied to her. Her parents were more likely to give her grief for not doing enough to lose her "baby" fat.

"Hey, you *are* beautiful," Jane protested loyally.

"Yeah, 'She's got such a pretty face,'" Ava quoted dryly. "What a shame she's so plump/heavy/hefty." *That* was a conversation she'd overheard more than once.

"You know Janie better than to think she implied that, Av," Poppy said. "She said you're beautiful—and you are."

"I love you both for saying so, but that would be you, Poppy, not me." With her Nordic blond hair and breezy confidence, Poppy was in a category all her own. She could've been part of the popular kids' clique if she'd given a rat's ass about that sort of thing. Hell, Ava thought proudly, Poppy could've *ruled* that crowd. She and Janie, on the other hand, would have never made the cut.

Not that Jane wasn't attractive, but it was a quiet

prettiness that sort of snuck up on you. She had shiny brown hair and really great legs, but the clothes she wore made Goths look colorful. Plus, she was a brain-iac—something most of the so-called in crowd were too stupid to appreciate.

Ava gave a mental shrug. Neither she nor Janie gave a rip any more than Poppy. The kids in that crowd were mostly asses, and the three of *them* had something worlds better than winning a high school popularity contest—each other. They were tight. BFFs. They'd met at this very school in the fourth grade and been a unit ever since.

Ava sure wished, however, that she were a size zero—okay, eight—like Janie and Poppy. Usually, in fact, she was fairly green-eyed over the knowledge that, no matter how nice her clothes, she always seemed to look like a sausage that had been packed too tightly into its skin—while her friends wore their Old Navy duds like runway models.

Today, however, it didn't matter. Because last night Cade Gallari had kissed her, touched her, made *love* to her. And since the moment she'd opened her eyes this morning, she'd felt almost skinny, wholly desirable and, yes, beautiful.

Not that her first foray into sex had been completely wonderful. If the truth be told, the foreplay had been awesome, but the actual penetration part…well, that had been uncomfortable and over so fast she'd never actually gotten the chance to cross the finish line. But hey, it had been her first time, so it wasn't as if she'd expected angels to sing or anything.

Still, Cade had made her feel special. Between kisses, he'd told her how gorgeous her lips were, how pretty her hair, how soft her skin, how awesome her breasts.

And afterward he'd held her as if she were more precious than platinum.

Which didn't prevent her from being blown away that she'd done it with *him*. She sure never would have predicted that. Up until six weeks ago, in fact, she'd have sworn it wasn't even a remote possibility, since she couldn't remember a time when Cade hadn't been a giant pain in her butt. They'd known each other since birth, practically—yet at the same time hadn't truly known each other at all. But the little she *had* known of him?

She hadn't liked. He was part of the crowd that reveled in ridiculing anyone who didn't fit their standards, which, face it, was nine-tenths of the student body. So when she and Cade had been assigned partners in Mr. Burton's year-end seniors science project, she'd seen *Titanic* stamped all over it. Because, c'mon, her and Gallari? On a project that accounted for a quarter of their grades?

When the two of them were eight, he'd pulled her hair and trod all over her toes in cotillion class. In the tenth grade the guy had looked up her skirt from beneath the bleachers, for God's sake, then told everyone she wore pink panties! Before last night, in fact, her blood had congealed at the thought of him seeing her fat thighs and probably laughing about them with those asshole buddies of his.

Yet over the past month and a half, she'd seen another side of Cade, a sweet, funny, thoughtful side she hadn't dreamt existed. And sitting across from each other in the library or at the coffee shop tables they'd taken to staking out to work on their project, an insidious attraction had begun to grow. Soon they were sitting in the dark in his car just talking, talking, reluctant to call it a day.

Until one night he'd kissed her. And once that frontier had been crossed, there was no going back. Every time he'd kissed her these past couple of weeks, every time his hands had grown bolder charting new territory, she'd just melted, finding it really difficult to call a halt as, little by little, he'd pushed the envelope on their intimacy level.

Until, last night, she just couldn't make herself say they had to stop. Her lips curled up in a secret smile.

"Okay, that's it!" Stopping in front of the cafeteria doors, Poppy grabbed Ava's arm. "What is *up* with you?"

She laughed.

Tried to keep the news to herself.

Then ultimately caved, because they were a sisterhood and she told them everything.

"I did it, Poppy. I thought for sure I was going to graduate—if not die—a virgin, but last night I..." Heat crawling up her chest, she suddenly turned shy at the idea of saying the words aloud.

Jane's mouth dropped open. "Oh. My. Gawd," she said slowly. "You did the deed?"

She nodded.

Poppy looked perplexed. "With who?" Then her eyes narrowed. "Oh, crap, please tell me it wasn't Buttface Gallari!"

"Don't call him that!" Okay, so she was the one who had given him the title way back when. But still—

"Just...don't, okay?" she said in a softer tone and shook her head. "Look, I want to tell you guys everything, and I will—after school when the potential to be overheard isn't so high."

"Yeah, all right," Poppy agreed. "But the minute we're clear of this place, I've got some questions for you, sister." Turning Ava loose, she pushed open the lunchroom door, and they walked into the chaos and bedlam of second lunch.

Trays and crockery clattered, voices reverberated off walls, and students seemed in constant motion as they either moved between the long tables or jockeyed for position at them. Peering around a couple of jocks tossing a baseball back and forth, Ava looked for Cade. Not wanting to appear too obvious when she didn't immediately locate him, she followed her friends to the lunch counter.

She'd picked up a tray before she noted an unaccountable lessening in the noise level. It was never quiet in here, yet except for a few conversations still going on at the farthermost tables, the usual babble had faded to near silence. She looked over her shoulder to see everyone looking at her.

Someone snickered.

She smiled uncertainly, so damn dumb that even *then* she didn't get that she was the butt of some joke. It wasn't until Dylan Vanderkamp, the biggest ass in Cade's crowd of mega-asses, rose to his feet, smirked at her and brandished a fat roll of cash that she began to get an inkling that this was not going to be good.

"Here you go, Gallari," Dylan said, "two hundred bucks." He extended it across the lunch table. "A bet's a bet, my man. You said you could bag the fat girl, and by God you did it." Giving Ava a slow up and down that left her feeling naked, he curled his lip. "I'd say you more than earned it."

It was a bet? a voice shrieked in her head. *I'm the "fat girl" he slept with on a bet?* Her hands went numb, her legs lost strength and sickness rose in a sour tide up her throat.

Dylan stepped to one side, and for the first time she saw Cade, who was lounging on his tailbone looking bored. He glanced at her, and for one crazy, hopeful second, she thought he'd slap the money out of Vanderkamp's mitt. But he merely raised a languid hand and plucked it from the other boy's fingers.

"Thanks," he said and tucked it in the front pocket of his jeans.

Everything inside her turned to ice. At the same time, all those eyes avidly waiting for her reaction seemed to burn pinprick holes everywhere they touched.

But she couldn't simply stand here, taking shit off Cade's group of over-entitled Neanderthals. Her chest might feel as if a two-ton rock sat on it, and God knew she desired nothing more than the ability to turn invisible—but she and her friends had always given back as good as they'd gotten from these idiots. Suckered by Gallari's sweet talk, she'd forgotten for a while who she was dealing with.

She sure as hell remembered now. And, dammit, she *would* get a handle on herself, if it killed her.

A bitter laugh almost escaped her. Because the treacherous, lying, two-faced bastard had gotten a jump on that, hadn't he? Still, if she was going down, she'd at least do so dealing a little damage of her own.

"I think I should get part of that," she managed to drawl past the huge lump in her throat. "One session with Quick Draw McGraw here pretty much put me off sex for life—and if that doesn't entitle a girl to a cut, I don't know what does."

It was the slightest balm to her wounded heart that a few people laughed at Cade's expense rather than her own. It wasn't enough—she'd prefer that his dick shrivel up and drop off—but it would have to do. That lump was growing and she couldn't force out another word.

As if she knew, Poppy placed an unobtrusively supportive hand on her back. "Yeah, what was it she told us, Jane?"

Jane shrugged. "That if she ever got over the trauma of Gallari's fumbling and worked up the nerve to try it again, it would be with someone who knew what the hell they were doing."

Cade continued lounging and looking bored, but Ava had the satisfaction of at least seeing a little dull color climb up his razor-sharp cheekbones.

She'd take more pleasure in seeing him experience a fraction of her humiliation, but God, she just hurt so bad. She felt shattered, as if her insides had been torn apart, then put back wrong. She would never, ever forgive him for setting her up this way, for lifting her up—only to slam her down.

Swallowing hard against a rising tide of grief, she turned her back on him, blindly grabbed a bowl of Jell-O and slapped it on her tray. No way would she be able to swallow a bite.

But damned if she intended to turn tail and run from Buttface Gallari. Even if, inside, a piece of her had just died.

CHAPTER ONE

I'm not sure if I just made a really savvy move—
or the biggest blunder of my life.

Present day, the ninth of November

THE BASTARD was late. Ava Spencer cursed the man she was waiting on as she paced the front foyer of the Wolcott mansion, alternately hugging herself against the cold and trying to rub some warmth into her arms through her coat sleeves. The place had been closed up for several weeks, and between the wind currently buffeting the mullioned windows and the rainstorm that had blown through earlier, leaving a Seattle-centric damp-to-the-bone chill in its wake, she was freezing her ass off.

She would've turned on the heat, but there was little point. If the guy ever deigned to get here, she'd be showing him the mansion from attic to wine cellar. And while Jane kept the front parlor and hidden closet in Miss Agnes's upstairs sitting room climate-controlled for the preservation of the Wolcott collections that weren't currently sold or on loan to museums, it would take until noon tomorrow to warm up the rest. And although she had turned on every light in the house, the illusion of warmth from the yellow glow of the lamps and overheads didn't come close to replacing the real thing.

A laugh that went a little wild escaped her. Like *that* was the crucial issue here. Because... *It's not some* guy, *Av. It's Cade Calderwood Gallari.*

Jeez Marie. She couldn't *believe* she'd agreed to this. So, yes, she was concentrating on the minutiae for all she was worth to keep from thinking about him. Because it was too freaking late to second-guess herself now.

Wasn't it?

She froze for an arrested second. Hell, no, it wasn't! The heavy feeling in her stomach lightening, she snatched up her purse and started down the hallway to the kitchen. Its exterior door was the direct route to where she'd parked her Beemer. Cade was late? She was *out* of here.

Headlights swept the east wall across from the kitchen archway, stopping her dead. "Shit."

Too late.

She did a little dance in place to shake off the tension that had her tighter than an over-wound watch, throwing in some yoga breathing for good measure. Exhaling a final gusty breath, she nodded to herself. "Okay. Time to pull on your big girl pants."

She forced herself to shove down her irritation over Cade's tardiness, over the fact that he *breathed,* and bury it deep. *It's been thirteen years, girl. He's a footnote, someone who no longer matters. Who hasn't mattered for a very long time.* So it probably wouldn't do to snap his head off first thing.

But, oh, boy. The temptation.

She watched him through the back-door window as he climbed the steps and stopped beneath the porch light, and her annoyance surged back with a vengeance. She fought it to a standstill once more, pushed out a final exhalation and reached out to unlock the door.

The knob turned before she could open it, and he blew into the kitchen, shaking himself like a wet dog and sending raindrops flying in all directions from his sun-streaked brown hair. Looking beyond him, Ava saw that it had begun to pour again.

"Man, it's wet out there!" He flashed her his trademark Gallari smile, white teeth flashing and deep creases bracketing his mouth. Only she noticed that this time the blue, blue eyes glinting between dense, dark lashes held…something. Wariness maybe or…calculation? Something cooler and edgier than the smile that for years had haunted her dreams.

It just bugged the hell out of her that she felt his impact like a cattle prod to the breastbone. Why was it like this every damn time she laid eyes on him: this immediate, visceral one-two to the heart? It was identical to the reaction she'd had around teenaged Cade—and even after everything she knew about him, everything he'd *done*—seeing him gave her that same hot punch to the solar plexus.

Well, it would be a cold, cold day in hell before she felt the least bit tempted to act on it. She raised an eyebrow. "And you call yourself a Seattle native?"

"I forgot how fast the rain can soak a guy up here."

She gave him a polite smile. "I suppose living in southern California will do that to a person." She made a show of glancing at her watch. "Tell me why you think I should give you the time of day—let alone rent you the mansion for a documentary."

"*O*-kay. No small talk." His mouth developed an unyielding slant that somehow looked more at home on his chapped lips than his old smile. "Sorry I'm late. There was a wreck on I-5 and it took a while to get traffic moving again."

She nodded her acceptance of his apology and watched as he looked around the kitchen. A small pucker of dismay appeared between his dark eyebrows. "It's been modernized."

When Ava looked him fully in the face this time, she found it less unsettling. "Surely you didn't expect it to be the same as it was back in the eighties?"

"I guess I'd hoped it would be."

"As soon as Poppy, Jane and I inherited it, we had the awful sunroom addition removed and, yes, modernized the place throughout. We were expecting to sell it, Slick, not rent it—and even that's not a done deal." She raised her brows. "Your pitch?"

"As my production assistant told you on the phone, I want to do a documentary on the Wolcott Suite mystery. But more than that, I want to feature Agnes Wolcott."

She had, and Ava had to admit that was the reason she was standing here. But—"Why? I mean, sure, the Wolcott diamonds gained urban legend status locally, but I doubt the story surrounding it is nationally famous."

"Maybe not, but I grew up in this town, and I've been fascinated by the mystery of it since I was a kid." His blue eyes lit with enthusiasm. "It's got everything, Ava—a cool old mansion, a fortune in diamonds that were never recovered, a murder…and a woman at the heart of it that I find more and more remarkable the deeper I dig."

She really liked that last part. What she didn't like

was him. "And I should care about what you want, why?"

"Because I can do justice to a woman I know you cared for. And because I'll give you and your friends thirty grand for six weeks' use, pay all the peripheral expenses for the time Scorched Earth Productions is here and landscape the grounds back to the way they were in the eighties."

Oh, low. The mansion had turned into an albatross around her and her friends' necks in this economy, and he undoubtedly knew it. Desperately, she wanted to spit in his eye. But she thought of her friends. Poppy and Jane had never complained, but she knew this place was a drain on them, too. So, sucking up her ire, wondering if she was making the worst decision of her life, she gritted teeth and said through them, "Fine."

"You'll do it?"

"Yes." What the hell. She wouldn't have to see him. "Have your assistant call me for my lawyer's number—you can send him the contracts—and if he finds it agreeable you've got a deal. Do you want a tour before you go? Since you seemed concerned about the work we had done, I'd be happy to show you. I think you'll agree our crew did a wonderful job of preserving the spirit of the original design in their restoration." She stepped back.

"One more thing," he said, halting her. "I want to hire you as the production company's concierge, as well."

She laughed in his face. "No. Do you want that tour or not?"

"Forget the tour—"

"Works for me. Send your paperwork to my lawyer." She turned to go.

"Look. I'll pay you two grand a week plus a fifty

thousand dollar bonus if the documentary comes in on time and on budget."

"Which somehow won't happen, right?"

"The bonus is a legitimate offer, Ava. I'll email my own contracts for your attorney to look over while he's going over yours, and you'll see I have a lot more to lose than you."

Doesn't matter. Because it's not going to happen. But damn him. Damn him, damn him, damn him! Not only had her trust fund taken a huge hit in the economic downturn, so had the finances of many of the clients who formed the foundation of her concierge business. And as one of the gazillion mortgage holders who'd been caught up in the subprime lending disaster, she was facing a huge balloon payment on her condo that was coming due in the not-nearly-future-enough future.

Well, too bad, so sad for her. She'd rather lose the place than spend six weeks in this bastard's company.

Seriously? her hardscrabble practicality demanded. She had to admit that was pretty cut-your-nose-off-to-spite-your-face idiotic. This could actually be the answer to her prayers. And hell, it wasn't as if she were worried about falling under his spell. Been there, done that.

"You'd be in place to make sure I do credit to your Miss Wolcott," he said softly.

She blew out a defeated breath. "All right. Contingent on my attorney's evaluation of the contracts, I'll do it—to see you do justice to Miss A's story." And if she was also doing it for the money, he didn't have to know. "Do you want that tour? We can start with the dining room across the hall."

She turned, only to feel Cade wrap a hand around her forearm to halt her. Heat seeped through the cashmere of her coat sleeve beneath his light grasp, and she promptly swung back around, twisting her arm free.

"Do not," she said with hard-fought calm, "touch me."

Releasing her, he stepped back. "I just wanted to tell you, before we get started, how genuinely sorry I am for what happened back in high school. I was—"

"Forget it," she interrupted. She *so* did not want to rehash the ugly details of the past with him. "I have."

"Really?" An eloquent eyebrow rose, surprise flashing in the depths of his cobalt eyes.

She gave him a regal nod. She had cut him off at the knees the other times he'd sought her out over the years to apologize, but if acknowledging his regret would move him along to a place where they didn't have to discuss the past, then, fine. She'd grant him his damn redemption.

"You forgive me then?"

No. Hell, no. That would be a snowboarding day in hell.

But she gave him a serene smile, knowing from this point on she had to be professional. "Let's just agree to leave the past in the past, shall we?" Not awaiting a response, she led him to the dining room and got down to business. "As you can see, great care was taken in here to preserve the integrity of the era in which the Wolcott Mansion was built—"

SHE MET JANE AND POPPY at Sugar Rush, her favorite neighborhood coffee shop/bakery, the next afternoon. As they took their seats at a round table by the play area, she sucked in a quick inhale, then eased it out. "I did something last night I hope you'll be okay with," she said to her two best friends amid the clatter of crockery and conversations. She hesitated for a brief second, then blurted, "I agreed to rent the mansion to Cade Gallari."

Okay, her ripping-off-the-Band-Aid delivery was clearly a little too abrupt, for Jane's blue eyes went round with shock. Then her friend slapped both hands onto the tabletop, came half out of her seat to shove her face closer to Ava's own and said, "You agreed to rent it to *who?*"

Ignoring the two women at the next table whose attention was drawn by Jane's incredulous rising voice and aggressive stance—a look at odds with her neat, shiny brown hair and dark-hued clothing that always looked so conservative at first glance—Ava focused on her friends. She knew perfectly well she'd been heard. Nevertheless, she repeated evenly, "Cade Gallari."

"Tell me you're kidding." Poppy's voice might have been calmer than Jane's, but as the curly haired blonde set her coffee cup down the expression in her topaz-brown eyes held identical disbelief. "Why would we let that douche anywhere *near* our inheritance?"

It was a fair question. Miss Agnes, the cool old lady who'd started having the three of them over to her mansion for monthly teas when they were twelve, who'd given them their first diaries and gotten them started on their lifelong journaling habit, had become a friend and a mentor. In Ava's and Janie's case, she'd been more parentlike than their own parents. And when she'd died a year and a half ago, she'd left a big hole.

Even in death, however, she'd been full of surprises, and Ava, Jane and Poppy had been astounded to learn she'd bequeathed them her estate. Miss A might well be rolling over in her grave at the thought of Cade in her home. God knows she'd played a large role in helping Ava pick up the pieces after his betrayal.

Feeling a little beleaguered, she stared at her friend. "It's not as if I would've chosen to let him use the Wolcott mansion, either, Poppy, given any other option. But I'm fresh out of those. I said yes because the market for houses in our price range is stagnant and we're paying through the nose for taxes, lights, utilities, yard maintenance and all the other crap that goes along with maintaining a place this size. He'll pay very well for the privilege."

She told them the terms. "And he'll pay even more if we decide to rent him a few of Miss Agnes's collections to use in his production—something I told him he'd have to discuss with you, Janie. You both know he produces documentaries about unsolved mysteries, right?"

The other women shifted guiltily, and she laughed, feeling tension she hadn't even realized she'd been carrying—in her neck, her shoulders, her spine—release its grip. "Relax, I don't doubt your loyalty—you guys have boycotted all things Gallari forever. But we'd have to live in outer Mongolia not to have heard something about the name he's making for himself."

"Okay—I confess—I saw one of his films." Poppy held her hands up in a *Don't shoot!* gesture when both Ava and Jane gaped at her. "*I* didn't pick it out—Jason ordered the damn thing from Netflix one night. He-who-shall-not-be-named is never mentioned in our house, so Jase had no way of putting the documentary maker together with the guy he saw upsetting you in that bar in Columbia City last year. Murphy'd just told him he had to see it."

Focusing on the sign next to the kiddie play area, Ava did her best to wrestle her curiosity to a standstill. Unsupervised Kids Will Be Given An Espresso And

A Free Puppy, she read. Usually that tickled her, but now the words simply bounced around in her head like Ping-Pong balls in a box—until finally, unable to help herself, she surrendered to her need to know. "All right, I give. Did it live up to all the hype?"

"Yeah." Her friend grimaced. "I'm sorry, Av, but it did. I've never liked the dramatization-type documentaries because the acting is usually abysmal. But apparently Gallari's gaining something of a cult rep as a star-maker. Several times now he's chosen unknown talent that he's gotten on the cheap from SAGIndie or university drama programs, who've then gone on to garner moderate-to-Ohmigawd-worthy success."

"And you know this how?" Jane demanded. "Jeez, what are you, Gallari's biggest fan now?"

"Seriously?" the blonde demanded right back. "Could you be any more insulting, Janie? Of course I'm not. Jase was so blown away by the documentary he insisted on watching the extras."

"Good God," Ava muttered. "The thing was *that* good?" As she watched Jane reach for Poppy's hand and say, "Sorry, babe," she wasn't sure how she felt about Cade's achievements. On the one hand, she would hardly cry a river if he tanked in every endeavor he touched.

On the other, his success might well help her and her friends' finances.

"I'm afraid so." Elbows on the table, Poppy skimmed back her cloud of curls with both hands. "He really does have an eye for talent. But he only used the reenactments in tiny doses. It was the interviews that really sold it. The whole thing was just so...compellingly presented."

Then her slender brows drew together. "Still. Why

the hell would he want to shoot one in the Wolcott mansion, which he had to know would be a hard sell, given it belongs to us now? Unless—?" Abruptly, she let go of her hair and snapped her spine erect.

"Ho-ly shitskis, Av. You said he'll landscape the ground back to the way it was in the eighties?"

"Of course." Jane, too, sat straighter. "The break-in where Miss Agnes's guy was killed and the Wolcott diamonds disappeared."

"That would be the unsolved mystery," Ava agreed.

In 1985, during a remodel of Miss Agnes's bed-and-sitting-room, her suite of diamond jewelry had been stolen. Late one night six months later, "her man, Henry," as she always referred to him, heard a noise and came out of the office where he'd been working to find Mike Maperton, the head carpenter from the remodel, inside the mansion. Henry tripped the alarm, but Maperton killed him before help could arrive. It was assumed the construction worker had been retrieving the jewelry from where he'd hidden it, but if so, it was never recovered.

Jane smiled crookedly. "I always got the impression, whenever Miss A referred to Henry, that he was a lot more to her than just a factotum or man of business or whatever the heck he was supposed to be."

Poppy shrugged. "We all did. What's your point?"

"Damned if I know, except that I can see the story playing out in a documentary." Jane hooked her hair behind her ears. "And I hate to admit it, but it would be nice to have the financial burden taken off our shoulders for a while. But Miss A was one of a kind—so, unless Gallari's scored Streep to play her, I can't imagine the actress who could do her justice."

"I'd like to talk to you about something that's

related to the Miss A part, but first I should probably tell you—" *okay, this is the tricky part* "—that I, um, agreed to work for him next week, then for an additional six weeks during the actual production, which starts around the first of the year."

"Are you out of your freaking mind?" Poppy kept her voice low to prevent two nearby little girls eating the frosting off their cupcakes from overhearing, but her tone held a fierce edge.

"Maybe." Tough to take offense when she'd been asking herself the same thing way too frequently since walking away from Cade last night. "Probably, even. My first impulse when he approached me was the same ole, same ole—to either spit in his eye or gouge them both out."

Straightening her shoulders, she looked from one friend's face to the other. "But that's just a knee-jerk reflex."

"One that totally works for me," Jane interjected in a dry tone.

Ava shook her head. "He's old news, Janie. I am so over him. But you know how dicked up my finances have been the past year." Her lips tilted wryly. "So when he made me an offer I couldn't refuse as the production company's personal concierge—I didn't."

Watching her with concern-filled eyes, neither Janie nor Poppy smiled back and Ava sighed. "What? You think I'm too fragile to handle it?"

"No, of course not," Jane said. "But I don't trust that bastard as far as I can throw him. We were there the last time he got up close and personal with you and had to watch you struggle to put yourself back together."

"It was a piece-by-piece process," Poppy agreed, "that took way too long and too much glue before it held together. And *then* you had to handle most of it on your own because of him screwing up our after-graduation plans—"

Yeah, getting shipped off to the fat farm didn't help hasten the process, she thought wryly. Which, okay, was more her mother's fault than Cade's. But screw that—the truth was, if she hadn't been so flattened by his betrayal, something her mother hadn't even seemed to notice, she would have dug in until she'd won that battle. So, for all intents and purposes, it was his fault.

She tuned back in to hear Poppy continue, "So I suppose that I, at least, am a little afraid for you. You worked like a demon to build yourself back up, and I just don't want to see all your hard work go down the drain because of Buttface Gallari."

"Neither do I. And I won't let it. I will never forgive him, Poppy—*ever*. But I'm through running away from him. Because you're right, I did work too hard building myself back up to keep doing that. I'm not surprised you might have reservations about my ability to handle myself—"

"I don't! You'll go down in the I-am-woman-hear-me-roar annals for your counterattack on Gallari during the worst moment of your life. You more than proved you can handle yourself."

"Since then, though, I've been more reactive than proactive whenever I've run into him. So maybe *I* feel I have something to prove—to myself, if no one else. It doesn't help that I looked in the mirror this morning and had a 'fat' moment."

"Dammit, Av," Jane said. "When are you going to let those go? You've been a size twelve for twelve years."

"Which *you* like to remind me would be a size four-teen if I'd buy my clothing at the less spendy stores where most women shop." She knew her friend was only teasing when she said that, but she couldn't honestly deny Jane was right.

"Please." The brunette made a rude noise. "You know I only say that because I'm jealous you have big boobs. *I* wanna have big girl boobs some day." She gestured at Ava's emerald-green cashmere sweater and the black pencil skirt she'd tucked it into. "Look at you!"

She glanced down at herself. "I know. Does this make me look rotund?"

"Oh, for God's sake, Spencer, snap out of it!" Poppy gave her a get-over-yourself glare. "As Janie said, you've maintained your killer bod for pretty much your entire adult life. And you *know* men trip all over themselves when you walk by. It's not because you're fat, girl-friend."

"Okay. Sorry." She shook out her hands and picked up her coffee cup—then merely held it for a moment as she gave her friends a rueful smile. "I backslid for a minute there. Jeez. I've been down Insecurity Road so many times it likely has a butt-shaped rut etched in it. But I'm good now."

"It's that damn Gallari, showing up out of the blue and shaking you up."

She shrugged. Seeing him again had contributed for sure, but it was really the telephone conversation she'd had with her mother earlier in which Jacqueline had made her usual crack about Ava's weight. Why was her mom always so sure that she could do better, diet herself thinner? Never mind that she was a busty, hippy, big-boned girl who could starve herself into an early grave and still not die a sylphlike woman.

Well, *she* mostly knew her worth. She also knew

she'd earned it for more than shedding thirty-nine pounds.

She knocked back a sip of coffee, set her cup on the table and, hands flat on either side of the mug, leaned into them in her intense need to make her friends understand why she'd agreed to do the last thing they'd expect from her. "Look, I'm not exactly raring to play personal concierge to Cade myself. But it's work I can do with my eyes closed and he'll pay me a weekly bundle for it, plus a huge bonus if the documentary comes in on time and on budget."

"Even if he's on the up-and-up, how on earth are you gonna deal with seeing him day in and day out?"

"By being the biggest professional you've ever seen. By reminding myself that if all goes well, I can finally pay off that frickin' balloon payment that's been hanging over my head."

Remembering a discussion with Cade last night that she had almost enjoyed, she flashed her dimples at her friends. "One of the things I'm genuinely excited about is an agreement I made to talk with Cade and his scriptwriter about Miss A to get her part as authentic as possible. So tell me what you guys would like to see included about her."

After an enthusiastic conversation about their mentor, Ava looked at her watch and pushed back from the table. "I know this is a bombshell and I'm sorry to drop it on your heads and run, but I'm meeting Cade again this evening at my lawyer's to go over the fine points in my contract and discuss my job description in more detail. Until that's taken care of, I don't plan to sign anything." Rising to her feet, she looked down at her two friends. "We good?"

"Of course we are." Poppy stood as well and gave

Ava a hard hug. "I just don't want to see you get hurt again."

"Not gonna happen," she promised.

"Don't forget dinner at Dev's and my place next week," Jane added as she, too, rose to give her a hug. "And you step carefully around that man, you hear?"

"I will," she said, pulling on her plum-colored Steve Madden wool peacoat, flipping up the collar and picking up the plum, blue and green scarf Poppy's mother had made her to wind around her neck. "Love you guys."

She headed for the door, but paused to shoot her friends a cocky smile over her shoulder. "And don't worry! I'm gonna kick some serious booty on this job."

CHAPTER TWO

I didn't think I'd ever get used to being in the mansion as an owner after Miss A died. So how weird is it that it feels so strange to suddenly be here as an outsider?

Nine weeks later

"SHE HERE YET?"

Beks Donaldson, Cade's production assistant, was slow to pull her attention away from the chart she was putting together at the kitchen table in the Wolcott mansion. By the time she craned around to look at him over her shoulder, he was seconds from tapping the face of his watch with his forefinger—that detested, time-is-money gesture his old man always used to use on him. Fuck. He'd sworn he would never do that to anyone else, so what the hell?

Annoyed by his slipping control, he found it didn't help his mood that while Beks didn't roll her gray-blue eyes, she somehow managed to convey the impression of doing so.

But all she said before turning back to her chart was a mild, "No." He noticed she also refrained from reminding him that he'd interrupted her work less than ten minutes ago to ask the same damn question.

"She's late," he growled at the feathered tips of Beks's Harley-Davidson shield n' wings tattoo showing on either side of her nape above the neckline of her sweater.

"Uh-huh."

Okay, he was being an idiot. But damn Ava Spencer anyway for keeping him waiting. He considered giving Beks a you-don't-even-wanna-mess-with-me look, but she didn't bother to turn around again. He had to settle for a stern, "Let me know when she arrives."

"You got it, boss."

He went back to the parlor where he'd been working on his own prep work—only to discover that he couldn't concentrate for shit.

Dammit, he *never* lost the ability to focus when it came to work. He'd bled too many buckets, poured too much of his heart and soul into carving out a place for himself in this industry, to allow himself the luxury.

Not that he didn't understand what the problem was, of course; he knew exactly where he'd gone south. He was always proactive, accustomed to working through every eventuality ahead of time to avoid spanners being thrown in his works during the actual production. Generally, by the time he was ready to dig in and really rock and roll, he'd worked out ninety-nine percent of the kinks, thereby sidestepping a lot of blunders. But he'd made a serious one with Ava that night back in November.

Yes, he'd owed her an apology for being such a shit in high school. But considering he'd attempted to *give* her one several times over the past decade, there had been no need to lead off with it the minute they'd come face-to-face. Her coolness that evening had made him rush the sorrys instead of waiting to get a feel for the emotional climate, a skill he'd developed early in his career and found handy in damn near every situation.

The trouble was, he had everything riding on this project. In order to get it funded he'd had to accept a couple of contract clauses he ordinarily would have avoided like a flaming case of jock rash. So he'd gone in knowing he had to talk Ava into renting him the Wolcott mansion. It was that or scrap the project, because if he had to build sets to duplicate it, his budget would be a bust before he even got started. And considering he'd already signed the damn contracts, that wasn't an option.

Not that he'd hamstrung himself entirely. Never one to go into anything blind, he'd investigated before he'd signed anything, then deemed the risk worthwhile when he'd discovered the extent of Ava's financial difficulties. And if securing the mansion had been his sole objective, things would have been business as usual.

But while he prided himself on always hiring efficient crews, for this project he'd needed not just efficient but the very best. That was a nonissue when it came to industry personnel. He'd known exactly who to hire: the professionals he'd worked with most successfully in the past. The ones whose visions meshed best with his own.

He always used a local as well, however, someone familiar with the area, to manage logistics and coordinate daily living for his cast and crew so he could focus his own attention where it belonged—on the production. To his dismay, not only had Ava turned out to be one of the owners, hers had also been the name that had kept cropping up when he'd started putting out feelers for a Seattle go-to, detail-oriented person with the best contacts. How ironic was that?

Karma sure was a bitch. Still, he had bet on himself. Because while the risks of this project might be greater than all his other ventures combined, so were the rewards.

The Wolcott documentary was his ticket to even bigger and better things. Velcro it to his past several achievements and maybe, just maybe, he'd finally get to take the script he'd been sitting on for three long years and turn it into the film he'd been dreaming of. The latter wouldn't have a blockbuster-sized budget. But that only meant it would be all his to do the way *he* wanted to do it.

Well, either that or it would be the flush heard around the world if his gamble failed and Ava Spencer decided to use the mansion or her position on his crew for payback. He had to admit it was a concern that had been scratching at the back of his mind ever since they'd signed the contracts. Yet, staring at the blustery weather outside the parlor window, he didn't see *how* she could do it, given that she needed money almost as badly as he needed this documentary to succeed.

Still, it had been naïve of him not to even consider the possibility that she had an agenda of her own before he'd all but handed her carte blanche to the most important project he'd ever worked. Which was surprising, considering naïveté hadn't been a part of his makeup since the day he'd found out his dad wasn't really his dad.

"Boss!"

Grateful for Beks's bellow yanking him away from the pit into which that last thought likely would have landed him, he stalked over to the open pocket door and stuck his head out into the hall. "Yo!" That subject was a dead horse he had *no* desire to beat all over again.

"Your concierge is here."

There was no good reason for his heart to start tripping all over itself. Snapping off a silent command for it to get the hell back to its normal steady rhythm, he muttered a terse, "About damn time," and headed down to the kitchen.

"You ever consider going into acting?" he heard Beks demand as he neared the room. "'Cause you're, like, a ringer for those amazing actresses that ruled back in the Hollywood studio system era. Same vibe, same glamour, swear to God."

He paused in the doorway to watch Ava peel off a pricey-looking coat as she smiled in bemusement at his production assistant.

Beks had that effect on people. If she harbored a single inhibition in her entire body, he had yet to discover what it was. A guy could rack his brain until it liquefied, in fact, and still never come up with an instance in which the younger woman had bothered to censor her thoughts before loosing them on the world.

He had to admit, though, that she was right on the money with her assessment of Ava. Between the concierge's flame-red thirties-style bob and her forties, knock-you-on-your-ass body, she had the retro glamour of a Hollywood golden age starlet. The impression was only reinforced when she finished removing her coat and revealed a black cashmere sweater dress that clung here and skimmed there, showcasing spectacular curves both above and below the skinny red belt that cinched in her waist.

Feeling a primal pull of attraction, he took a step closer to the threshold.

Then she tipped her head back and laughed in genuine amusement, and he stopped in his tracks. Because he remembered that sound. Remembered it from that long-ago time before he'd made one of the dumbest decisions of his life.

"Me, an actress?" Even in profile he could see a dimple flash. "No, I can honestly say I've never considered that as a career choice." Another laugh burbled up her throat. "Really, *truly* never considered it. I couldn't act my way out of a paper bag if my hair was on fire."

"Which the color sorta suggests it is," Beks said.

"Yes, well, that's the curse of the redhead for you. Trust me, given a choice, I'd much rather have black hair like yours. But no one who knows me would ever put me and acting in the same sentence. I'm supereffective when it comes to making people's lives run smoothly. But be scintillating in front of a camera?" Her quick grimace produced another dimple. "Not so much."

"Yeah, I can't act for shit, either," Beks admitted gloomily. "Otherwise, I'd be all over gettin' into the star groove."

Stepping to the side of the archway out of Ava's sight, Cade watched as she studied Beks's skim-milk skin and dark hair, which the younger woman wore in high, fan-shaped, burgundy-streaked pigtails. Ava's lips crooked up in the faintest of smiles as she took in the Goth eye makeup and bloodred lipstick, both of which presented a stark contrast with the Catholic schoolgirl uniform and knee socks Beks wore, yet tied right in with her black lace-up, patent leather ankle boots with their clunky heels and three inch, correction-shoe-looking platforms.

Ava's smile grew wider, punching dimples deep in her cheeks. "Yeah, speed assessor that I am, I kind of guessed right away that you're not the repressed type."

Cade frowned. They were obviously in the throes of one of those instant bonding moments females were so freaking fond of—and he hadn't hired Ava to hang out with Beks.

He stepped into the room. "Good of you to finally make it, Spencer."

Her dimples disappeared as she turned to give him the same cool, detached look that had been a trademark of their previous meetings. "Mr. Gallari," she said coolly. "I said I would be here, didn't I?"

"Yeah, at one-thirty." He resisted the urge to drive home the fact she was an hour and a half late. He didn't doubt for a second that she was every bit as cognizant of the fact as he.

"Oh, gosh, you didn't check your messages, did you?" Her tone was easy, friendly, but her gaze seemed to say something else. "I called last night to let you know that, although I'd secured the house for your crew that I told you about last month, I had a last-minute opportunity to strike a better deal, so I would be late." Reaching into a vintage alligator briefcase, she extracted a handful of papers and extended them to him. "I had a meeting with the owner this afternoon and I think you'll be happy with the results of my negotiations."

Accepting the stack without looking at it, he gave the pocket where he kept his cell phone a surreptitious pat, only to find it empty. Shit. He knew he should own up to the dead battery he'd discovered when he'd turned his cell back on after debarking the plane this morning, and the fact that he'd plugged it into the rental car power source—where he'd undoubtedly left it. He absolutely should, but he was irritated with her even though it wasn't her fault.

Still...

If he were to be honest about it, his and Beks's arrival into town had been extremely smooth—maybe even the smoothest ever. The town car driver had been there with Cade's name printed on a sign when they'd reached Baggage, the key to the back door had been exactly where Ava had said it would be and her instructions to disarm the security alarm clear. Unlike the last time he'd been here, the mansion had been warm and inviting, and they'd found the refrigerator stocked with cheese, meats, fresh fruit and an assortment of drinks, both hard and soft. On the counter had been two different kinds of crackers and a box of Fran's Gray and Smoked Salt caramels. So she'd done her job—and then some.

He let his irritation go on a quiet breath. "You've met Ms. Shy and Retiring here, I take it?"

Ava smiled at the nickname but said, "Yes and no. We've been talking for a few minutes but never got around to the actual introductions."

"In that case, let me present Rebekka Donaldson, my production assistant."

"Okay, there's a name I haven't been called in a while," the younger woman said as she reached out to give Ava a firm handshake. "It's been so long, in fact, that unless you're my grandmother, it's unlikely I'll respond to it. Everyone except Granny Louise—and maybe Mom when she's unhappy with me—calls me Beks."

"Come to think of it, except at our own introduction I've never actually heard anybody call you Rebekka," he agreed. "So, Ava, Beks. Beks, meet Ava Spencer, our local concierge."

"What does a production assistant do?" Ava asked, folding her coat and laying it over the back of an antique oak chair. As she looked at Beks with bright-eyed interest, she smoothed the soft fabric with a long, pale hand. Her fingertips bumped one of the turned spools that rose on either side of the chair's back and she traced its shape between her fingers and thumb.

He looked away, jolted all over again by her unconscious sexuality. He'd felt it when they were kids but had always assumed that was merely because *A:* she had a way of moving that made him think of sex and *B:* sex was all he *had* thought about at the time. Hell, he'd been a teenage boy, ready and willing to nail anything with tits. And God knows she'd always had great breasts.

But that didn't explain his reaction to her now.

"I'm half gofer and half coordinator," Beks said. "Cade's giving me my big break."

Clearing his throat, he shook the reaction aside. "Beks is our detail woman. There are a million attached to filming and she's a genius at keeping track of 'em all."

Beks nodded. "That whole 'making people's lives run smoothly' thing you said you do?" she said cheerfully. "Well, I am to the running of a production what you are to people's lives."

Turning back to Cade, she waved at the papers in his hand. "Go ahead and look over the contracts, boss. I'll show Ava what I'm working on at the moment."

It wasn't a quick tutorial he heard, however, as he turned his attention to the rental agreement. Instead Beks mentioned that while the weather up here would take some getting used to after L.A., at least she didn't have to worry about getting a sunburn.

Ava laughed but then said that even in Seattle in the winter women with skin as fair as theirs required a good sunblock.

Which promptly segued into a spirited debate over the best brand.

Shaking his head, he searched the contract for the bottom line, flipping through the pages until he came to the one that had the clause disclosing the monthly rent. He read it swiftly. Then went back to read it again more slowly.

And blew out a breath. "No shit?"

Ava turned her head, raising her brows at him. "I assume that meets with your approval. In fact, a nice little gift certificate to my favorite spa for my negotiation skills wouldn't be out of line."

"It really wouldn't." He read the clause again, then looked up at her, feeling some of the she's-gonna-blow-my-big-chance-all-to-hell-and-gone knot he'd been packing for the past couple of months dissolve. "How the hell did you talk the owners down to a rent this reasonable?"

She shrugged. "By being the best at what I do," she said lightly. "Which is why you hired me. Although I did have to give the owner my word that if he finds someone interested in seeing the place while your crew is still in residence they'll be reasonable about allowing it to be shown—with the strict understanding, of course, that it's not available until your lease expires." Leveling those green eyes on him, she said, "I also promised that your crew would leave it in as good, if not better, condition than they found it."

"We will," Beks agreed, and Cade nodded.

"If there are any small repairs that need doing—and they have time and the union allowing—I'll talk to the guys about taking care of them," he said, then gave her a solemn, head-on gaze. "Good work."

Ava INCLINED her head. "Thanks," she said. But she wasn't as uninfluenced by his approval as she might have wished.

Not that she wasn't over Cade, because she *so* was. It was more that…she hadn't expected to still feel this pull of unwilling attraction.

She supposed that was precisely what she should have expected, given she'd had a similar reaction at their earlier meetings. But perhaps because she'd handled the first face-to-face pretty well and had felt reasonably removed when she'd had to see him again at her lawyer's office, then again during the summit with his scriptwriter in the beginning of December, she had assumed she'd gotten the whole oh-my-gawd-am-I-really-going-to-work-with-the-bastard thing out of her system.

Apparently not.

Still, that was all this was, a sort of knee-jerk what-the-hell-am-I-doing-here vibe at being thrown together again with the author of her worst insecurities.

Which she had worked her way through, thank you very much, more than a dozen years ago. She didn't discount the great deal of effort it had taken on her part, but damned if she intended to go back there again. Squaring her shoulders, she dug two sets of keys out of her briefcase. She handed the larger one to Beks. "These are to the house. I think I have enough for everyone who's staying there, but if you need more let me know and I'll have the landlord make them up."

The other set she handed to Cade, along with an additional contract. "I wasn't able to get as good a deal on the Belltown condo you requested, because short-term leases on units in that area have a built-in demand. I did, however, talk them down two hundred and forty bucks from the original asking price, since historically

January is a postholiday lull month." She shrugged. "It's not much, but I imagine every little bit helps."

"You *rock*, girlfriend," Beks said and offered up her palm for a high five.

As Ava slapped it, Cade gave her an unsmiling nod. "It does, yes. Thank you." His fingers, brushing hers as he accepted the keys, were warm and hard.

He was harder and tougher-looking all over, in fact, than he'd been at eighteen, his shoulders wider, his chest brawnier. The sleeves of his blue sweater were pushed up, revealing silky dark hair that feathered tan, muscular forearms. And his face, which was more angular and less…pretty…than it had been in high school, sported even darker stubble around his mouth and along the inflexible lines of his jaw.

He also seemed a great deal less carefree than he'd been back in the day, more somber-mouthed and watchful-eyed.

Not that she gave a great big rip one way or the other. Who didn't change after high school? She was just interested in discovering the kind of man she'd be working with in the here and now. The more she knew, the better prepared she'd be to keep him at arm's length, right where he belonged. Because while a whole lot had changed in thirteen years, the fact that he couldn't be trusted remained the same.

But speaking of work…

"As you requested, several of Miss Agnes's collections are in a vault here," she said briskly. "If you'll give me some times that work best for you, I'll coordinate them with Jane's schedule so we can discuss which ones you want to use for your documentary. Once you've made your decision, we'll arrange to have the rest moved to off-site safekeeping."

He nodded. "The sooner the better works for me."

"Let me call her."

She set up the appointment for that evening, then left to take the staples, supplies and extra linens she'd bought earlier to the two rentals. When she got back, Cade's director of photography, a beefy, bald guy named Louie who looked to be in his mid-forties, had arrived. She also met the night watchman, a tough-looking older man named John.

It was full dark when the van she'd arranged for pulled into the driveway and disgorged the production's soundman, the lighting engineer and a film school student who was the light man's assistant. She pulled out her iPhone and added notes to the ones she'd already jotted down on Louie and John to keep everyone straight in her mind.

For the soundman she thumb-typed: Kyle. 40-smthing. Never seems 2 b w/out Bose in-ear headset.

The lighting engineer rated: Jim Short. 60s? size matches name. Asst Ryan. Blond surfer boy. Somthg they call Best Boy.

Over time she would add personal preferences to their files, because information like that was what had contributed to her success over the years.

Jane arrived a short while later, and Ava escorted her down the hallway, the two of them chatting nonstop. Finding the pocket door to the parlor open, she glanced in to see Cade sitting at the desk, poring over the papers spread across its surface. A rich brown lock of hair fell over his forehead, the desk lamp picking out its subtle streaks of bronze and blond. And her friend's voice promptly faded to a background murmur.

Because, for just a second, she had a vision of that silky hair brushing her stomach.

She jerked in shock and slapped a new vision in its place—this one of letting herself into her Alki Beach condo, kicking off her heels, lighting a few candles and turning on the fireplace. She'd love nothing more than to climb into her nightie and maybe pour herself a nice glass of wine. To flop down on her big, overstuffed couch and know that this day was finally over.

She couldn't deny she was intrigued and excited at the opportunity to be part of a documentary featuring Miss A. It was a world outside her normal experience and she was fascinated by the idea of learning about it.

But a big part of her was already exhausted by the push-pull of her emotions, which kept flip-flopping all over the place whenever she was in Cade Calderwood Gallari's company. And for now she just had a need to escape.

So she cleared her throat and leaned into the room. "Jane is here and I'm gonna take off."

Janie grabbed her by the arm at the same time Cade jerked his head up to stare at her in alarm.

"Are you crazy?" her friend demanded. "Leave me by myself with this clown and I won't be responsible for what I say."

"That is not an option," Cade agreed. "We need you to stick around so you can handle the details."

Both were clearly determined that she wouldn't leave, so postponing her home-sweet-home fantasy, she blew out a quiet breath and gave in with reasonable grace. "Very well," she said and preceded Jane into the room.

Where, steeling herself, she took the farthest seat across the desk from the man and his damn vision-inducing pheromones. "Let's get this done."

CHAPTER THREE

Lord. I didn't realize how crazy the next six weeks were gonna be until I wrote down everything I need to get done.

Later that evening

IT WAS NEARLY NINE when Cade let himself into his rented Belltown condo in a renovated 1914 brick building on First Avenue. Dropping his keys into a burled wood bowl on a tobacco tin–sized table, he didn't bother feeling for the light switch. Instead he made his way down the abbreviated hallway and into the body of the living space by the glow of the city lights pouring through a good-sized triple-pane window that blocked most of the downtown traffic noises. He went directly to the gas fireplace in the corner of the room and flipped on the switch.

With a soft whoosh, flames leapt to life and began licking at the artificial logs. Turning on the table lamp, he looked around his new digs.

It was a short tour, since the place had a single studio-style bedroom, a galley kitchen and a bathroom boasting an oversize shower, which all by itself made it worth twice the price he was paying. It would definitely do.

It had been a long day, however, and he was past ready for a little kick-back time. So he toed off his shoes and padded in his stocking feet to the kitchen, where he delved into the fridge Ava had stocked, grabbing the first thing he saw: the half gallon of milk. Opening it, he gulped down a quarter of it straight from the carton, then bent to study the rest of the refrigerator's contents.

She'd bought him chicken tenders, a skewer of grilled Alaska salmon, cut veggies and fruit, a tub of kalamata olives, a wedge of aged Beemster Gouda, salad fixings and a container of some New Agey–looking salad made of couscous or quinoa, or some such shit. But it was the container of deviled eggs he pulled out.

He wondered if she'd remembered how much he liked them or had just gotten some for everybody.

Probably the latter.

Taking the lid off, he tossed it on the counter, grabbed the carton of milk and took his booty over to the chair by the fireplace. He set the milk on the little table at his elbow, swung his feet up onto a footstool, fished out an egg half and popped it in his mouth.

"Damn." He didn't know if Ava had made these herself, gotten someone else to make them or picked them up at one of the upscale grocery stores that seemed to liberally sprinkle Seattle these days, but he had to hand it to her—they rocked.

So far, at least, she seemed to be good at her job.

Yet here it was, not even the first official day, and he already needed a break from her. That didn't bode well for the next month and a half.

When he first got the brainstorm to hire her, he'd considered himself fricking brilliant. It was a win-win: Ava was the choice most highly recommended and he could finally pay off the debt of his high school screwup, which until last November she'd refused to even let him apologize for. As an added benefit, she was providing the food services and seemed to have a strong knowledge of the town's players. All of which would save him money in the long run.

In that aspect, and given the quality of her work, he *was* brilliant. But he hadn't thought things through. He hadn't considered how being constantly thrown into contact with her would make him feel.

He'd forgotten how much he'd liked her back in the day before he'd thrown her to the wolves in order to keep a bunch of friends, who hadn't been worth what he'd sacrificed.

"Shit." Losing his appetite, he set the container of deviled eggs aside, dropped his feet from the stool and sat up. Jamming his fingers through his hair, he stared at the flickering flames.

Let it go, Slick. What was done was done, and going over it for the hundredth time sure wouldn't help him unwind after a day crammed with traveling and trying to get things organized. And hungry or not, he needed to fuel up. Tomorrow was the first full day on the set, and he needed to be on top of his game.

So he reached for another egg. He'd eat his food, drink his milk and just veg in front of the fire for a while. What he wouldn't do was obsess over old mistakes.

Especially not the one he'd made with Ava Spencer.

SLOW TO PULL her attention from the lists she was compiling when the landline at her elbow rang the following morning, Ava reached to pick up the receiver without bothering to check caller ID. She brought it to her ear and murmured an absentminded hello as she ran her gaze down the list she'd been assembling on her Grocery iQ app. Grey Poupon! *That* was what she'd forgotten—she'd known there was something.

She added it to her list.

"Ava, I need you to plan your father's birthday event."

Well, hell. That got her attention. Abandoning her iPhone on the breakfast bar, she straightened on her stool. "Hello, Mother. I thought you and Dad were still in Chicago."

"Yes, yes, we are." Impatience laced Jacqueline Spencer's tone. "Which is precisely the problem. We'll be here until early February—which allows me no time to arrange your father's birthday myself. So you need to do it."

Ava counted to ten. "Do you remember the documentary job I told you about?" She didn't hold out much hope, since usually the things that were important to her went out of her mother's ears as quickly as they'd gone in.

But Jacqueline surprised her. "The one with Allan Gallari's son?"

"Yes. I just started it yesterday and between that and some jobs for a few of my longtime clients, I'm afraid it's going to take up all my time for the next several weeks. But I can refer you to a fantastic local party planner I met at the conference in New York last summer."

"I don't want some second-rate caterer! This is your father's *sixtieth birthday* we're talking about, Ava."

Crap. The guilt card. No wonder parents played it so often—it was so freaking effective. Sighing, she picked up her iPhone again and opened a new app. "How many people?"

"I'm keeping it small. I thought seventy-five. At the house."

Small. Uh-huh. "On Dad's actual birthday?"

"Don't be silly, darling—how many people will turn out on a Wednesday night? Make it the following Saturday."

"Winter theme okay?"

"Yes, that would be lovely. And engraved invitations, of course, with the RSVP to you, no gifts. I'll get you the guest list."

Ava made a note to contact the calligrapher she used as soon as she had that in hand. "What do you have in mind for food? The guest list strikes me as too large for a sit-down unless you want me to rent a tent for the back lawn."

"Not in late February—the weather's too iffy for that."

"My thoughts exactly. Were you thinking circulating waiters with hors d'oeuvres? Or a buffet?"

"I thought an open bar and hearty hors d'oeuvres, served by, yes, the wait staff. Then a dessert buffet with, of course, a spectacular cake as its centerpiece. Tiered, not sheet. Champagne fountains at either end."

"I will need to hire one of my caterers, because I don't have time for that part and I know you want the best for Father's party."

A sigh came down the line, but her mother restrained herself to a stern, "I expect you to supervise them carefully."

"Uh-huh." Didn't she always? "An eight to midnight timeframe, then?"

"Yes."

"All right." She made note of that as well, added additional reminders for a few things she'd have to follow through on, then shut down her app. "That will get me started. I'll send you an email to confirm what we just talked about, but I need to hang up now, Mom, or I'm going to be late for my real job."

"Mother," Jacqueline Spencer corrected her automatically. "And really, dear, you're a businesswoman in high demand—must you sound as though you're off to flip hamburgers on the weekend shift?"

Ava laughed. "Sometimes I think that would be more relaxing."

"What am I to do with you?" Jacqueline said, and Ava could envision her mother shaking her head. "Well, I shall let you go, I suppose. But do keep an eye on the mail—I'm going to send you an appropriate dress to wear to your father's party."

Ava's smile dropped from her lips as ice rimed her veins. "I'm not twelve anymore. I can find my own dress, thank you."

"You'll like what I select," Jacqueline said serenely, ignoring, as she always did, Ava's wishes on the matter.

"No, Mom, I won't. You constantly buy me things that I don't have a prayer of fitting into and I never wear them. Save your money."

"You simply need to lose a few pounds and my money won't be wasted."

She tried counting to ten again but only got as far as six. "How I handle my weight is not your decision to make. I have curves. I'm always *going* to have curves and will never be rail-thin like you. Deal with it."

"I don't believe I like your tone, Ava."

"And I don't like being treated like an incompetent child."

"I don't do that!" Jacqueline sounded both shocked and affronted. A heartbeat of silence passed before she added stiffly, "I was merely trying to help."

God save me from your help, Ava thought in despair,

but only said, "I appreciate that. But I'm thirty-one years old. Allow me to dress myself."

The pleasantries they exchanged after that were few, awkward and doubtless left her mother feeling, as they did her, not so pleasant. It was a relief to finally ring off, and Ava carefully reseated the receiver in its stand on the kitchen counter.

All the while painfully aware that her first inclination was to hurl it across the kitchen.

God, she was tired of this. She knew her mother loved her, in her own self-absorbed way. But wouldn't it be nice, just once, to get through a conversation that didn't leave her achingly aware of the conditions Jacqueline placed upon that love? That didn't raise the issue of her damn weight?

Instead, their conversations generally left her feeling anywhere from vaguely to DEFCON Alert–level dissatisfied. Not to mention not all that great about herself.

She knew it was ridiculous—that only her opinion ought to count. It didn't change the fact that when she swiveled on her stool and caught a glimpse of herself in the sound-facing bank of windows that the interior lights and stormy weather darkness outside had turned into a mirror, she saw herself through her mother's eyes and thought, *Cow.* Didn't change that—

"*No,* dammit." She wasn't going down that road again. She had things to do—even *more* things, given the addition of her father's party, than she'd had fifteen minutes ago. She didn't have time for this inadequacy crap.

Turning back to the counter, she tossed her cell phone into her purse and plucked her black draped cardigan from the back of the stool to pull it on over her wrap-front beach-blue dress. She stepped into her heels and crossed to the closet for her coat.

Then, picking up her Kate Spade purse as she sailed past the tiny entry table, she let herself out of the condo and, bypassing the elevator, headed down the stairs to the parking garage.

SINCE AVA was the last person Cade wanted to see, naturally she was the first one he clapped eyes on when he let himself into the Wolcott kitchen. She was bent over a table she'd set up against the wall, putting what looked to be finishing touches on the spread she'd set out.

It looked like something out of a magazine—a considerable step up from the usual food services arrangement—and he wondered if he'd congratulated himself too soon regarding the anticipated money he'd save by having her take over the job.

It was a hard thought to hang on to, however, when her butt was bumping in tune with some bluesy, jazzy song about not treating a dog the way the singer thought a woman had treated him, which purled out of an MP3 player on the counter. She'd always been a kick-ass dancer—even back in their prepubescent days when they'd had to learn all that formal stuff in cotillion class. Nor had she ever been the least bit self-conscious about dancing down the hallway at Country Day.

Except for those last few weeks of their senior year.

He cleared his throat. "I didn't realize you were here. I didn't see your Beemer in the drive."

Her hips ceased swiveling as she looked at him over her shoulder. "I drove a client's car today."

"The Audi A6?"

"Yes. I'm taking it to be detailed on my lunch hour."

"You're working other jobs?"

"On my own time, yes." Turning slowly to face him, she crossed her arms beneath her breasts, plumping up the creamy cleavage in her blue V-neck dress from what had been a mere hint to an impressive flash of the real deal. "You didn't seriously expect me to blow off my clients who've been with me through the good times and lean for six weeks of working for you, did you?"

Yeah, he supposed he had. But when she put it that way...

Kyle walked into the kitchen before he could respond, which was probably just as well. The soundman gave Ava's cleavage an appreciative glance. But even before her arms dropped to her sides, restoring the generous swell back to its original hint, his focus had switched to the food she'd laid out. His brows furrowing as he crossed the room to pour himself a cup of coffee from the industrial coffeemaker at the end of the table, he scrutinized the offerings.

And turned accusing eyes on her. "No bear claws?" he demanded.

"Sorry, no." Ava picked up a plate and grabbed a pair of tongs that she left suspended above a plate of long rectangles of lightly sugared pastries as she glanced over at Kyle. "Try a galette. Are you an apple or a blackberry man?"

"Blackberry, I guess." He watched suspiciously as she scooped the pastry onto a plate. "That looks like one of those girly tea-party desserts."

She grinned at him, her dimples punching deep. "Just try it. If you don't like it, I'll get you some bear claws when I go out this afternoon."

"Yeah, okay," he grumbled and took a bite. He swore as several blackberries tumbled from the pastry back onto his plate, but chewed and swallowed the portion that had made it into his mouth, licked a crystal of sugar from his lip, then met her gaze. And smiled sheepishly.

"Damn." He took another bite and said around it, "That's better than an orgasm."

Ava laughed. "Or almost, anyway."

It was all Cade could do to bite back a growl. But enough with the sex talk, already!

"Hey, I smell coffee!" Beks burst into the room, then went on point like a German shorthair spotting a pheasant. "Food! Wow, look at that!" She flashed a smile at Ava. "You've got some seriously mad skills, girl."

"Try the galette," Kyle said around another mouthful. "It's even better than bear claws."

"Shut the front door!" Beks gawked at him. "I thought you didn't think anything was better than bear claws. This I gotta taste for myself. And ooh, God, lookit this fruit! *Seriously* mad skills, I'm telling ya."

The next thing Cade knew, all of his team who'd shown up this morning were swarming the food table, making a huge dent in Ava's arrangement. And she just laughed while they did, refilling coffee cups and urging them to try this, that or the other treat. Apparently she got off big-time on seeing to it that everyone was fed.

He waded in to grab a few things for himself before the locusts formerly known as his crew reduced it to crumbs, a few apple cores and orange peels.

But when he told them a few minutes later that it was time to get to work, the swarm reverted to the professionals he knew and cleared out to get back to their various tasks.

AFTER EVERYONE LEFT, Ava happily puttered around the kitchen, clearing up the dishes and coffee cups, replenishing the fruit tray and bringing out a vegetable platter to place beside it, along with a bowl of dip she would refrain from telling Kyle had a yogurt base.

She made a trip out to Mrs. Hoffert's Audi and retrieved the plastic crate that cradled her big Crock-Pot, which she had transferred from her own car earlier. She had slow cooked a tortellini soup overnight, and she brought it into the kitchen, plugged it in and turned it on to warm. She put out spoons and a stack of bowls next to the pot. Then, pouring herself a cup of coffee, she sat down and went over this morning's offerings, checking each item and making adjustments to the amounts she'd need to buy for tomorrow.

She also made some notes on ideas she had for switching things up so the crew didn't get bored the next few weeks.

This was her element. She loved seeing a need and filling it. She liked feeding people, liked doing what it took to make their day-to-day lives easier. It was what she was good at.

It was purely a bonus that performing those functions made it easier for her to ignore Cade.

The back door banged open, making her jump. Cold, damp air gusted into the room, and a lean man in a black watch cap and parka blew in along with it. He probably only topped off around five-eight or so, and taken feature by feature should have been average-looking. But his spectacular aqua-blue eyes and the overall way all those features were put together added up to an attractive package.

At a glance, Ava would say he knew it, too, for he grinned, said, "Hey ya, beautiful," and nodded at the alarm box keypad. "What's the code?"

"Considering I don't have a clue who you are, I'm not inclined to tell you that," Ava responded calmly, keeping to herself that the alarm wasn't armed at the moment, since one of the discussions Cade's crew had had while eating her food was that between all the comings, goings and equipment deliveries throughout the day, it would be a major pain to have to constantly set and reset the alarm.

Obviously figuring for himself that it was turned off, the man crossed the room to her. "Anthony Phillips," he said by way of introduction. "But everyone calls me Tony. I was hired as security for Scorched Earth Productions."

Ava raised a brow at him. "I was under the impression that was John."

"Whoa. Suspicious much? He's night security. I'm the day watchman."

She rose and went to the archway to stick her head out into the hall. Power cords and cables snaked the normally pristine hardwood floor, and for a second she merely blinked at them. Then she collected herself. "Beks!"

"Yeah?"

"Your day security guy is here."

"Thanks, Ava. I'll be down in a sec to get him."

She turned back to catch Call-me-Tony eyeing her butt. "Have a seat. Or coffee's over there if you'd like a cup."

"Thanks, doll, a cup of Joe would be nice."

"You and I will get along a great deal better if you don't call me doll."

"Right. Got it, doll—uh, Miss."

"I'm Ava."

His big flashy smile returning, he stepped forward and stuck out his hand. "Nice to meet you, Ava."

Beks came in and crossed to Tony. "You Anthony Phillips?"

"That I am," he agreed. "But *you* can call me Tony."

Ava conceded his flirtatious charm might not be premeditated. It was possible he was just one of those guys who couldn't help themselves.

In any event, Beks wasn't charmed. "I'm the PA and the coordinator," she said, all business, and introduced herself. "Follow me." She turned on her chunky heel, clearly expecting him to do as she directed and asking as they exited the room, "You got your papers and ID?"

Ava watched them disappear, thinking how interesting it was to see Beks at work. The crew was going to be testing audio and lighting today, so she likely had a lot on her plate. It would be fun to be a fly on the younger woman's wall and observe more of her interaction with Mr. Charm in the midst of all that.

"Right," she murmured with a little laugh. "Like you've got so much time to be watching someone else work."

And shrugging, she went back to her own.

CHAPTER FOUR

*This is turning out to be a lot harder than I
thought it would be.*

THE MINUTE AVA got home that evening, she kicked off
her heels, washed off her makeup and changed into her
navy, white and orange Moroccan-tile-patterned sleep
pants, topping them with a cotton knit camisole and
cardigan. She made herself a quick bite to eat and was
seated in front of the fireplace with a glass of chardon-
nay a short while later, trying to decide if she wanted
to select a recorded program from her DVR to watch or
simply continue staring at the flames, when her doorbell rang.

She blew out a breath. "Crap." She was so not in the
mood for company.

But since she was currently in a dating slump, it was
likely Poppy or Jane, and adjusting her attitude, she set
aside her wineglass and rose to answer the door.

The last person she expected to see on the other side
was Cade, and for a second she could only gape at him.

"Whoa," he said, looking just as startled. Except that
didn't make sense. Not when, unlike her, he had known
perfectly well he was coming here.

Damn him, anyhow. Here she was all naked-faced,
not a spec of makeup to give her pale complexion a little

color or hide her freckles, while he, even under the hall-way's fluorescent fixture, looked like a million bucks, his eyes blazing brilliant blue in that lightly tanned, angular face. The harsh light also picked out the rain-drops spangling his hair and dampening the shoulders of his worn leather bomber jacket.

His expression smoothing out, he gave her a slow once-over and raised his eyebrows. "Modeling for Victoria's Secret in your spare time?"

She glanced down at her unfastened cardigan, which exposed the fact that she was naked beneath its match-ing light orange tank top. *Crap.* She pulled the car-digan's sides together to add another layer of fabric between his too-seeing eyes and her unbound breasts.

And made a rude noise even as she buttoned it. "Like I *have* free time. Aside from this half hour I was trying to snatch for myself, that is." She gave him a pointed look. "I'm off duty, Gallari. Why are you here?"

"I wanted to remind you that the makeup and hair people will be here day after tomorrow, as well as three of my interview subjects, so you'll have additional people to feed."

"I know. I talked to them about their transportation needs, remember? Which, since the hair and makeup women are local, were nonexistent. And I've arranged drivers for the interviewees." She waved a dismissive hand. "But that's neither here nor there. The real ques-tion is, you couldn't have *called* me about it?"

"I could have. Except I also need to talk to you about doing an interview for the documentary—and that's better done face-to-face."

"You want me to—?" Wondering if she looked as blank as she felt, she gave her head a little shake and admitted, "Okay, I'm clueless. Surely you have more qualified people to do whatever it is that needs doing."

"I don't need your help conducting interviews, Ava— I'm talking about you *giving* an interview."

"Like the three people you have lined up for tomorrow, you mean? You want to interview me? On *camera?*"

"Kinda hard to let people know your take on Agnes without it," he agreed with a slight smile. "I'd like Jane and Poppy's participation, as well."

There was no need to speculate about her expression this time—no doubt it was every bit as horrified as she felt. "No. *Hell,* no. Janie and Poppy might have a different take, but for my own FYI...*are you out of your mind?*"

"I prefer to think of it as doing my job. I have a thousand and one details that need my attention, and you and your gal pals are one of the biggies." He raked his hair off his forehead, leaving damp furrows in the wake of his fingers. "Look, do you think I could come in? This is important to the documentary, and I'd really appreciate a few minutes to explain why."

Her first inclination was to say no. She didn't want him in her place. And please, she was off the clock— did she really have to carry the professionalism she'd been so carefully maintaining into her personal time and space?

Only if you want to maintain a civil working relationship for the next month and a half, girlfriend. Damn. With a resigned sigh, she stepped back, opening the door wider. "Come in."

"Thanks." He stepped inside and shrugged out of his jacket as he followed her into the living room. When she didn't offer to take it off his hands, he slung it over the back of one of the breakfast bar stools they passed.

She was tempted to ignore the fact she had a glass of wine waiting for her while he did not, but she had already strained the manners that had been drummed into her since birth by willfully ignoring his coat. With a genuine attempt not to sound as grudging as she felt, she said, "Would you like a cup of tea or a glass of wine or something?" She drew the line at coffee. She was *not* offering to make a pot for one cup.

"Water would be good."

"Have a seat and I'll get you some."

It only took her a minute to grab a bottle from the fridge and bring it out to where he stood in front of the fire. After handing it to him, she settled back into her seat on the couch.

Cade unscrewed the cap and chugged the water down in one throat-working, attenuated swallow. He set the empty bottle on a magazine on her coffee table, looked around, then dragged an armchair over to face her. Sitting, he planted his forearms on his thighs and leaned toward her.

"This production isn't just about the murder of Agnes Wolcott's man of affairs and the mystery surrounding the disappearance of the Wolcott Suite," he said, his eyes intent. "It's first and foremost the story of Agnes. I admit it started out primarily about the mystery, since that's what I've built my name doing. But once I started researching and realized how ahead of her time and larger than life she was, I widened the scope of the story. It was also her personality and accomplishments that sold it to the network."

He made an uncharacteristically awkward motion, as if to touch Ava's knee, but then pulled the hand that had started to reach out back again, letting it dangle between his spread knees. "It was you, though, who really got me fired up when you talked to me and Karin about Agnes when we met to discuss the script. Your enthusiasm brought her to life in a way she hadn't fully been before."

"Trust me," she said dryly, "nobody will be enthused when I turn out to be a big stiff in front of your camera." Her heart skipped a beat at the mere thought of having one trained on her.

Cade looked skeptical. "This from a woman who isn't the least bit shy about breaking into a dance whenever and wherever the mood hits her? I'm not asking you to strip naked in public, Ava. All you'll be doing is having a conversation with me, one-on-one."

"Yeah, that oughtta make me less self-conscious," she muttered. "Being on camera with the man who told the world I was a big fat joke."

He froze, his face losing all expression. Then he slowly straightened until his wide shoulders brushed the back of the seat. He met her gaze with a level one of his own.

"I have apologized and apologized for that, but I'll say it again. I'm sorry. I can't change what I did, but I am—swear-on-a-stack-of-bibles, strike-me-with-lightning-if-I'm-lying—sorry."

Then he leaned forward once more and planted his elbows on his knees. "Admit it, though, Ava—even then, even that day—you weren't intimidated by me. You know damn well you gave as good as you got. Hell, I was known for what was left of our senior year as Quick Draw."

She shrugged. "You came, you went."

"Yeah, I'm painfully aware of the fact. I'd apologize

for that as well, but I was eighteen frickin' years old and you had me hotter 'n a pistol. But, hey." His blue eyes glinted a second before his mouth quirked up in a self-deprecating smile. "If you want a do-over I'd be more than happy to demonstrate how much I've improved since then."

Her stomach hollowed. Assuring herself she'd simply eaten too fast, she said coolly, "What a generous offer. Thank you, but I'll pass." And yet… *You had me hotter 'n a pistol?* His friend Dylan-the-asshole had made sleeping with her sound more like an onerous chore than an act of unbridled lust.

Before she could figure out if Cade really meant it, however, or if he was simply saying what he thought she wanted to hear now in an attempt to get his own way, he gave an indifferent shrug and returned to the original subject.

"Look, I know you may not like me, but you can take one thing to the bank—I am dead serious about making Agnes's story the best damn representation of her that I can."

"Then I'll say it again," she promptly retorted. "Putting me on camera won't aid your project."

"I've heard you talk about her, Ava, and you obviously loved her. Then there's the fact that I've seen you and your friends together. As a unit you're invincible and you know it. Once the three of you get going on Miss Agnes, as you called her with me and Karin that day, you won't even remember the camera is there. Hell, you likely won't need me to guide the conversation at all. Not to mention all three of you are probably photogenic as all get out." He seemed to look inward for a moment. "The trick is gonna be sound. It's always more difficult when you have more than two subjects." Then he shook his head. "But that's why we have Kyle—he's the best sound mixer I've ever worked with."

Eyes sober, he leaned deeper into her space. "Tell you what, I'll make you a deal that I never make with my subjects. If you don't like the way I capture you, I'll edit you out entirely. I strongly believe that by doing so I'll be doing your Miss Agnes an injustice, but you have my word that I'll bite the bullet and do it anyway. I'll put it in writing," he added quickly before it even occurred to her to make a snide remark about his word. "You have an opportunity here, though, Ava—a chance to round out Agnes's story by telling the world about a woman who had an impact on your life. In any good documentary, it's the personal knowledge of a film's subject, the anecdotes the people who knew her tell, that in the end add the texture and richness to that subject's story."

"Why have a scriptwriter at all, then, if you think unscripted reminiscences add so much?"

"I'm approaching this project like a feature. There are a lot of very visual aspects to Miss Agnes's life and I have a budget like I've never had before. So I'm shooting the interviews in HD, but shooting the re-creations with the actors on film to give that lusher look of an earlier era. It will give her story a larger, richer look." Slowly he straightened back into his chair and for a moment simply looked at her. "I hope you'll agree to be part of it. But even if you don't, would you give me your friends' numbers so I can see about getting their input? I want to capture the woman who befriended three girls not just for a single tea at her mansion, but for years' worth of teas and other important landmarks in their lives."

Ava knew he was right, that he was offering her an

unprecedented opportunity. She hated to admit, even to herself, that a big part of what was holding her back was the knowledge of how that bugger-all camera would add ten pounds. God, how shallow could she get? She'd rarely even thought about Cade during the past decade and now she was worried about what he'd think when he saw her on film or digitized or whatever? What the hell was *that* all about?

"I'll do it," she said before her vanity could sink its claws even deeper.

"You'll give me their numbers?"

"I'll participate in your documentary. It would probably be best if I called Jane and Poppy, myself. They're not exactly your biggest fans."

His mouth crooked. "You don't have to pretty it up. You can say they hate my guts."

"They hate your guts. But they loved Miss Agnes, so even if the request came from you they'd likely do it for her. But it'll probably fly better coming from me."

"Thank you."

She rose to her feet. "You do understand I'm not doing this for you, right?"

"Oh, yeah. I get that." He, too, stood up. "But thanks, anyway. When I was researching Miss Agnes, she struck me as a woman who was not only fascinating, but unique. I'm happy for every opportunity to showcase as many facets of her character as I can fit into ninety-nine minutes."

"I'm starting to believe that." She plucked his coat off the back of the stool and held it out to him. "It's the only reason I've agreed to do this."

"Yeah." He shot her a crooked grin. "I figured it wasn't for my dazzling smile."

It could have been, Ava thought.

Once upon a time, before he'd wrecked everything, it really could have been.

CHAPTER FIVE

I thought I knew everything about Miss A. But I'm learning all sorts of new things.

AVA MADE HER WAY through the mansion's crowded salon to the silver-haired gentleman whose interview Cade had just wrapped up. Beks had passed along a request from Cade earlier to hold herself ready to escort the finished interviewee out of the room so they could get the next interview rolling without delay. Or as the younger woman had put it with her infectious smile: "I'll haul 'em in, you haul 'em out."

She'd snatched the opportunity to watch the shoot from an inconspicuous vantage point at the side of the room, hoping to get a feel for what she, Jane and Poppy could expect when it was their turn. Her attention had drifted from the interviewee to Cade way too often, but as she approached the two men, she did her best to ignore his half of the duo.

"Mr. Tarrof?" She brushed the man's gray tweed jacket sleeve to get his attention. "I apologize for interrupting, but—"

Both men turned to her. The older man was nattily attired in a beautifully tailored suit, gray shirt and a yellow tie that matched the impeccably folded handkerchief peeking out of his coat's breast pocket.

Cade, by contrast, was casual in a royal-blue sweater he'd no doubt chosen to match his eyes and a pair of jeans almost disreputably worn. "This is Ava," he said with a smile that included them both. "She'll be your guide navigating the land mines out of the room."

To her, he said, "I was just thanking Stan for his awesome interview," then turned the full power of his attention back on the older gentleman. "And I can't do that enough. You gave me some seriously good footage. So, again, thank—"

A sudden bump from behind sent Ava stumbling. She felt Mr. Tarrof reach out to steady her, but his cool, dry hand slid off her forearm without finding purchase. It was Cade, taking a long-legged step toward her, who stopped her forward momentum.

But it wasn't a pretty landing. She smacked up against the hard wall of his chest, and the impact flattened her breasts and knocked the breath from her lungs.

The lack of oxygen wasn't the worst of it, though. *That* would be the instant heat, instant awareness. Like déjà vu, it was eerily familiar. Yet the body she was pressed up against was different—bigger now than it had once been, harder and tougher.

Shit! Sucking in a breath to replace the air she'd lost, she leapt back, and Cade's hands, which had grasped a hip and her shoulder, dropped to his sides.

"God, Miss—Ava—I'm sorry," a man said from behind her, and Ava turned to see the grip named Collin with a long stepladder in his hands. He set it up a short way from the "set" they were using for the interviews. "I was trying to dodge Ryan and I misjudged. Are you all right?"

No. "Yes, sure. I'm fine." *Except for this shook-up, out-of-control feeling.*

The thought snapped her spine erect. Because that was just plain dumb, considering her history with Gallari.

Cade cleared his throat, and, beginning to feel like a wind-up doll turning this way and that, she jerked around once again.

"See what I mean about land mines?" he was saying to Mr. Tarrof, then to her added, "I'm putting Stan in your hands, so give him your best."

"I always do," she agreed, curving her lips up without actually meeting his gaze. Yet she was conscious of his tanned forearms with their dusting of dark hair below his pushed-up sleeves. Aware that her hands could still feel the cashmere softness of the sweater they'd gripped. Turning to the older man, she cleared her mind of everything but him. And gave him a real smile.

"I can see why Cade was so pleased," she said as she led him away, pointing out various cables snaking across the floor for him to avoid. "I had the chance to see most of your interview and you were fabulous."

"Well, I don't know if I'd go that far," he said with a half pleased, half rueful smile. "I'm mostly just glad it's over. I was a bit nervous."

"I hear that. My friends and I are scheduled for the day after tomorrow and my stomach keeps doing flip-flops at the thought of having a camera recording my every mistake." She flashed him another smile. "If it helps, though, your nerves didn't show. You came across as very natural."

Putting out a staying hand, she avoided a collision between them and the best boy Ryan as he rushed by— and made a note to have a word with the gaffer about the kid's need to be more aware of the people around him, since they had just narrowly avoided what would have been two accidents within as many minutes.

"I did notice, though," she said as they continued on, "that you didn't eat beforehand. How about a cup of coffee or tea or maybe a soft drink? And I still have some fabulous pastries. They're a huge hit with the crew, but I managed to squirrel some away so the rest of us might have a shot at enjoying them."

He gave her an appreciative smile. "That would be nice. Thank you. My appetite's returned now that I've got the interview behind me."

She laughed, knowing exactly how that went, and guided the older gentleman around Collin, who was now moving a light under Jim Short's direction. Once they'd steered through the beehive of activity and made their way out to the hallway, it took only seconds to reach the kitchen.

She waved at the service table. "Help yourself to whatever appeals to you. I'll just get some of those pastries I told you about."

Mr. Tarrof poured himself a cup of coffee and lifted the Crock-Pot lid to Ava's soup of the day, releasing taco-scented steam into the air. He glanced over to where she was arranging pastries on a platter a little way down the table, the bunch of grapes he'd just picked up suspended over the fruit platter. "Do you mind if I ask how you knew Agnes?" He gave her a smile and transferred the grapes to a small plate, next to a few cubes of cheese. "You're much too young to have run with her crowd."

"Miss Agnes befriended me and my two best friends back when we were only twelve." Her lips curved up at the flood of fond memories. "From our first encounter, she was always there for both our achievements and our failures." She brought the plate of pastries over. "Here, try one of these."

Comprehension dawned in his faded blue eyes as he stared at her. "You're one of those young women she left her estate to."

Ava slid one of the galettes that were so popular with the crew onto his plate, removed the dish from his hands and put everything on a tray. "I am, yes." She led him over to the small grouping of tables she had arranged near the door to the pantry.

"Well, I'll be damned," he said, following her. "The kitchen of a documentary shoot isn't exactly where I'd expect a Wolcott heiress to be working."

Ava placed his tray on a table, pulled out a chair and waved him into it with a pleasantly bland smile. He wasn't the first to think what she did for a living was beneath her station in life.

That honor went to her mother.

Tarrof made a face as he slid into the seat, obviously realizing he hadn't been very diplomatic. "I'm sorry, Miss, that was tactless. I meant no offense."

"None taken." She deftly removed his items from the tray and arranged them in front of him. Tucking the tray beneath her arm, she winked at him. "I suppose I could say I'm here to keep an eye on my property, but the truth is I'm a personal concierge—which is a fancy title for a jack-of-all-trades. Today I'm providing escort and the hospitality service for Scorched Earth Productions. Tomorrow?" She shrugged. "I might walk someone's dog or arrange a ski trip for a party of twelve. It isn't everyone's cup of tea, but I find it immensely rewarding."

He studied her closely. "I've heard of you," he said

slowly. "I didn't put it together before, but you're Ava...
ah, Ava..." His brow, which had furrowed in concentration, suddenly cleared, and he snapped his fingers.
"Spencer, right? Donald and Jacqueline's girl?" Picking up his coffee, he wrapped both hands around it and
gazed up at her. "You're Mitzy Kemper's gem."

She laughed aloud. "Is that what she calls me? She's
such a sweetheart."

"Small world." He took a bite of the pastry, swallowed and said, "Wow. You're right. This is great." He
gave her an appreciative smile. "I might have to avail
myself of your services myself. Do you have a card?"

"I do. Let me just grab one for you." Going into the
pantry where she kept her purse, she fetched a card from
her case and took a moment to record a quick reminder
on her phone to bring additional ones tomorrow, as well
as a holder to display them in.

Hey, a girl had to take advantage of whatever promotional opportunities came her way.

She handed Tarrof the card a moment later, then went
to pour herself a cup of coffee. Rejoining him, she immediately went back to the subject on her mind. "About
your interview. Do you mind if I pick your brain?"

"Not at all. It's not every day an attractive young
woman solicits advice from an old duffer like me."

She made a scoffing noise. "Old duffer, my ass...
terisk. I bet you have to beat the ladies off with a stick."

They grinned at each other, but Ava's slowly faded.
"I'm anxious about my interview and was wondering...
you indicated you were nervous about yours as well, yet
you came off sounding genuine and relaxed. How did
you manage that? You honestly looked as if you could
have talked for hours. And you did it all before breakfast."

"Oh, from your lips—but I thank you for the compliment. I think it was actually due to Mr. Gallari's interviewing technique." He essayed a wry facial shrug. "During the preinterview on the phone, I kept trying to get him to give me a list of the questions he'd be asking so I could practice a little. I didn't want to come across as an idiot."

She nodded fervently. "I *so* get that desire." And the last person she wanted to sound foolish in front of was Cade Gallari. "Is that what I should be doing, then? Asking Cade for questions I can put some thought into before I have to answer them on camera?"

"Unfortunately, no. He was pretty firm about not wanting rehearsed answers. I don't mind admitting that wasn't what I wanted to hear, but as it happens he's quite easy to talk to. He has a way of making you feel as if he finds everything you say of vital interest."

Ava nodded. "It did look like he has an easy style." She had watched Cade pull his chair close to Mr. Tarrof's the way he had done at her condo the other night— and had wondered at first if the mannerism was simply a well-practiced all-purpose gambit that he'd discovered worked for him.

And yet...

If it were contrived, he was certainly one world-class actor and could probably make serious money facing the camera rather than working behind it. As reluctant as she was to think anything nice about the guy, she couldn't deny that he'd appeared genuinely fascinated by what Stan Tarrof had to say.

"I must say," the old gent went on, "in the end he asked me about the very things we had discussed. So it turned out to be much less stressful than I'd anticipated."

"Well, rats." With a sigh, she climbed to her feet. "I

guess there's no secret handshake or magic bullet, then. I'll simply have to muddle through somehow." She gave Tarrof an appreciative smile. "I can only hope I come across a fraction as interesting as you did."

CADE DIDN'T GET right back in the groove of things after he heard Ava laugh that deep belly laugh that managed to grab him by the short hairs every time. Beks ushered in the next interviewee, yet instead of putting the woman at ease while Kyle fitted her with a lavalier microphone, the way he normally would, he found his mind wandering.

That laugh was never directed at him. He shouldn't give a damn—yet for some reason he did. Why, he didn't know. It wasn't as if he'd pined for her for these past however many years.

So wouldn't you think the truth of that might have kept him from damn near groaning aloud when she'd slapped up against him and he'd felt her lush roundness shifting to accommodate his harder planes, when the heat that emanated from her in waves had sunk straight into his muscle memory, his *bones?*

On the other hand, what red-blooded, hetero guy *wouldn't* have had the same reaction? This was a woman who had it all, with her creamy skin that didn't need a goddamn thing except the dusting of cinnamon freckles that came stock, her vibrant hair and dimples, her knock-your-socks-off individualistic style.

And that *body.* Jesus. That body.

The truth was, even back in the day when he'd been a popular member of the in crowd and she'd been a denizen of the invisible fringe, he'd always had a sneaking fondness for Ava and her attitude, had always looked at her and seen *woman* in the ripeness of her breasts and ass, in the way she moved, even when she carried extra weight. Yet he hadn't hesitated to throw her under the bus anyhow. So, yeah, in all likelihood what he was feeling here was a little residual guilt.

She was sure as hell nobody's victim, though. She'd hit back hard when he'd sacrificed her back when, then had gone on to hone herself into a fucking *goddess*.

If there was one lesson he'd had drummed into his head, however, it was that the only person he could depend on was himself. God knew Ava was never going to be in his corner. So why the hell was he allowing himself to be bugged by a little thing like a laugh that wasn't intended for him?

Gritting his teeth, he manipulated his head to stretch the kinks out of his neck. He *wasn't,* dammit. And it didn't bug him. He was just having a nostalgic moment, that was all. Give him a minute and it would pass.

They always did.

Turning to the woman whose dress Beks was currently making immaculate with her lint roller, he signaled the cameraman to start shooting.

"So, Mrs. Sandor," he said warmly, taking his seat, scooting his chair forward and focusing on her. Putting everything else from his mind, he prepared to go mining for the thrill he got with each and every new interview, that gratification of discovering people's stories and helping to bring them to life. "When we talked on the phone, you told me that you and Agnes Wolcott would have been debutantes together in 1946—if she hadn't refused to participate. Could you tell me a little more about that?"

TONY PHILLIPS, the day security guard, looked around the upstairs hallway and, seeing the coast was clear,

headed to the sitting room of Agnes Wolcott's bedroom
suite. His nerve endings buzzing with anticipation, he
could almost feel the eager rush of the blood through
his veins. So what if it wasn't the long con he was more
familiar with?

According to Uncle Mike, this was something a
helluva lot better: a one-way ticket to Easy Street.

Tony shrugged. He didn't know about that, but at
least he had the upstairs to himself. Which didn't mean
he was gonna go get cocky. Getting *into* the room was
the easy part. It was getting back out again with the
Wolcott jewels in his pocket that was uncertain. But if
he could pull it off, if he could really get his hands on
the old lady's long lost diamonds, then a huge-ass ticket
was exactly what the old man's information would turn
out to be. And all he'd have left to do was stay cool for
a few short hours until John the night guy showed up
to relieve him.

Knowing that, knowing that once he had those spar-
klers and could blow this pop stand, that he could just
keep on trucking and never look back…well, that made
him feel…it made him feel so—

Day-umn.

Like he could start planning for a life of leisure on an
as-yet-to-be-determined tropical beach. So what were
a couple of hours compared to that?

As soon he entered the sitting room, however, all his
pretty fantasies went up in smoke. Standing as though
someone had superglued his shoes to the highly pol-
ished, long-plank fir floor, unable to step forward or
back, he stared in dismay at the wall to his left. "Son
of a bitch."

He should have known it was too good to be true.
But he had cut his eyeteeth on the legend of Mike

Maperton's coup back in the eighties. He had grown up hearing about how his uncle had copped the suite of Wolcott diamonds and set in motion an urban legend so fricking juicy it was still widely known to this day.

Hell, it was the goddamn basis for the documentary all those marks downstairs were busy getting underway.

As much as he'd like to bring the old man back to life just for the satisfaction of killing him again, he had to give Mike his props. The bastard had taken brilliant advantage of the whims of fortune that had dropped—bing/bam/boom—in his lap back in '85.

First, while heading up the renovation here and in the adjoining bedroom, the man had stumbled across a secret compartment. Although he claimed he'd considered doing what unimaginative people liked to call "the right thing," and actually report his discovery to the Wolcott broad, that very evening Agnes Wolcott had changed history forever when she'd gone and left a diamond necklace, bracelet, earrings and hair clips out on her night table instead of stashing them in her safe like she always did when she came home from an event.

Clearly she'd been *looking* to get fleeced. Mike had simply obliged her by stashing the jewels in the new-found hidey-hole.

Then—and this was the part Tony loved—the old dude had tracked her down to tell her he'd seen them when he'd gone in to take some measurements and warn her she should put them away before something happened to them. In the wake of discovering them missing, everyone's belongings, including Mike's, had been searched before they were allowed to leave. Yet he had been the *only* one who hadn't been a serious suspect.

Tony couldn't help but chortle to himself. Because, please, that was seriously funny. The Mikester being such an honest guy and all.

Too bad his uncle's luck had run dry when he'd gone back to retrieve the jewelry he'd concealed. It should have been a cakewalk. It wasn't as if the old guy hadn't been überpatient—hell, he'd waited more than six months for the place to be empty. Miz Wolcott and her man of business, Henry Somebody-or-Another, were supposed to have been on a trip to Europe.

No one had ever really explained to Tony's satisfaction *why* good old Henry hadn't been in Europe with Agnes Wolcott. All he knew was that when his uncle had come face-to-face with the man he had believed to be safely halfway around the world, he'd panicked, shot first and asked questions later. The reflexive action might have worked in Mike's favor—had he actually killed Henry outright. But he hadn't, and that failure had landed him in the state pen at Walla Walla when the butler dude had managed to cling to life long enough to finger him.

To Tony's family's eternal dismay during the near-quarter of a century since, Uncle Mike had remained stubbornly mum about where he'd hidden the loot. Then, out of the blue, the old man had summoned Tony to his side at the penitentiary, said he didn't have long to live and told Tony exactly where he could find the to-this-day-never-recovered Wolcott diamonds. Behind the fancy carved part of the north wall in the room attached to the old lady's bood-wah, he'd said.

Fat lot of good *that* information did him. Tony stared in disgust at the boudoir's sitting room. Because what Mike had neglected to add before croaking in the middle of their conversation, which had already been interrupted a dozen times by the old guy's lifelong four-pack-a-day-habit's wet, hacking cough, was that the entire fucking *wall* was ornately carved. Or half of it was, anyway. It was that whatayacallit stuff—wainscoting.

Finally getting his feet to move, he crossed the room and inspected the floor-to-midwall carvings.

And heaved a sigh. He was going to be here for a while.

Well, what the hell, he was a confidence man by trade. His own usually consisted of bilking women out of their cash, but a con was a con. He sure as shit hadn't gotten this far just to throw in the towel at the first setback. Not when the potential payoff made his previous takes look like peanuts in comparison. He was the only person alive who knew the diamonds were still here in the freaking house after all these years. That shooting the Henry guy had panicked Mike into running before he could retrieve them.

And that was just too delicious to walk away from.

So squatting in front of the farthermost bottom corner, he started palpating the ridges and swirls of the rich, carved fir. He had no idea if he was warm, hot or cold.

But a guy had to start somewhere.

CHAPTER SIX

Maybe—and I'm only saying maybe—Cade's not all bastard, all the time.

GESTURING at her black dress, Jane stormed into Miss Agnes's bedroom where Ava and Poppy were getting their makeup and hair done. "I don't see why I can't just wear this."

Looking over from the chair where she sat draped in a voluminous silver cape, Ava watched Jane stomp across the room to the closet and rattle through the dresses she'd brought from home. As she watched, the disgruntled brunette selected one and yanked it, hanger and all, from the rod, holding the sheath out to inspect.

Ava smiled, because nerves affected everyone differently. In her case, it was a jittery stomach from an iron-clad conviction she was about to come across as plump and stupid on Miss A's documentary. "I did warn you not to bring anything black, Janie," she reminded her friend gently.

"Which pretty much wipes out three-quarters of her wardrobe," Poppy said dryly with a nod at Jane's current selection.

Tossing the blonde a sullen look, Jane stuffed the sheath back on the rod.

Ava gave Poppy—who probably didn't suffer from

nerves—a wry smile even as she said, "Sorry, I guess I should have shared the reason behind the No-Black rule. They're gonna seat us on that old black-and-gold tapestry settee-and-chair arrangement you always liked so much, and apparently dark clothing will just make us disappear into it."

Jane's face got an arrested in-*that*-case look and, reading her like a book, Ava hurriedly added, "No whites or beiges, either, babe. I'm told those will wash us out."

"Shit," Jane muttered.

Ava gave her a baffled look. "I don't get it. You know this kind of stuff—it's exactly the sort of thing you take into consideration when you put together your exhibits at the Met. So why are you being such a baby about it?"

Jane mumbled something.

"Speak up, girlfriend. I didn't catch that."

"I'm just more comfortable in black, okay?"

"Yet you look so pretty in colors. But yeah, I totally get the comfort level thing." Jane's folks were flamboyant actors, and her mother's penchant for screaming colors had long ago driven Jane to adopt the opposite end of the spectrum. It had only been since falling for Devlin—and especially since marrying him—that color had begun creeping into her wardrobe.

"Try the sage one Dev bought you," Poppy suggested. "Or better yet, that beautiful sapphire one that matches your baby blues. Just look how well Av's green-to-bring-out-my-eyes works for her." Then a wry smile ticked up the corners of her lips. "Or *recall* how, I guess I should say, since Molly's got her covered from stem to stern."

"We don't want powder all over her beautiful dress,"

Molly said as she worked makeup into Ava's T-zone with small circular strokes. "But you're right. She totally rocks green—and I'm about to make her eye color pop even more." Setting the powder brush down, she selected an eye shadow brush and a subtle lavender shadow.

"Close 'em," she directed, and the instant Ava lowered her lids, the makeup artist brushed color from her lash line to just above the crease of her right eye. She repeated the process on the left eyelid.

When Ava heard the soft clicking sound of Molly trading brushes, she cracked open her eyes. A new eye shadow brush shimmered with the palest of pinks, and the makeup woman swept its soft bristles along her brow bones below the arches of her eyebrows.

Poppy caught Ava's gaze from across the space separating them as Molly traded the lavender shadow for a darker plum and grabbed yet another brush for lining and accentuating the creases of her eyes. "How about you, Av?" she inquired. "How are you doing, nerve-wise?"

"I subscribe to the Jane Kavanagh school of being on camera. I've got some serious stage fright going."

"You, too?" Jane demanded, pulling the blue dress on over her head. "Bless you, that makes me feel better." She grimaced as the fabric cleared her face. "Not that I want you to be nervous. It's just nice to not be the only one." She jerked a thumb at Poppy. "You know *she's* not."

"What's to be nervous about?" their friend demanded. "We're here to talk about Miss A—there is no downside to this. But I know what will help Ava relax, at least, and likely give you a smile, too. That's good enough," she said in an aside to the woman fussing with her wild curls and climbed out of the chair. "There's not a whole lot you can do with this mop."

"There's nothing I can do for any of you," the woman muttered. "You and Ms. Kavanagh don't want any changes to your styles, and Ms. Spencer has a two hundred dollar haircut that needs no help from me."

"So you get an hour off." Poppy shrugged. "I'd bask in it, if I were you."

"Well, you're not," the stylist snapped. "I'm an artist. I don't bask."

"Alrighty then," Poppy said cheerfully, glancing around the room. A moment later she turned back to the hairdresser. "You guys have any music around here?"

The stylist shrugged, but Molly said, "Beks will know," and pulled her cell phone out of her smock pocket. She hit a few buttons, talked into the device for a moment, then disconnected and returned it to her pocket. "She'll be up in a second."

Poppy flashed a big smile. "Now, *you* are helpful, girl. Thank you."

"I hear you're looking for music," Beks said as she breezed into the room a few minutes later, decked out in a tight black girl-T, a short, swingy skull-decorated skirt and black lace fingerless gloves. She headed to the dresser to set up a laptop. "I've pulled up my iTunes. I'm not sure if my taste will do it for you, but you're more than welcome to check it out."

Poppy joined her and bent to study the selections, then gave Beks a quick grin. "You've got an interesting collection for a Goth girl."

Beks shrugged good-naturedly. "My mama raised me to embrace all music."

"What a coincidence, so did mine. You mind if I

make a playlist? Ava's feeling nervous about being on camera and we need some dance music to distract her."

Ava snapped upright in her seat. "This is where I work, Poppy—I'm not gonna dance here!"

Poppy gave her a *yeah, right* look. "Yes, you will."

"She will," Jane agreed.

Poppy shot Beks a conspiratorial smile and gave her a friendly bump of the hip. "She won't be able to help herself. She hears anything with a good beat, she's gotta dance. It's a conditioned response."

"Kind of like Pavlov's dogs," Jane agreed.

"Oh, for God's sake." Ava rolled her eyes.

Beks laughed. "I'd definitely put this one on your playlist, then. And maybe this," she added, pointing out another, then turned to Ava when Poppy nudged her aside to pore over the music for herself. "Why on earth would you be nervous?" she demanded. "I've said it before, girl, and I'll say it again, you were *built* for the camera. You are so gonna shine."

"That's really sweet of you to say, but being the focus of a movie is outside my comfort level."

"Oh, this one!" Poppy said. "Beks, you *are* an eclectic chick. I'll save it for—let's see. Yeah, after this."

Beks leaned over her shoulder to look. Raised a brow. "Really?"

"Oh, yeah. Trust me. This is her version of crack cocaine—she won't be able to resist."

Molly completed Ava's eye makeup with two coats of reddish-brown mascara, then applied an apricot blush to the apples of her cheeks, brushed a dusting of gold atop it and turned away to paw through a selection of lipsticks, stains and glosses. As Eve and Gwen Stefani's "Let Me Blow Ya Mind" purled out from the computer's speakers, she held out two colors. "What do you think? Nude Beach? Or Summer Rose? You've got those yummy full lips, so you can pull off neutral or dramatic."

"Let's go with the neutral."

"Nude Beach it is. We'll add a touch of drama with a tiny dot of gold gloss in the center of your lips."

By the time Molly whipped the cape away, Ava was beginning to sway in time to the music. The makeup woman traded wry smiles with Poppy but merely said, "Who's next?"

"Me," Jane said, coming over. "Av, you look amazing. I think Beks is right, you're going to totally shine on camera." Climbing onto the bar stool Ava had vacated, she smiled at Molly. "If you're even half the genius with me, it might cut my anxiety in half, too. So work your magic."

"Oh, please!" The hairstylist surged to her feet. "If the kumbaya, everyone's-just-wonderful-wonderful saccharine levels in here rise any higher I'm gonna go into a diabetic coma." She blew out a disgusted breath. "I'm going out for a smoke."

Ava watched her stride from the room, then turned to Molly. "Is she always this cheerful?"

The makeup woman made a face. "She was okay with Mr. Tarrof yesterday but a little rude to Mrs. Sandor when the old lady indicated she was uncomfortable with the way she was styling her hair."

"She the artist she claims to be?"

"She's good," Molly promptly agreed, then shrugged. "But I know several stylists who are just as good if not better, *and* they've got better people skills. There's one in particular who's brilliant. She has a knack for listening to what people want instead of pushing her own agenda on them, so everyone winds up pleased by the time she's finished."

Ava turned to look at Beks and raised a brow. "You thinking what I'm thinking?"

"Yeah. Cade's whole deal is for the people who make this documentary possible to leave here with a positive experience." She turned to Molly. "I imagine the brilliant listener is probably booked solid, huh?"

"Actually, she's on maternity leave—and bored. You want me to call her?"

"Yes."

"I should warn you, she's seriously preggers. But she's not due for like another six weeks, so I doubt she's gonna go into labor in the middle of a session or anything."

Beks grinned. "If you don't mind giving me her number and lending your name as a reference, I'll call her myself. It's easier to lay out the terms of our offer without having to go through a middleman."

"Not a problem." Molly pulled out her cell phone again. As she relayed the number, the music changed to an Al Green song.

Several bars into the tune, Beks suddenly snapped around to look at Ava.

"Omigawd." She laughed out loud. "Do your friends know you or what? Poppy said this would be your crack cocaine."

A half smile curving her lips, Ava shrugged as she swiveled her hips and moved her arms, her shoulders, to the insistent beat. As long as she could remember, she'd heard certain songs and just *had* to move to their siren rhythms.

"What can I tell ya?" Arms overhead, she bumped

her hips left, right, left, her head turning side to side in sync. "Who can hear 'Love and Happiness' and *not* dance?"

CADE STEPPED BACK from seating Ava and her friends on the little grouping of antique furniture he'd had Collin arrange in front of the fireplace in the formal living room and making them comfortable. Ava and Jane were obviously struggling with some apprehension over being on camera, but even anxious, the three women shared a connection that made their interactions electric to the casual observer. They had for as long as he'd known them, and it clearly hadn't lessened any.

He wondered for an instant what it would feel like to have that sort of bond with someone. The *famiglia* Gallari hadn't exactly been warm and fuzzy—for a damn good reason, he'd discovered toward the end of his senior year in high school.

He shook the unbidden memory—and the depressing feelings it dredged up—aside. *Was a long time ago, in a galaxy far, far away, Obi-Wan,* he reminded himself dryly and focused on the issue at hand. Given the infectious enthusiasm Ava had already demonstrated for Agnes Wolcott, he didn't doubt for a minute that both she and her brunette friend would shake off their nerves once they got started sharing reminiscences.

Then there was the visual impact, which he could see on the large monitor the grip had set up near him was going to be huge. After Louie, his director of photography, got them well and flatteringly lit, Cade asked to see his wide shot, medium, close and extreme close-ups of all three women. Finally he turned to grin at his DP. "If they're coming across even half as good as I think they are, this is gonna be great."

"Dude." Looking through the viewfinder at the three women, Louie thrust out one of his beefy hands to give him a thumbs-up. "More like *twice* as. They're gonna be off the charts."

Cade watched as the boom operator fitted them with the lavalier mics and had the women clip on additional radio mics whose wires he helped them thread through their clothing. Each woman's voice would then go directly to the camera on separate channels for his soundman to mix.

"Whoa, mama!"

Cade stared at Ava, who'd started shifting in her seat. She suddenly reached into the scooped neckline of her emerald-green, black-belted dress, her hand disappearing up to the wrist into her generous cleavage before reemerging with the radio mic.

"The little bugger came unclipped and was making a break for it," she said, holding up the large-vitamin-capsule-size microphone and laughing that contagious belly laugh of hers.

His boom operator laughed along with her. "Here, let me give you a hand with that," he offered, making Cade take a hot step forward in instinctive protest.

Then he caught himself. *Jesus, Gallari, get a grip,* his sensible, grown-up, professional self commanded. *Guy's just doing his job.*

He stayed put and found his faith in Justin's professionalism immediately borne out when the boom operator directed Ava to clip the microphone to her bra strap near the upper part of the dress's neckline, then hold it in place while he checked that the wire, which had been threaded down her dress and out through her hemline, had enough slack for her to move around a bit without pulling it loose again.

Eventually everyone was in position, good to go, and he walked over to join the women. "Okay, ladies." Focusing primarily on Poppy and Jane, who had been civil, if cool, since he'd entered their orbit, he said, "Ava probably told you how blown away I was when she talked to me about Agnes last November. Her enthusiasm made your friend come alive for me, and I'm pumped to hear your stories of her, as well. So we're gonna get started in just a minute.

"First, though, I want to go over a couple of things while the camera gets up to optimum running speed. You all met Justin while he was wiring you for sound. What he's holding now is a boom mic." Justin held up a big black microphone attached to the end of a twelve-and-a-half foot fish pole for them to see. "It's going to be overhead during the interview and will be moving back and forth to catch what each of you says while you're saying it, so do your best to ignore it.

"And speaking of ignoring, let me introduce you to our director of photography. Ava, I know you two have already met, but Jane, Poppy, this is Louie. Louie, meet Poppy and Jane." They exchanged greetings, then he said, "Now I want you to ignore him."

"Well, that's rude," Poppy said.

"I know, and people tend to be polite, which means including the cameraman when they're telling an anecdote or answering questions, because he's right there in their line of vision. But trust me when I tell you it doesn't play well, so look at me and only me."

Unless it's each other if you get a dialogue going, he silently added, but didn't bother saying aloud. Because face it, that would only happen if they could forget that the camera was there—and then it would be instinctive, not something he'd need to choreograph. The fewer directions he gave, he generally found, the better.

Scooting his chair a little closer to them, he felt that little buzz he got whenever he started a new interview. He nodded to his AD, who called out, "Quiet on the set, please."

Conversations ceased and while his key grip, gaffer and makeup girl stayed handy in case they were needed, everyone except the DP cleared away from the camera. He glanced at Louie. "Roll camera, please."

"Speeding," the DP replied, and Cade turned back to the women.

"How did the three of you meet Agnes Wolcott?"

"We met at a musicale when we were twelve," Poppy said.

"At Ava's," Jane added before turning to Ava. "Remember how jazzed your mom was that Miss A was attending?"

"Pretty hard to forget," she agreed, then looked back at him to explain. "Miss Agnes was renowned for turning down more invitations than she accepted, so it was a big deal coup when she RSVPed that she'd attend my mother's event."

"The three of us likely wouldn't be sitting here, though, if Ava'd had her way," Poppy said with a crooked smile. "She thought the musicale was the dumbest idea ever and campaigned to blow it off and do an overnighter at my house instead."

"Well, it was very Jane Austen, wasn't it—that whole music in the parlor gig?" She flashed her dimples. "I was heavily into Kurt Cobain at the time, so singers accompanied by harpsichords and violins just struck me as so last millennium. Plus, Poppy's parents always let us have s'mores and told us to have fun. My mother's events were always accompanied by endless rules." She grimaced. "Don't eat more than one tea cake, Ava. Don't spill anything, Ava. Make sure your friends are quiet, Ava. And for God's sake, don't embarrass me in front of my guests." She shrugged. "The usual, in other words. I was expected to be one of those throwback kids who was seen but not heard—

"Crap." She looked at Cade in dismay. "What am I thinking? Can you edit that out?"

Even as he agreed, then asked Louie for a change in framing, Cade studied her, seeing in his mind's eye the overweight kid she'd been then. Knowing the role he'd played in contributing to her miseries didn't stop him from disliking her mother and her fucking rules. Who said money bought happiness? He and Ava could sure as hell dispel that myth.

"Still, you gotta give your mom props for drumming those beautiful manners into you," Poppy said and grinned at Cade. "Since that's how we *really* met Miss A."

Jane nodded agreement. "Ava dragged us over to where Miss Agnes was sitting, kind of off by herself, and introduced the three of us." She got a reminiscent look in her eye, and Cade signaled Louie to go in close. "She was different than any grown-up we'd ever met— and I'm not just talking about that foghorn voice of hers, which God knows was distinctive."

"We thought she was nice enough at first, but nothing really special, you know?" Poppy said.

"Then she asked us what we thought of the music," Ava contributed. "And those manners Poppy likes to razz me about? I followed the party line and gave a standard, polite response." She grinned, all bright eyes and dimples. "And Miss Agnes blew us away by saying that personally, she found it nice…but it was certainly no 'Material Girl.'"

Poppy laughed. "We discovered over time she had the driest sense of humor. She said things with this kind of deadpan delivery that just cracked us up. And that first night, almost before we knew it, we'd spent the whole evening talking to her."

"Yeah, my mother wasn't thrilled with me for monopolizing her guest of honor," Ava said. "But I didn't care. Miss A had liked us. *Really* liked us—she'd made us feel as if *we* were the fascinating ones. And before she left that night, she invited us to join her for tea at the Wolcott mansion."

"Which turned out to be the start of almost twenty years of teas with her," Jane said. "Like I said, she was different from any grown-up we'd ever met."

"And she was sooo interesting," Poppy added. "She'd been to places I'd only ever heard of—hell, to places I've *still* never seen outside of movies or books."

"No fooling," Ava agreed. "And not just the usual places, like Paris or Madrid or London, either. She'd been to Africa and Madagascar and the Amazon and… oh, just everywhere."

"And she'd done everything," Jane added. "Did you know she flew her own plane? I always regretted we didn't meet her until a few years after she'd given that up, because wouldn't that have been a kick in the pants? To soar through the sky with her? And her collections! Oh, my God, those fabulous collections."

"Yeah, it's because of Miss A that Janie's a curator." Ava gave her friend an affectionate smile. "She's not exaggerating, though—Miss Agnes did have the most amazing stuff, not the least of which was her wardrobe. She was a total clotheshorse and had suits and gowns and dresses from every couture house you've ever heard of." Her eyes went dreamy, and again Cade sent Louie a hand signal for an extreme close-up. "My favorites were her vintage gowns."

"She let all of us dress up in them," Poppy said. "But she particularly liked dressing up Ava in her thirties, forties and fifties gowns. Ava would sometimes get down on herself about her appearance, but Miss A always said that she was simply born in the wrong era—and was exquisite just the way she was." She shot Ava a stricken look. "God, I'm sorry. I shouldn't have said that on camera."

"No, it's okay. She did make me feel beautiful," Ava concurred. "This style you see today?" Her fingers traced an elegant outline in the air above her voluptuous torso. "Admire it or detest it—it got its start upstairs in Miss Agnes's dressing room."

Cade was thinking that he, for one, admired the hell out of it when Poppy said, "She let me paint her walls in colors of my choosing."

"Yeah, this place was all white inside before Poppy got her hands on it," Ava said. "But that was the genius of Miss A. She encouraged our passions and helped us to build on our strengths."

"In my case it was allowing me to spend hours messing about with her collections," Jane said, then laughed and shook her head. "It wasn't until I was in college that I understood how much they were worth—and she just let me play with them like they were Wal-Mart toys."

Remembrances tumbled out with nonstop gusto, one piling atop another as the three women discussed their friend and mentor with unbridled affection. "That first time she had us for tea, she called us a sisterhood. I thought that was so cool."

"She gave us our first diaries that day, too. We all still keep one to this day."

"She was in attendance at every event that had any meaning in our lives."

Cade was jazzed as he directed the DP to go wide to catch Ava leaning forward with smiling intensity as she related a memory, or Poppy wedging herself into the corner of her seat and folding a leg under her on the settee, talking with her hands as she described an event. He signaled him to pull in close when Jane, the quietest of the three, threw back her head and laughed as if someone had just told her a really great dirty joke.

Since he wouldn't be a part of the finished product, which meant the audience wouldn't hear his questions, he often needed to repeat them in order to get complete, powerful sentences out of his subjects regarding something they'd already talked about. But except for follow-up questions to flesh out a newly introduced topic and some queries that got the three women talking about how they'd felt when they'd discovered they were Agnes Wolcott's heirs, he rarely interrupted, instead letting them take their reminiscences to organic conclusions.

"Are you getting all this?" he demanded sotto voce to Louie as Molly stepped in for a moment to powder Jane's forehead and Ava's nose.

"Yeah. Jesus, Mary and Joseph, dude. They sure were crazy about that woman. And their enthusiasm…? We've got some stuff here that's beyond good."

"That's what I'm seeing, too." He could already envision spots where he could cut away to some kind of visual: to one of Agnes Wolcott's richly textured collections or some articles of her haute couture. It would be cool to find some old pictures of Wolcott with the three girls at different stages in their relationship, as well. He made a mental note to ask Ava if any old photo albums existed and to sic Beks on them if they did.

They went back to the shoot but wrapped up a short while later. When Cade called the final cut, the entire crew whooped their appreciation for the interview, and he thanked the women with wholehearted sincerity.

As his crew immediately began to get ready for the next interviewee and Beks led away Poppy and Jane, he pulled Ava aside to ask about the albums.

"I'm sure there are," she said. "Miss Agnes was interested in everything, and that included photography, so she took lots of pictures. Let me talk to Jane—she's most likely to know."

"Thanks. And I know I've said it before but I just can't say it enough—you and your friends really rocked that interview. You can take it from me, Spencer, you look incredible on camera." He grinned when she actually flashed her dimples at him with obvious pleasure over either the compliment or maybe just the fact that the shoot was over and had been an unmistakable success. "I promised I'd let you see for yourself, though, so if you'd like to see how you came across, I can probably get to it later this week."

"Later this week! What's wrong with right now?"

"Aside from the fact that we're moving right on to the next shoot, you mean? Look, I'm not shining you on here. If I finish up before you're ready to go home, I'll see if I have time to go over it with you. But don't hold your breath, Ava. I've got a feeling I'm going to be putting in a long day."

She studied him for a moment, then nodded and blew out a breath. "Fair enough. But I'm dying to see how I turned out." She grinned. "It was a lot less stressful than I anticipated, and I gotta admit, I'm totally revved up. So I'm going to go feed my friends and celebrate having it behind me. I'll let you get back to work. Oh, by the way—" she gave him a smile "—you were right. You are a good interviewer."

And about-facing on a black stiletto heel, she headed across the room to where her two friends awaited her at the entrance to the hallway, leaving him staring after her and listening to that damn infectious laugh that trailed in her wake.

CHAPTER SEVEN

I'm so lucky to have Jane and Poppy. But there are still times when I just feel so damn alone.

"Thanks again for dinner, you guys," Ava said to Jason and Poppy as she stood in their front doorway the next evening, hugging two fat leather albums to her breasts. She shot her blonde girlfriend a wry smile. "The apple sure didn't fall far from the tree when it comes to cooking—your stroganoff's every bit as mean as your mama's." Then, noticing Jase pulling a jacket out of the closet and shrugging it on, she zeroed in on him.

"You better be telling me you got called in to work," she said, narrowing her eyes at the tall, dark-eyed man she and Janie had dubbed Detective Sheik, because he had that same compelling air about him as the fantasy man the sisterhood had created to titillate themselves in their tweens.

"I'm walking you to your car," he said with the authoritarian don't-mess-with-me voice he probably used on the snitches and burglary suspects he came into contact with. "Deal with it." Reaching out, he relieved her of the albums.

She knew him well enough by now not to fight him for possession. The man was programmed to protect—and was downright implacable once he got his mind set on something. Plus it wasn't as if she'd ever once won the you-don't-need-to-walk-me-to-my-car arguments. So, knowing it drove him crazy, she gave him the Big Sigh instead. "You are such a cop."

That merely earned her an incredulous stare and an, "Uh, *yeah*."

Laughing, Poppy raised onto her toes to give her husband a peck on the lips. She grinned at Ava when she settled back on her heels. "If you think telling him *that* is going to rattle his cage, you picked the wrong boy. Being a cop is Jason's entire reason for living."

Jase softly stroked the tips of his long fingers down his wife's temple and along her jaw. "No, Blondie, that would be you."

"Oh." Poppy, a woman not normally given to blushes, rosied up and her brown eyes glowed with pleasure. "Good answer."

Ava was struck dumb by the sheer tenderness in Jason's gesture, in his dark eyes when he gazed at his wife. It gave her a sharp pang of loneliness. But forcing a smile, she shoved it aside, kissed her friend and allowed him to escort her to her car.

She quit fooling herself on the drive home, however. She was so happy for Poppy and Jane because both her friends were wildly happy with their lives, and she wanted that for them more than anything. Yet she couldn't help the pea-green envy she occasionally felt around them. They both had such good men who loved them unconditionally, while she had…nothing, really. God, it had been forever since she'd even been out on a date.

But she could change that, she thought determinedly. It wasn't as if she wasn't asked out on a regular basis—

she just got busy and tended to let that portion of her life slide. *And "nothing" is a bit melodramatic.*

She had her friends, and it was no small deal that the group had grown by two great guys. Plus she loved her home to pieces. Which, okay, maybe wasn't the best example, considering she was currently fighting to hang on to it. Casting about for something else, for an affirmation to hoist her out of this abruptly pessimistic mindset, she latched onto the obvious. There was her job.

The instant she thought it, however, a wild laugh escaped her. "Oh, God, my job," she sputtered.

Working for the guy who'd slept with her on a bet.

"Crap." If this were thirteen years ago, the downturn in her mood would've called for a hand-packed half gallon of Husky's Mocha Almond Fudge.

She sat up taller in her seat as she took the Harbor Avenue exit off the West Seattle bridge and turned right toward the Duwamish Head. Because this *wasn't* high school and she knew her current case of the poor-pitiful-me's would soon pass. She did adore her job. And she would save her condo. Plus, she was almost home. Just a few more minutes and she could climb into her jammies, grab a Skinny Cow ice cream sandwich, or—hell—go hog wild and make herself a cup of cocoa. Then she'd light a few candles, turn on the fireplace and put on some music to help her unwind.

Tomorrow, she would likely wonder what the hell she'd been all worked up about.

Right this minute, however, she just felt so knee-walking lonesome she could cry.

IT HAD BEEN another long day. Cade was dog tired but had no desire to go home to his empty rental. So he headed over to West Seattle to see if he could talk to the owner of Easy Street Records. Every L.A. music buff who'd heard he was heading to Seattle had instructed him not to miss it, an opinion that had been endorsed by Ava just this afternoon when he'd asked her what she considered the best music store in town. Everyone seemed to agree Easy Street was one of the most highly regarded independent record stores in the U.S.

According to Ava, in the nineties when various members of Pearl Jam, Nirvana and Soundgarden lived in the West Seattle neighborhood, the record shop had been the go-to spot for the thriving Seattle grunge movement. And apparently more than a few big-name bands still stopped by for impromptu jam sessions when they were in town.

Cade hoped to cop a few minutes with the owner to pick the guy's brain about some music ideas he had for Agnes's documentary. And knowing Ava lived a mile or two from the record shop and having time on his hands—not to mention his Mac with yesterday's footage in the back of his rental—he decided he might as well swing by her place and show her the great job she and her friends had done in their interview. Strictly so he could check that task off his to-do list.

Hey, he knew how anxious she was to see the results of the shoot for herself.

This time, however, it would probably be smarter not to drop in unannounced. Pushing the phone button on the OnStar program in his rental car, he gave Ava's name at the automated prompt. As he waited for it to connect him, he crossed California at Alaska Street, cruised past Easy Street's forties-era brick building and started looking for a place to park.

Then she picked up, he heard her voice…and felt something beneath his skin strum.

Ignoring it, he said, "I took your advice and am stopping by Easy Street."

"Really? Matt's working tonight?"

"Damned if I know, but—"

"Wait. You didn't even call first?"

"No, but that's not the point. *That* would be the fact that I'm in your 'hood, and was thinking that after I talked to the guy—"

"If he's even there," she interrupted.

"Yeah, yeah, if he's there," he agreed impatiently. "Jeez, you're a buzzkill. I thought as long as I'm in the area anyway, I might as well stop by your place when I'm done and—"

She cut him off yet again. "Tonight's not good for me, Gallari."

"Why, you got a hot date?" Then he jerked upright in his seat. Because, Jesus, maybe she did.

Not that he'd care or anything. But it would sure blow his bagging two crows with one bullet agenda.

"No," she said in a civil tone several degrees chillier than it had been a second ago, "I do not have a date, hot or otherwise. But neither am I in the mood for company. Especially *your* com—"

"I've got my Mac in the back, Spencer," he said, happy to be the one doing the interrupting this time. "And it's got some seriously good footage of you and your posse on it."

He heard her swear under her breath. Then she gave one of those big, attenuated sighs only women were really good at and said begrudgingly, "Okay, fine. Whatever."

"*There's* those beautiful manners I've heard so much about."

She invited him to do something men simply weren't built to do and, laughing, he hung up.

Less than an hour later, he was in the foyer outside Ava's penthouse condo, jacked up on the conversation he'd had with the record store proprietor.

"*Thank* you," he said as soon as she opened the door. Barely giving her time to step back, he strode into her place. "I stopped by Easy Street like I said I was gonna and you were wrong, Matt was there. But you were also right in what you told me this afternoon—he couldn't have been more helpful. The guy's knowledge of music is amazing and he gave me some great ideas for Miss Agnes's sound track."

Remembering the owner's directive, Cade shot her an I-know-your-secrets grin. "He told me to say hi, by the way. Said you were an excellent customer and confirmed what you told us yesterday—that you really *were* a freakin' huge Kurt Cobain fan."

"Did he rat me out for going all fangirl on him the first time I went into his store?" She charmed him by blushing as she invited him, with a sweep of her arm, into her living room.

Then she laughed when he nodded his agreement. "Well, color me officially embarrassed. I'd heard he was tight with that whole grunge/punk scene, so when I met him I went on and on ad nauseam about how much I'd loved Cobain. He delights in not letting me live it down."

As she spoke, her gaze traveled to his MacBook Pro and latched onto it with bright-eyed interest. Without taking her attention off the only thing that had gotten him through her door, she asked, "Would you care for something to drink?"

She clearly wanted him to say no and get on with showing her the footage. Now that he was here, however, he found himself in no big hurry to jump straight into the business that had landed him on her doorstep. Not when he knew damn well he'd just have to turn right around again and head back to his quiet condo as soon as he had. "That'd be great," he said, carefully setting the laptop on her coffee table. "Got any beer?"

"No, sorry. I'm not a beer girl. Well, except for a Belgian maybe once a year." She waved a hand in a but-that's-neither-here-nor-there erasing movement. "I've got a nice Cab from a Yakima winery and I've got tea, club soda or water."

"Well how 'bout that, we've got a lot in common. I'm not a wine or tea guy—not even once a year."

"And this gives us a common interest, how?"

"We're both not-a-somethings. I'll take the club soda."

He watched her walk away, noting her softly draped black loungewear with its wide-legged bottoms and the band of semi-see-through lace that showed hints of ivory skin where it circled the tunic just above her waist. Remembering his last visit here, he'd put money down she'd put her bra back on in the wake of his phone call.

And wasn't that a crying shame.

He wandered around her place while she was in the kitchen. It looked like her, all lush and warm and built for comfort. Although the sun had long since set, between the buttercream walls, white woodwork, golden hardwood floors and the bank of windows overlooking the sound and Olympic mountains, he knew it would be light and airy during the day. Even with those windows shuttered, it had a spacious feel that opened a guy's lungs and made it easier to breathe.

She'd furnished the place in an uncluttered medley of styles that had nothing in common yet somehow worked together. A big overstuffed couch in a black-and-white print and two surprisingly comfy-looking midcentury modern ruby chairs created a conversational area around a three-drawer, leather-trimmed silver metal steamer trunk that she used as a coffee table. The dining area was defined by a beautiful Persian rug, on top of which sat a glossy Stickley-style dining set from an earlier era than the arrangement of starburst clocks on the wall above it. Other retro accessories mixed happily with antique collectibles, plants, pictures and girlie stuff on a series of multilevel bookshelves. Eclectic art provided pops of color over the fireplace and couch.

"Here you go." She plunked his drink down on a coaster on the steamer trunk. "Have a seat. Drink up. Let's see that seriously good footage you promised me."

Wondering if he should be insulted that she clearly wanted to see the footage and get him the hell out of here—or be grateful that for once she wasn't killing him with her damn unsmiling, meticulous courtesy, he joined her at the couch. Dropping down in the middle in front of his computer, he pulled his Mac over. Ava sat at the far end. "You've got a nice place here," he said as he booted up the laptop.

"It's the same stuff that was here the last time you showed up."

"I guess I didn't pay much attention to it that night." He kept to himself the fact that once he'd seen she was braless, he'd been pretty much blind to everything else.

"But this is awesome. You've got a real eye—it's much homier than my place in L.A."

"Thanks. I love it."

He patted the cushion next to him. "Move down here. It's a laptop screen. You're not going to be able to see anything from that angle."

He kept his attention on the program he was bringing up as she scooted closer, but was conscious of her warmth when the cushion he sat on depressed as she moved in to see the screen. For a second, the side of her shoulder, hip and thigh pressed heat against his. Then it was gone as she shifted to put an inch or two between them.

"Because it's on my laptop instead of the main computer, these are only 1K reference movies. But it should still give you a clear idea of how you and your friends came across, which was kick-ass excellent. Keep in mind that it's rough. I don't edit until I've pieced together all the interviews to tell the story. That's why I kept asking you the same questions in different ways during yours—to get the strongest, most complete answers without inserting myself in the documentary." He turned his head to look at her, and discovered she was close, her eyes alight as she leaned forward.

"Rough," she agreed impatiently. "Got it."

"But still rocks. You ready?"

"Yes!"

He couldn't help but smile at her eagerness as he hit the key to start the QuickTime player.

"Wow," was the first thing she said as she leaned further forward to take everything in. "We do look pretty good."

"Told you. Louie knows how to light. And it doesn't hurt that you're a good-lookin' bunch to begin with."

He didn't bother to give the screen more than an occasional glance himself. He'd seen most of the women's interview on his monitor as it had been unfolding and had checked it out after he'd transferred the footage from the RED camera's hard drive to his computers—he knew it was good. He watched Ava as she watched it instead. Heard her laugh at something Poppy said on-screen. Saw her eyes go round and her lips quirk up when something delighted her—usually in regard to one of her friends. Listened to her gasp, then breathe, "Oh, look at Janie," when a particularly good close-up of the brunette appeared.

When the final footage had played and the player went black, she turned to him. And flashed him the biggest, friendliest smile he'd seen since he'd shot their relationship down in flames in the high school cafeteria back when.

"Okay, I admit it," she said. "I'm glad I participated. You really captured something here. This—" she flapped a hand at his now sleeping screen "—my God, Gallari, parts of this are just incredible. Jane and Poppy's memories were so vivid it was almost like having Miss Agnes back for a couple of minutes."

"So were yours. In fact, I think the definitive moment in the whole interview was when you said the genius of Agnes was the way she encouraged all your passions and helped you build on your strengths. That was a very telling, powerful statement."

Ava stared at him for a second, then gave him another deep-dimpled, goofy smile. "Aww." She got up off the couch. "Just for that, I've got a present for you. I was going to bring these to the mansion tomorrow, but you might as well take them with you tonight." She shot him a crooked smile. "Better you have to pack them than me."

She strode over to a leather purse sitting on the breakfast bar and plucked a set of keys from it. "I'll be right back," she said, then disappeared out the front door before it sank in that she was leaving.

"What the hell?" He, too, climbed to his feet. Where had she gone?

Somewhere close by, he guessed when he saw that she'd left the door ajar. But she wasn't in the tiny foyer outside her penthouse apartment, the elevator door was closed, and he hadn't heard it chime between the time she'd walked out and now.

The light above it lit up a moment later, however, and an instant after that it did chime as the doors slid open. Ava stood inside, a stack of what looked like albums in her arms.

"Oh, man," he said, anticipation building as he stepped forward to relieve her of the burden. "Are these what I think they are?"

"If it's the albums you asked for, then yes." Ava led the way back inside and closed the door behind them. "It turned out Poppy had them. She gave them to me when I had dinner with her and Jase tonight, so I had them in my car."

"Mind if I flip through them real quick?"

She hitched a shoulder. "Knock yourself out."

He carried what turned out to be two fat albums over to the breakfast bar, where he dumped them beneath an overhead directional light from the kitchen. Sliding the topmost album to sit alongside its twin on the counter, he reverently opened its leather cover.

Excitement rose as he flipped through page after page, his imagination catching fire with the variety of ways he could use some of the pictures. Agnes Wolcott had been as good at photography as she had been at everything else she'd touched. The biggest problem might be whittling down his choices, since in the one album alone there had been a good dozen or more evocative photos he wouldn't have a problem finding a use for.

He looked over at Ava. "These are amazing."

"Wasn't she something?" she agreed fervently. "I know you only asked for the ones that had us with Miss A, but we've got more. We inherited all her albums, and they range practically from her birth to her death."

"Are you messing with me? Because that would be like my birthday and Christmas all rolled into one."

"I'm serious as cancer, Gallari. I want Miss Agnes's feature to be the best it can be."

"Sweet!" Laughing, he snatched her up and swung her around before laying an enthusiastic kiss on her.

It was an impulse…one that, had there been any thought behind it, would have been intended as a quick, friendly peck. But at the first touch of her mouth, at the feel of those soft, cushioning lips beneath his, all thought fled as the chemistry that had always simmered between them ignited. He hauled her close.

A soft grunt of arousal escaped him when her full breasts flattened against his chest. *Lemme in,* was the only thought in his head, and he opened his mouth over those lush lips, kissing her with hot, suctioning authority. *Open up, lemme in.*

Ava couldn't have been more blindsided if a truck had T-boned her out of the blue. *What? No,* flashed through her head. *This is crazy.* She had been enjoying the fact that Cade had driven away her lonelies—but she hadn't signed on for this.

The thought shorted out, however, as her brain began

sputtering like a faulty fluorescent light. Seduced by the urgency of his kiss, she wrapped her arms around his neck and opened her lips beneath the insistent demand of his.

With the barriers dropped, it was all bold exploring tongues. She felt both energized and languorous. Nerve-rich and sensitized. And so...damn...*hot*.

Hot blood.

Hot skin.

Hot, mindless purpose meeting what was clearly even hotter purpose.

Cade's hand speared into her hair and gripped, arching her neck as he tugged her head back. Her lips quickly cooled and felt naked when his mouth suddenly slid away from hers to press damp, blistering kisses down her throat.

His free hand slid up her back, then around her side and up her rib cage to encage one breast in furnace-hot fingers that splayed wide to contain the generous curve. They curled to mold to her shape.

Rubbed its fullness in a circular motion against the wall of her chest.

Turned light as a feather as he finessed his palm over her rigid nipple—making her head go light with need. If she could have, she would've blinked her top and bra away to feel the full effect of his bare skin touching hers.

God! Just the thought had her arching to push her aching flesh more firmly into that authoritative hand, and they both groaned.

It was her own *do-me* moan, so brazenly carnal, that shocked her back to her senses. Horrified to find herself about to repeat the biggest mistake of her life, she slid her hands down his chest and shoved him away.

"What the—?" Obviously still in the moment, he blinked at her. "Ava, no..."

She did her best to suck in equanimity—rickety as it was—with every breath she inhaled. If she'd had a second to consider Cade's actions, surely she would have repudiated them. But she hadn't—she'd neither had that second nor done any repudiating. Instead she'd practically climbed him like a cat in heat. "You need to go," she said around the ground glass of shame in her throat.

"What?"

She took a step back. Felt her fragile composure threaten to crack and grabbed another calming breath. "You need to leave now."

"You're kicking me out? *Now?*" His eyes, which had been hotter than napalm, abruptly morphed to cerulean ice. But he visibly reined himself in and gave her a charming little half smile. "We're not even going to discuss it?"

"Seriously?" she demanded hotly, then took vicious pride that she, too, could bury her temper almost as quickly as it had surfaced. Refusing to admit how bone-deep shaky she felt, she used all the edgy, achy dissatisfaction making her skin feel a size too tight to channel her mother. She wrapped her manners around herself like armor. Looked at Cade with Jacqueline's coolest you're-the-shit-on-the-bottom-of-my-shoe-but-I'm-much-too-well-bred-to-say-so demeanor.

"Excuse me if I'm not buying this again," she said with a calm she was inordinately proud of, given she was about to implode at any minute. "I got sucked in by you once—I'm not doing that again. And our history aside, this is a bad idea on so many levels I can't even begin to count them all. I will tell you this, though—I don't mix with my clients. Not this way. So, I'm sorry if I gave you the impression that I might be amenable to starting something with you, but that's never going to happen."

And ignoring the fact that there had been a moment there when she'd wanted nothing more than to sink into the sensations he'd made her feel, ignoring his dissatisfaction and the anger she could feel radiating beneath the easy-come-easy-go exterior he'd slapped over it, she found his coat and helped him gather up the damn albums that had started this whole fiasco.

Then she hustled him the hell out of her house, trying to get rid of him before he had a chance to see through the bum's rush to the raw nerves propelling her.

CHAPTER EIGHT

What is WRONG with me? Cade has no business messing with my head this way. I have got to put him out of my mind once and for all.

CADE DROVE downtown in a red haze of wrath, arriving at the pay lot down the street from his temporary Belltown digs without any recollection of his trip from point A to point B. Finding a single, barely adequate parking spot, he maneuvered into it. Then he merely sat staring at a patch of antiquated bricks where the foggy glow of the lot's spotlight illuminated the back side of the building in front of him.

Okay, he thought moodily, *what the hell was that all about?*

He'd gone at her with all the finesse of a bull in rutting season. And maybe he didn't like it, but she'd had every right to say no. But, dammit—

"'I'm sorry if I gave you the impression I might be *amenable* to starting something with you,'" he mimicked in an acidic falsetto. Hearing himself, however, he unclenched his fingers one by one from the steering wheel, blew out a breath and took a shot at clearing his mind.

Until—finally!—for the first time since laying that kiss on her, he felt his brain kick into gear.

Hell, yeah, she'd been amenable—there'd been no "might be" about it. He'd tasted her amenability on his tongue, had felt it like a diamond bit drilling a hole in his palm. So she had given him the kiss-off once she'd pulled out of his arms. It was on him that he'd allowed it to sidetrack him for a while—but he was through reacting like a frustrated teenager.

It was time to set aside his knee-jerk fury at her you're-the-shit-on-my-shoe delivery. And it was *way* past time to stop thinking with his dick.

Because his big head knew damn well she had wanted him every bit as much as he'd wanted her. They'd had some serious combustive chemistry going on tonight, and no way had it been all one-sided. A woman who was only tolerating a man's kiss didn't wrap her lips around his tongue and suck on it as if she were fellating a different appendage. She didn't plaster her luscious body against his from chest to knees.

And she sure as hell didn't push her plush, gorgeous tit into his hand in a wordless demand for more.

"Don't tell me it's never gonna happen, baby." *That* was a phrase she would've been smarter not to use on him. He'd built a career by proving tougher people than Ava Spencer dead wrong when they'd told him he would never do this, that or the other. Hell, Allan Gallari himself had told him he'd never amount to anything.

It had only given extra impetus to Cade's determination to succeed—and was the last time he had ever talked to his old man.

Because tell him no and it just kicked into gear his built-in "watch me" machine. It drove him to find ways, to use damn near any means at his disposal to accomplish precisely what he'd been told he couldn't do. It had worked in his professional life, and it would work with Ava, too.

For thirteen damn years, every time he was in Seattle he had knocked himself out trying to get her to hear his apology. He'd told himself it was merely because he was tired of beating himself up for what he'd done to her. But as much as he hated to admit it—and God knows he'd been denying this since senior year—they had some unfinished business. And it wasn't all his—they both needed to face up to it.

He got it already that he'd hurt her and she hated him. He really did.

But she also wanted him—and he was about to take advantage of that to get what *he* wanted.

Her.

"Jesus, woman." Shaking his head, he climbed out of the car and walked around to open the back hatch and retrieve his computer. "It's not like you to issue me a bald-faced challenge like that. What were you thinking?"

Because she of all people ought to know he wasn't above playing dirty.

THE NEXT AFTERNOON Tony strolled past Agnes Wolcott's bedroom suite on his security guard duties—or so he was prepared to claim if anyone asked why this was his third pass-by today. Not that anyone would. That was one of the things that made cons possible: people pretty much saw what they expected or what you put out there for them to see. It was a huge positive in his line of work.

Too bad for him, he was dealing more in negatives these days. Because once again the sitting room portion of Agnes's suite was filled with people, just as it had been not only during his previous two pass-bys, but every other time he'd checked it the past several days.

"Ladies," he said, poking his head into the room to give the females inside his most charming smile. "Gent." He shot the man sitting in the makeup chair, wrapped in a silver cape and looking chagrined to be caught having makeup applied to his face, a commiserating man's-gotta-do-what-a-man's-gotta-do nod. "No one's seen anyone around who doesn't belong, I take it?"

They agreed they hadn't, and, giving the carved wood wainscoting a quick covetous glance, he withdrew, traversing the hallway on light feet.

His tread was considerably heavier as he stalked down the stairs.

Shit! They couldn't use a different room to get the interviewees ready for the sonuvabitching shoot? The old duffer Molly was working on had been some pubescent kid with a crush on the Wolcott broad back in the day, or so he'd heard this morning. The bitchy hairstylist's replacement, a brunette named Sarah who looked scarily as if she was about to pop out a kid at any minute, was discussing with the woman in her chair how she liked her hair styled. He hadn't caught what the stylee's connection to the Wolcott broad was.

Like he'd give a flying fuck if he knew.

Dammit, this sucked large. The potential payoff here was huge, but he was on this gig with forged or borrowed credentials. He hadn't really perused them too closely, since he hadn't anticipated being around long enough for it to matter. Yet it upped the risk factor.

His chances were more than decent that no one would ever discover the fact. But he'd just as soon not test the theory. Not when Gallari had the look of a guy just a *lit*-tle too intelligent for Tony's liking.

On the other hand, he was nowhere near ready to pack up his bags and go home. His threefold goal was simple. Get the damn sparklies. Blow this pop stand. Live a life of leisure.

It sure as hell wasn't to go to jail for fraud. Or even to be taken in for questioning, since he couldn't afford to be scrutinized too closely. Not with his long list of aliases. And not when there was undoubtedly an outstanding warrant made out in one or more of those names. In possibly more than one state.

But this day-shift thing wasn't working out the way he had hoped. It would have been excellent if Uncle Mike had just cut to the chase and been more specific about where on the wall the goddamn hidey-hole was located. Had *that* happened, instead of the old man rambling on and on before abruptly going tits up, Tony would have been long gone by now. But it hadn't, so he had to deal with the facts as they stood.

Landing this job had taken a mix of blind luck, fast talking and hard work on his part. As usual, there was a woman involved—since charming the ladies was his stock-in-trade. In this case it had been Mildred—Christ, who named their kid Mildred in this day and age?— Westing, the painfully plain chick in charge of hiring at the company his meticulous research had discovered filled the security positions for Scorched Earth Productions. He'd wined her, dined her and casually dropped in conversation one night that he was looking for a new job as his money from the last one was starting to stretch thin.

Which reminded him. He stopped in the hallway and pulled out his BlackBerry. After texting her a quick note, he sent it winging off into cyberspace. Replacing the phone in his pocket, he continued down the hall.

It always paid to keep useful connections up to date—you never knew when one might come in handy again.

For all that he was grateful to Mildred for getting him this gig, however, he saw now that he needed the night shift. It would be quiet and a man would only have to perform an occasional pass through the mansion—leaving him uninterrupted hours to go over that complicated woodwork inch by inch.

Trouble was, John held the position, and it wasn't as if he could just ask the guy to switch shifts with him. So what did that leave him? To shove the night watchman in front of an oncoming bus? To rig his brakes or hit him over the head with a baseball bat?

He blew out a disgusted breath. He was a con artist—the emphasis here on *artist*—not some hit man or no-neck enforcer. Not that he *couldn't* do those things if the situation called for it. But he was pretty sure there was a better solution.

There was Beks, for one thing. He couldn't figure out if she was just a glorified gofer or had some actual clout. But he did know she was someone that everyone, including Gallari, liked. In fact, the producer-director indulged her a lot more than you'd expect from the usual power player in his position. Hell, for all Tony knew, maybe the guy just wanted in her pants—or was already doing her. She wasn't *his* type, but maybe he'd been overlooking something here. He was all about the simple solutions if there was one to be found.

He headed downstairs to check her out.

Gallari and crew were in the midst of yet another shoot, so he knew he'd have to work fast, since one of

Beks's jobs was to usher people into the interviews. Tony didn't know how long the one in progress would last but there were at least two more interviewees upstairs. After checking a few other rooms on the main floor, he tracked her down in the kitchen.

"Hey," he said, coming up to the service table where she was filling a plate.

"Hey, yourself. Taking a break?"

"Yeah. Aside from patrolling to make sure no one's where they're not supposed to be, there's not much to do with the place filled to the rafters. I've been wishing lately I'd taken the night shift instead."

"Why?" She studied him with raised brows. "Seems like there'd be even less to do then."

"True." He shrugged. Gave her his patented ladykiller smile. "But the trade-off for boring is peace and quiet. At least I could get some homework done."

"You're a *student?*" Her voice was so incredulous it was hard not to feel a little insulted.

But he hadn't been doing this for as many years as he had to let it show. Only rubes made newbie mistakes. "Yeah." Giving her a self-deprecating smile, he cocked his eyebrow at her. "Why do you find that so amazing?"

"Sorry." She grinned at him. "It's just—you seem a little old to be in college."

"I'm thirty," he agreed with a shrug, shaving seven years off his actual age without hesitation. Making lightning-speed adjustments to fit situations was second nature. "I've had to get my education in stages as I can afford it."

"Oh, man, I hear that. I got mine in the usual four-and-a-quarter years, but had to take out student loans to finance it. I'll probably be fifty before I pay the suckers off. So what's your major?"

He talked with her another five, ten minutes, but it quickly became apparent that he was no more her type than she was his. Mostly because—and this part pinched—it was clear she viewed him as too old.

Man, when had that happened? He was used to charming women of all ages, so it was hard not to wince. Never mind that when he was on the grift it mostly involved more mature women, since the young ones rarely had the resources to make them worth his while. Hell, yeah, never mind that. Nobody wanted to be thought of as *old*.

The built redhead strolled in a moment later. She greeted them both with a smile.

Now, her he wouldn't mind doing—*plus* she was closer to his age than the punk or Goth or whatever the hell type chick Beks was. But he dismissed the notion in almost the same instant it occurred to him. Red had seriously nice tits, but she ran the kitchen, for God's sake. What use could she possibly be to his cause?

Maybe he oughtta put some thought into creating a diversion that would get people the hell out of here for a bit instead. Not that he had a clue what kind of disruption would allow him the luxury of time to go over the carved wall undisturbed.

But he was definitely going to bend his mind to the problem. Because he *was* going to find the damn jewelry. And he'd prefer to do it fast, then get the hell out of Dodge.

Not that he was particularly hopeful right this moment about his chances for the desired fast find-and-leave. He had a feeling he'd either need the as-yet-undetermined diversion or some seriously good luck to further his cause. Without it, he feared he'd just end up empty-handed. And now that he knew what he stood to lose?

No fucking way was he allowing that to happen.

AVA CLEARED the platters off the food service table, packaging up what could be added to tomorrow's offerings and discarding the rest into the yard waste cart outside the kitchen door. She wiped down the counters and tables. All that remained then was to empty and clean the industrial coffeemaker, and she could hit the road. She'd been on her feet nearly all day, so she was more than ready to go home.

It was quiet in the mansion, which felt *off* somehow, even though the production company hadn't occupied it that long. Funny how quickly one could get used to the controlled chaos of a typical day on a shoot.

No, she corrected herself, the shoot itself wasn't chaotic. It was more that the production in general was often a beehive of activity. Or maybe an ant farm, since everyone performed assigned tasks with near-military precision. Either way, it was usually busy and noisy while they were setting up, then with one simple, "Quiet on the set," it went silent as a chapel.

She found herself fascinated by the process. Seeing Cade and his cameraman in action was sort of like watching a ballet for the deaf. He sometimes talked softly to Louie, but often their communication was done through hand gestures, while crew stood nearby ready to jump in to do their jobs with swift efficiency if they were called upon.

Now, however, most everyone had gone home. Cade was probably still around somewhere, since he tended to be one of the last people—if not the last person—to leave most evenings. She wouldn't know, though. She hadn't seen much of him for the past three days.

And that was fine with her. Would that she could arrange it like that all the time, because she'd thought of that damn kiss way too often as it was. She sure didn't need his annoying presence to remind her further.

John is around as well, she thought, determined to change the direction of her thoughts. He was probably making rounds to ensure no one had managed to slip in and secret themselves in the mansion while everyone was busy. There was a lot of very expensive equipment locked in here every evening, and both security guards took their jobs seriously.

She emptied the remaining coffee into a thermal pot that would keep it hot for John's shift and washed out the coffeemaker. Then, needing dishwasher detergent anyway, she kicked off her heels, bent from the waist and folded into a satisfying yoga stretch that eased the tension from her hamstrings. Releasing her loose grip from one ankle, she opened the cupboard and felt around under the sink for the Cascade.

"Sweet view."

Crap. Wouldn't you know it? Damn that Mr. Murphy and his stinking laws. Slowly straightening with the green box in one hand, she stifled a sigh. Well, she had known intellectually that her luck wouldn't hold forever. Didn't mean a girl couldn't still wish that she'd been two lousy minutes more efficient. Or, failing that, had at least been discovered in a less embarrassing position—one that didn't include her big butt sticking up in the air.

"Glad you like it," she said coolly without turning, and stooped this time to fill the little dispenser in the appliance, "considering I've put considerable effort into making it so." She leaned to put the box back under the sink, then slowly rose to her feet.

And found herself brushing along six feet of warm, hard body all the way up.

She froze at the apex of her rise, awareness exploding along her nerve endings.

"Trust me," Cade's husky voice murmured in her ear. "It's worth every minute you spent on it."

Her heart pounded like a bongo drummer on speed, but she fought to keep her voice steady when she said, "You wanna do us both a favor and step back there, Gallari?"

"Yeah, let me just get—" His voice trailing away, he reached overhead to open the cabinet, his inner arms and the sides of his biceps brushing her own arms and shoulders with the motion. The shivers that zinged down her arms from the point of contact were so electric she was amazed lightning didn't shoot from her fingertips. What the hell was he up to?

And why was she falling right into whatever dodge he was running?

Tipping her head back to see his expression in hopes of figuring out what his angle was, she felt his chin brush her hair as he grabbed one of the clean mugs she'd just put away. She was highly aware of his muscular chest against her back, the hard spread of his thighs bracketing her hips.

Damn, damn, damn. She *so* didn't want to be, but she couldn't deny the get-with-the-program responsiveness spreading warmth deep in her core.

Then he slapped the cupboard door closed again, and she started.

"There." He stepped away, leaving her scrambling to convince herself she did not feel chilled with the sudden loss of his body heat. "Sorry about that. I thought I had time to grab a cup while you were fooling around under the sink." He reached for the thermal pot on the counter and poured himself some coffee.

Did you, really? Ava narrowed her eyes at him. *Or are you just messing with me?* Because she knew this man. He looked way too innocent, and she didn't trust him as far as she could shot put the guy. "Well, enjoy your coffee." She started the dishwasher, stepped back into her shoes and turned away. "I'm taking off."

"Before you go, I need to give you some information so you can make some arrangements for me."

"Sure." In fact, she was all over the idea—why, just the prospect of doing a job she knew well drained most of the tension from her shoulders. Feeling her normal poise return, she flashed him a professional smile over her shoulder. "Hang on. I'll grab my phone."

He shook his head. "Yeah, God forbid you don't have your CrackBerry in hand."

"Please." Turning to face him, she gave him her best the-queen-is-not-amused pursed lips and nose in the air. "I'm a Mac girl. And Mac girls do not use those inferior brand-X products." She accessed the recorder. "Okay, tell me what you need done."

"We're gonna start shooting the re-creations next week. And since they're bigger and more complicated than doing interviews and we're gonna be shooting them in film, I've got more people and equipment coming to town in a few days." He reached into his back pocket and withdrew a many times folded piece of paper. He smoothed it out before passing it to her.

"Beks wrote up a who's who for you. If there's any room at the house you got for the crew, maybe the extra grips can stay there. But I need hotel rooms for the wardrobe woman and her assistant and the actors."

"Easy peasy. I don't think there're any major events going on downtown next week, but let me double-check." Waving him into a seat at one of the tables, she finessed her iPhone for the information.

"Looking good," she reported and poured herself a cup of coffee. She joined him, prepared to hunker in until she had everything she needed to do the job. "So give me the particulars." She rattled the paper he'd given her. "Is this everyone who's coming?"

"No. Actually the actress I found to play Agnes is from here. I discovered her through the U-Dub's School of Drama. I found a couple others there, as well."

"Give me everyone. Even if they don't need accommodations, *I* need the head count. Things could get ugly around here in a hurry if I ran out of food."

He laughed, and for just a minute she was thrust back to the brief period in her life when they'd been friends in tune with each other.

Then she shook her head. "I need details to have a better idea of what we're dealing with." She looked across the table at him, pleased to be back on an all-business footing. It was *so* preferable—this she understood. Hot feelings for the last man she should be having them for—and one, moreover, she was pretty damn sure was deliberately working to generate them—made her feel like a Grade A chump.

That was so not a sensation she enjoyed.

CHAPTER NINE

Black? White? Freaking shades of gray? How are you supposed to tell? God, I'm confused.

AVA DID NOT sleep well that night. She couldn't seem to stop obsessing over Cade's actions in the mansion's kitchen. How unfair was it that now, when it was too late to matter, everything she *should* have said kept spinning through her brain as if it were on some kind of endless loop? Where the hell had her quick wit been when it might have actually done her some good?

At two in the morning she flipped from side to goddamn side on her Tri-Pedic mattress.

At three she lay on her back, tapping her fingers on the coverlet and alternated flexing and curling her toes against the bedding she'd kicked loose, while staring up at a ceiling she couldn't even see in the impenetrable dark.

At three forty-five she switched on the bedside lamp and tried to read for a while. She couldn't concentrate for beans, however, and after fifteen minutes of rereading the same two paragraphs over and over, the sole result of which was a tear-producing case of burny-eyes, she turned the light back off, punched her pillow into what she dearly hoped would be a more comfortable configuration and attempted sleep once more.

"Shit!" Twelve minutes later she pushed up on her elbow, fumbled her iPod out of the nightstand drawer and slid its earbuds into her ears. She started the first song in her sleepytime playlist at a low, soothing volume and practiced deep, even breaths in counterpoint with Bizet's *Carmen,* John Barry's theme from *Midnight Cowboy* and Delibes's *Lakmé.*

Only to discover the usual soporific effect of combining soothing music with regulated breathing had apparently taken a vacation.

At five-fifteen she threw in the freaking towel. This was getting her nowhere, so she might as well get up. Tossing back the covers, she swung her legs over the side of the bed and sat up, reaching to snag her robe from the footboard.

Pulling its snuggly warmth around her and tying the belt, she trudged into the living room and opened the shutters. She didn't see any raindrops in the light cast by the streetlamp across Alki Avenue, so she headed back into the bedroom to don her firmest sports bra and pull on a wicking Tee and her thermal running pants. She made her bed, dropped down onto her slipper chair to pull on a pair of socks and her Adidas Supernova Adapts, then went into the kitchen to make herself a cup of tea and eat an orange and some yogurt. When she was finished, she rinsed her cup and stretched for ten minutes to warm up her muscles.

Finally, she pulled on a jacket, slipped her key and mini canister of pepper spray into its pocket, then let herself out of her condo. Bypassing the elevator, she jogged down the stairs to the ground floor.

Pushing through the building's security door, the first thing she noticed were the stars hanging in a clear, carbon dark sky. The air was still, which was nice, since that meant a morning that was crisp and cold but not freeze-your-ass-off frosty. Crossing the street to the bike and pedestrian paths that ran along the water, she plugged her iPod back into her ears, selected a jazzier playlist than the one that had failed to help her sleep and pointed her shoes toward the Duwamish Head, starting out at a slow jog until she built up her wind and rhythm.

She couldn't claim to be a big lover of running, but she did find it to be one of the more efficient methods for keeping her weight down, so a few times a week she made herself tie on her Adidas whether she wanted to or not—and, okay, mostly she didn't. Yet there was something peaceful about being out before dawn when all was quiet and she had the entire stretch of Alki to herself except for an occasional car and the biker who whizzed past her on the path with a warning of, "On your right."

Watching the latter disappear around the head, she increased her speed as she, too, neared the point. Then she rounded it and felt her heart lighten as she saw downtown Seattle across Elliot Bay, sprawled out in a mosaic of lights against the stygian sky. From the Space Needle to the north to the lit-up monolithic orange cranes at the never-sleeping Port of Seattle stretching along the southeastern end of the waterfront, it was a sight that never failed to raise her spirits.

With only the bay between her and the Seattle skyline, she could hear the trains coupling new cars over in the Sodo district and the mournful two-note wail of their horns as they rolled out of town in both directions. Woven beneath it were distant snatches of the clack and clatter of iron wheels rumbling along the tracks.

Then the sounds and diamond-bright cityscape disappeared as she ran past Salty's and the high berm that separated Harbor Avenue from the Port's busy Customs Exam station. And without the view to distract her, she had to face what she'd been avoiding all night.

Yes, she had spent sleepless hours coming up with all the brilliant, sardonic I'm-onto-you things she should have said both before and after that full body press with Cade in the kitchen last night. But mostly she'd been busy dodging what she *shouldn't* have said following the damn kiss that had no doubt driven Cade to initiate said FBP.

Which was telling him she didn't mix business with pleasure and then pushing the envelope by making it crystal clear that even if she did, it would be a cold day at the equator before *he'd* ever be the one to change her mind.

What the hell were you thinking? Yeah, yeah, big deal, she *did* have an unwritten policy of not mixing sex and the clients who employed her. She still should have just shrugged off those few moments of insanity in Cade's arms and kept her big mouth shut. What she shouldn't have done was issue what he of all people might construe as a challenge.

Dammit, she *knew* how competitive he was. She ought to—she'd seen it as far back as the freaking fifth grade. That was the first time she'd called him Butt-face Gallari, a name that had just slipped out after he'd accidentally-on-purpose splashed punch all over her pretty dress and in her hair at a yacht club cotillion. Not that he'd appeared all that disturbed by the name-calling. No, it had been when she'd sworn she would never dance with him again that he had made it his mission to prove her wrong.

Which he had done, the bastard—just the first of the

victories he'd racked up over the years whenever she'd challenged him.

Scowling, she stopped to catch her breath and maybe get a peek at the inhabitants of Kitty Harbor. Unfortunately, this early in the morning the doors to the big, clean courtyard where the rescued cats often lounged and played were still closed, so she couldn't distract herself by watching the always charming and amusing feline antics. Shrugging as she reached the intersection where the West Seattle freeway curved to the south overhead, she started back the way she had come. And finally quit dodging the issue.

She might have come a long way the past few years, but she was always going to be the sort of woman who issued challenges. Some deliberate, some not. And Cade being Cade, he would likely always be a jerk and push, push, push at her to prove her wrong.

Well, she wasn't wrong—not about refusing to get involved with him. They were grease and water and, chemistry be damned, getting physical with the man would be disastrous. Yes, she was drawn to him—there was just something about him that acted on her like catnip. That didn't mean she couldn't say, "Want it, not gonna grab it." God knows she'd been doing that very thing for more than a decade when it came to food.

So she *would* be ready for him the next time he tried to mess with her. Because she didn't try to fool herself. Cade wasn't going to just say, "Oh, what the hell," and let it go at that.

There would definitely be a next time.

SHE MADE BETTER time back from the Spokane Street turnaround than she had getting there. The phone was ringing when she let herself back into her condo, and, glancing at her watch, she wondered who on earth would be calling at six-thirty in the morning.

She sighed when she saw caller ID but dutifully picked up. "Hello, Mother."

"Why have I yet to see the invitations, Ava?"

"And a good morning to you, too," she said dryly. "You need to check your email more often than once every week or so. I sent you a JPEG of the invitation last week."

There was a moment of silence. Then, "I hate this newfangled technology. What happened to the days when people corresponded by mail like civilized men and women?"

"They discovered a faster, often more efficient way. It's what I, at least, seem to have the most time for these days. My job is keeping me pretty busy, Mom."

"Mother," Jacqueline corrected.

"Right." Drawing a calming breath, she unclenched her teeth. "Hey, speaking of my job, I met an acquaintance of yours on the set recently. Stan Tarrof?"

"For heaven's sake. I haven't seen Stan for…goodness. Probably four or five months. What an odd place for him to be—what on earth would a man like him be doing on a movie set?"

"Being part of Miss Agnes's documentary. Apparently he lived a few blocks away from her when he was growing up. He also knew her socially, but like many of your set was younger than she, so he wasn't a close friend or anything. His main claim to fame is that his grandfather built the Wolcott mansion."

"He did? I never knew that."

"Neither did I before watching the interview. That's one of the fascinating things about being even a small part of this production. I get to hear bits and pieces of all sorts of interesting stuff. Like Mr. Tarrof telling everyone how much he treasures all his grandfather's old blueprints." And more amusingly, in her mind, hearing him talk about when he and his brothers were kids. They hadn't revered the grandfather's work then—they'd just thought the Wolcott was a spooky old mansion and had dared each other to run up, ring the doorbell and run away. She found it such an interesting juxtaposition hearing it told by the dignified man of today.

The clock on the dining room wall caught her eye, and she dragged herself back on topic. "I still need to grab a shower and get ready for work, Mother, but you're right that we need to get going on the invitations. So pull up my email while I have you on the line. If you approve my choice I'll push for a rush on the order and get them to my calligrapher ASAP so we can mail them out right away. I have the guest list addresses you sent me on file, ready to be taken to Jessamine along with the invitations the minute the printers let me know they're ready for pick up."

It was silent on the line for several seconds. Then Jacqueline said, "It's not perfect, but it will do."

Ava rubbed at a little ache between her brows. "All right then. I'll send you an email as soon as I mail them out."

Another pause, then her mother suddenly said, "Actually, Ava, this is…quite nice."

A little spark of something lit in her stomach. "Yeah?"

"Yes. Really quite nice."

"Thanks, Mom."

"Mother."

She sighed. "Of course. I'll email you later."

Hanging up, she bent to pick up the shoes she'd toed off while she was on the phone. When the hell was she going to quit looking for the crumbs of her mother's affection? She was thirty-one years old, for God's sake. How pathetic was it that she was still so needy for Mommy's approval?

"Oh, well." On the bright side, she was at least better about it than she used to be. There might be hope for her yet. Straightening her shoulders, she blew out a breath.

Then headed down the hall to lose herself for ten or fifteen minutes in a nice hot shower.

BEKS STUCK her head in the mansion kitchen later that morning. "Hey. Loved those savory turnovers—they were totally tasty." She grinned. "Who woulda thought a turnover without sugar could be so yummy?"

Ava looked up from the fruit platter she was refilling. "I'm glad you liked them. They seemed to go over pretty well. At least no one left them untouched on their plates—that's usually a good sign that I made an okay choice." She flashed a smile at Beks, whose clunky boots were firmly braced against the hallway floor as the younger woman gripped the doorjambs with both hands and leaned into the room. Her perky pigtails were streaked with orange today. "You gonna just hang there or come in?"

"Dude, I would love to take a little coffee break and visit with you. But I've got stuff to do. And I'm here on a mission—Cade asked me to check if you've got a few minutes. He wants to see you in the dining room."

Shit. "Yes, sure. Let me just finish this platter and wash my hands and I'll be right in."

"I'll tell him." And whirling on her Frankenstein boots, the PA was gone.

Ava finished up, then gave herself a couple additional minutes by working some lotion into her hands and reapplying her lipstick as she waited for that little kick to her heart rate to settle back into an acceptable level. Finally she blew out a breath, which she seemed to be doing a lot of this morning, and crossed the hall to the dining room.

She found Cade standing with his back to her, his knuckles braced on the dining room table on either side of an open photo album. Several more were stacked nearby.

"You summoned?" she said dryly. But inside she was growling like a cat confronted with a raccoon. Because, dammit, why—even from the backside—did he always have to look so damn good to her?

He twisted to look over his shoulder. "Yeah, thanks for dropping what you were doing. I could use your help if you've got any free time between the jobs you're already working on."

Okay, sue her, she was a sucker for being needed. She simply loved being useful and adored performing the tasks that made people's lives easier. Well, except bathrooms. She didn't do bathrooms.

Which so wasn't the point. *That* would be that she wasn't a complete idiot. This was Gallari, who had slapped the moves on her just last night. She wasn't sure why yet, but there were no two ways about it, that was exactly what he'd been doing with that whole caging her between the counter and his body routine—and the subtlety of his maneuvers be damned. "To do what?"

"Come take a look at these."

She crossed to stand by his side and looked down at the open album. And smiled in delight. "Oh, look! What wonderful old pictures of Miss A—especially this one." Her fingertip traced a snapshot's serrated white edges and the black photo corners that secured it to the page. It was a black-and-white shot of Miss Agnes in front of a small airplane. Ava didn't have the first idea what kind of plane, but Miss A looked all Amelia Earhart in a light-colored jumpsuit, leather helmet and a long white scarf.

"That's the one I liked best, too," Cade said, pulling her back to the present. Hooking the toe of his shoe on the cross brace between a dining chair's legs, he pulled it away from the table. "After seeing your place, I knew you'd have a good eye. Here, have a seat." When she took it, he grabbed another chair for himself, whirled it around until its back faced her and dropped down to straddle its seat.

"Snapshots of this caliber will be a bonus for the documentary," he said, his blue eyes bright as they met hers. Folding his arms atop the chair back, he rested his chin on his stacked forearms. "The faded patina speaks to the bygone era and I'll get movement and texture when I cut away from them to the ones I'm having taken of Agnes's collections—as well as any old film on her I can find. I harvested several snapshots from the two albums you gave me the other night, but I'd appreciate it if you'd take a look through this bunch Jane delivered."

He climbed to his feet and leaned over her to turn the album's page, his other hand braced, fingers spread, against the glossy tabletop. "You've participated in one interview and watched several more. See what strikes you as fitting to the conversations. For instance, the one we both liked of Agnes and her plane would fit seamlessly into Jane's talking about how she wished she'd known Agnes when she was still flying her own planes.

I'm still on the search for old photos of the mansion for Mr. Tarrof's interview—all I have so far is bits and pieces that I've come across in the albums, but nothing that shows the whole thing in one frame."

Ava sat still, aware of being surrounded by him yet again. Dammit, was he making another move on her? In order to avoid touching him, she tried not to shift. The guy was so enthusiastic about his subject, though, that she wasn't even sure he was messing with her this time.

And because she didn't doubt his enthusiasm for the project was genuine, she said, "I might be able to help you with that." Then she let out a surprised shriek when the chair she sat in was suddenly tipped onto its back legs, and she found herself looking up at Cade's upside down face as he leaned to hang over her.

"Are you kidding me?" he demanded.

She ought to tell him to set her down. She ought to tell *herself* to ignore the flutter in her stomach at his delighted upside-down smile. Instead, she just stared up at him, transfixed.

"No." She swallowed. "When Dev was starting the remodel here, he brought a huge stack of photographs of the place that he'd gotten from…I don't know, the state archives or some such, over at Bellevue College. I don't have a clue if he checked them out like in a library or bought copies, or what. But I could find out."

"Damn, you *so* are worth every penny I'm paying you. Yes. Please. Do that." And, leaning down, he laid a fast, smacking kiss on her, his top lip to her bottom and vice versa, then snapped back to a standing position and lowered her chair onto all four legs. "I'll leave you to see what else you can find in these albums. I've said it before, Spencer, but I'll say it again. You rock."

His long legs took him to the hallway entrance in a few short strides, but he paused to look at her where she'd twisted in her chair to stare back at him. "Seriously *rock*." Then he strode out the door.

Well, dammit, unless she was mistaken, he'd just fired another volley in their personal war. And she'd sat there like a damn statue and let him do it.

Straightening in the chair, she lifted her chin. Okay. So maybe he'd won this round. But that wasn't going to happen again.

No freakin' way, no freakin' how.

CHAPTER TEN

*I've thought long and hard about this. And enough
is enough. I am so nipping this sucker in the bud.
No, I'm more than nipping. He is going to* suffer.

"THAT'S *TWO* NIGHTS' sleep you owe me now, you bastard."

For the second morning in a row, Ava threw back the
covers of her thoroughly torn apart bed, madder than
a wet cat to be hauling her butt out of bed *again* at the
crack of o'dark thirty. Well, screw running this morning. She had battle armor to prepare.

Because the one positive aspect of the night's tossing and turning was her newfound resolve regarding
the big issue she'd been chewing over since she'd allowed Cade to mess with her again yesterday. Being a
redhead, her natural inclination tended toward impul-
siveness. A trait her mother had always abhorred. Since
high school, however, Ava had bent so far backward to
avoid making brash choices she might later regret, she
sometimes paralyzed herself into making no decisions
at all.

Well, after the restless night, she had finally reached
one, and wouldn't you know it? It was exactly what her
immediate gut reaction had urged her to do.

Quit playing nice. Drop the freaking manners. Fight fire with fire.

No one could say she hadn't tried her damnedest to be adult, to be professional. Unfortunately it wasn't enough that she'd determined to keep her sexual distance from Cade. A decision like that only worked if the other party was willing to respect your boundaries.

Clearly Gallari was not. And wasn't that just typical?

Because, thinking back to their first go-around in high school, she realized he had always been the one in control.

He'd pursued her.

He'd seduced her.

God knows he had dumped her.

While she? Dammit, she so, so hated to own up to this, but back in the day she had fallen much too easily into the role of supplicant. Sexually awakened for the first time, thrilled with the attention he'd paid her, she had willfully ignored their adversarial history and been idiotically happy to do whatever he'd suggested. And just look where that had gotten her.

Well, guess what, honey?

Those days were gone.

She had left that insecure, overweight, self-doubting girl behind some time ago. Oh, not that she didn't occasionally still have her moments, but for the most part she knew her worth. So *this* go-round?

She was bringing the man to his knees. Cade Calderwood Gallari would rue the freaking day he'd ever messed with Ava Spencer.

Striding across the room, she switched on the light in her walk-in closet. Lips pursed, already planning which shower gel, lotions and makeup she'd use, she perused the contents, shelf by shelf, hanger by hanger.

And flashed a smile she didn't doubt for a minute would make Cade's balls crawl right up inside his body if he could see it.

"Hello, mama," she murmured. "You're a bit much, but then that's what I'm looking for, isn't it?" Pleased with herself, she reached for the padded hanger. Yes, indeed.

It was time to bring out the big guns.

CADE AND LOUIE were standing at the foot of the mansion's sweeping staircase, discussing the technicalities of the upcoming segments they'd be shooting in film soon, when Louie's jaw suddenly went slack.

"Ho-ly..." His voice trailing away, he leaned farther and farther to the left, clearly craning to see around Cade. "Jeeeeee-zus." He breathed reverently and licked his lips. "*Damn,* that girl is built."

Cold premonition crawling up his spine, Cade turned, knowing exactly who he'd see. Preidentifying the problem, however, didn't prevent the sensations that hit him like a freight train.

No.

Not like a train; he felt like he'd been Tasered. His skin buzzed, his heart pounded. God, his damn *lips* had gone numb.

All he was missing here was the drool.

Ava was sauntering down the hallway toward them, and he could practically hear a drum-heavy sound track in his head keeping time with the slow oscillation of those hips. She was shrink-wrapped in a dress that— Jeezus—oughtta be outlawed.

At least on that body.

It looked as if it had been constructed out of a red-and-black spandex ace bandage. Several bands of black overlapped each other to circle her thighs; several red ones bound her hips. Then another, wider portion of the black bands swathed her to her waist. From that point the red fabric played a game of peekaboo with various sized and angled Vs beneath two black multi-layered bands crisscrossing her upper torso from waist to breasts before squaring off to her shoulders and into sleeves that hugged her arms to the elbow.

And, God. Those breasts. The largest red V filled in what the crisscross didn't cover, but its piped-in-black top edge stopped well below the squared-off point of the dress's upper half.

The entire thing was the shortest, lowest-cut little piece of nothing he'd ever seen on her.

Okay, so it wasn't porno short or low-cut. But it sure as hell displayed more leg and freckled cleavage than anything he'd seen her wear at work before. Legs that were long-thighed and firm and cleavage that jiggled subtly with every lazy stride she took.

Drawing closer, she gave both men a sleepy smile. "Mornin' boys." Stopping just shy of them, she hooked a hand around the newel post and, bending her right knee to lift her foot behind her, reached back to adjust the strap of her heel. Her dress slid up her thighs a couple of inches. "How are you?"

"Feeling better by the minute," Louie said with a grin, giving the newly exposed portion of her legs an appreciative look.

Cade centered a steely stare on his director of photography, and when Louie diverted his attention long enough to catch it, he promptly performed an about-face.

"Guess I'd better get back to work," he said over his beefy shoulder as he walked away.

"See you later," Ava called softly to his retreating back, then turned back to Cade when the cameraman disappeared into the parlor. Her tone, as always when she was addressing him, became all business. "Is Beks upstairs?"

"No." The buzz-and-numb sensations fleeing, he said sourly, "She might have been, if she hadn't had to run an errand for me because you weren't here to do it."

"Yes, I apologize for being late. I forgot to set my alarm." She tugged down her hem. "Well, if she's not around I'd better get to work, too."

Catching himself watching the subtle rise and fall of her breasts, he belatedly got his act together. *What are you, thirteen?* He gave her a slow once-over and, forcing amusement into his expression, met her gaze with raised eyebrows. "Interesting outfit."

Clearly unabashed, she merely glanced down at herself, slicked long-fingered, bloodred-tipped hands over her hips and thighs. Then laughed low in her throat. "I know. It's a little over the top, isn't it? But I've got a hot date tonight and zero time to go home to change."

Shock reverberated in his gut and zinged down the nerve rich column of his spinal cord. Taking a hot step forward, he demanded before he could stop himself, "With who?"

She gave him a cool look, clearly wondering what the hell business he thought it was of his. Still, she answered him, which he hadn't actually expected.

"Eduardo," she said, drawing the syllables out, her lips caressing them as if they were made of Godiva chocolates. "He's an—" Cutting herself off, she shook her head. "Well. You don't give a rat's rear end who he is."

"Sure I do," he forced himself to say in a bored tone, dismayed to discover that part of him was seriously tempted to grab those spandex-wrapped arms and shake the information out of her.

With a little yeah-right laugh, she ran a finger down his forearm. Even through the sweater sleeve separating her skin from his, he felt it like a low voltage buzz of electricity. "How uncharacteristically kind of you to pretend an interest." Then she waved an impatient, forget-that hand. "Eduardo's an Argentinean I met a few years ago when he was up here on business. He's back in town for the next—I can't remember exactly how many days. I was so excited to hear from him that I'm afraid I didn't pay the strictest attention when he told me." She smiled dreamily. "God, I love—" She broke off once again. "Sorry. I'm babbling on and on and keeping you from work. I'll let you get to it."

She started to turn away, but he reached out and stayed her with a hand on her arm. Her skin was warm and velvet soft beneath his fingers. "What do you love?"

"Trust me," she said with a wry smile, "you really don't want to know. Men *hate* these kinda conversations."

"I'm tough, I can take it. What do you love?"

"Argentinean men. They have so much—" She hesitated, then said on a happy sigh, *"Stamina."*

You just had to ask, didn't you, chump? Because hearing that was like a kick to the balls, considering how little staying power he'd had during their one and only time together.

His back stiffened. Jesus, he'd been eighteen years old. So, big deal, excuse the hell outta him if he hadn't yet learned how to pace himself when he was totally hot and randy for a girl.

Ava gave herself a little shake, which did interesting things to her cleavage. "Well, as I said, I'd better get busy. I'd hate to cause a riot because I didn't get the food out on time."

And turning on those heels that made her legs look a mile long, she sauntered back toward the kitchen.

Causing the sound track in his head to start up again as he watched the left-right-left twitch of her hips the entire way down the hall. *Boom-ba-ba-Boom-ba-ba*—

Wait. A damn. Minute.

He ran a hand down his arm. Since when did Ava voluntarily touch him?

The answer to that was simple. Since goddamn never. Which could only mean one thing.

Shit. He didn't frickin' believe this.

He had just been played.

There may or may not be a go-all-night Argentinean named Eduardo that she was seeing tonight. But there was no question she'd played him. And damned if he hadn't fallen for it, too.

Hook, line and sonuvabitchin' sinker.

AVA HAD TO stop herself from laughing out loud several times as the morning rolled into afternoon. She contented herself with dancing around the kitchen instead.

Now *this* was more like it. It was about damn time Cade got a taste of his own medicine. She refused to feel anything but tickled to be enjoying the heck out of being proactive for a change. God knows she had wasted far too much time reacting since he'd blown back into town.

During the odd spare moments here and there, she

arranged for VIP privileges for one of her clients at a downtown nightclub and finalized hotel accommodations and airport transfers for a party of six for another. At one point she called her favorite bakery to order the cake for her father's birthday party.

Just after three, her phone rang. She didn't recognize the number, so she simply opened the line and said hello.

"Miss Spencer?" a male voice said. "This is Stan Tarrof."

"Mr. Tarrof, hello! How are you?"

"I've been better, dear. I've had a trying day and night. My house was burglarized last night."

"Oh, my God. Are you all right?"

"Turns out I am, but I got—what's that expression? Oh, yes, coldcocked. I walked in when the robbery was apparently still in progress and got hit over the head from behind. I was just released from the hospital."

Shock that a such nice man had been the victim of violence rendered her speechless for a moment. When she regained her voice, she said, "I am so sorry! Is there anything I can do for you?"

"That's why I'm calling. I have a regular cleaning woman, but the cleanup needed in my office and, to a lesser extent in a couple of the other rooms, is beyond what she can or would care to handle. Also—and of more immediate concern to me—are the drawers full of original blueprints from my father's and grandfather's practices that got tossed around. Many of them are quite old and will require a careful touch to be put back to rights. I wondered if you know someone capable of doing that for me."

"Yes." Running a quick mental finger down the list of the outfits she used most often, she pinpointed the one most likely to do a good job of both this scope and delicacy. "I know a detective in the Seattle P.D. burglary department, as well. I'll call him to find out when we'll be free to go in, then arrange a crew to be there the minute we receive the authorization. Do you have family to stay with until we can get it cleaned up?"

"No. My brothers are gone now, and my daughter's in Boston."

"Would you like me to arrange for a hotel room, at least for tonight?"

He blew out a shaky breath, the first sign of nerves she'd heard him display. "That would be nice. I'm a little uncomfortable at the idea of going back there tonight."

"Of course you are. I can only imagine what a frightening experience that must have been. Let me make a few calls and I'll get back to you. Would you also like me to get a security company to drive by your place a few times tonight or perhaps a guard to patrol the grounds around the house?"

"Yes. The former, I think." The line hummed with silence for a brief moment, then he said, "Mitzi was right. You are a gem."

"Aww. What an incredibly lovely thing to say when you're smack in the middle of such a traumatic ordeal. Does a downtown hotel suit you or would you prefer another area?"

"Downtown sounds nice. I'm in the mood to look out and see people and activity."

"Where are you right now?"

"In the lobby at the Swedish Medical Center."

It broke her heart a little that anyone should be so alone. "Why don't you let me send a cab over to get you? You can come back here and hang out in the kitchen with me until we get you set up."

There was an instant of silence, then he said, "I'd like that. Thank you."

When she hung up a moment later, it occurred to her that she probably should have consulted Cade before extending the invitation. The mansion might belong to her and her friends, but Cade was paying them rent. And that made it technically, if temporarily, his.

She nevertheless called the cab company to go collect the older man before she went looking for Cade.

She found him talking on the phone in the parlor. "You've got it penciled in for the day after tomorrow, right?" he said. He listened, then gave a decisive nod, even though the other party clearly couldn't see. "Good. It's a go. Ink it."

She stood quietly until he disconnected a minute later and looked up at her. Then she stepped forward. "Have you got a minute?"

His eyes were slightly wary but his voice easy when he said, "Sure. What's up?"

She explained about Mr. Tarrof and how she'd sent a cab for him to come to the mansion until she could get him settled. "I hope that's all right."

"Hell, yeah, it's all right. What a shitty thing to happen."

"I know, isn't it? It must be awful to have the home you've always felt safe in be violated like that. And that's *before* getting hit over the head. I just hate the thought of what he's going through by himself." It felt strange to be on the same page with him for a change, to talk so easily.

And for this minute, at least, she set aside her new agenda. Because strange or not, it was also nice. "Thank you, Cade. I admit I forgot while I was talking to him that this isn't my place at the moment. So I appreciate you being reasonable about it."

"Not a problem." He shrugged, then gave her a leisurely up and down. "You might wanna find an apron or something, though, to slap over that dress. Mr. T doesn't need a heart attack on top of everything else he's been through. He's probably seen all he cares to of hospitals."

She had to bite back the laugh that tickled the back of her throat. Instead she made a production of sighing. "So much for the detente. Still, while you're being so understanding and all, can you spare me for a half hour, forty-five minutes, to go to his place and pack him a bag? I don't think it's a good idea for him to go back in his house until I can arrange to have it put back to rights."

"That shouldn't be a problem. Just let me know when you're ready to go."

"Fair enough." She faced him squarely. "This is very nice of you."

"I can say the same of you. You're taking care of a guy you only met once."

"Ah, well, but then that's what I do." Hitching a shoulder, she gave him a crooked smile. "I like taking care of people."

They stared at each other for a moment, then she shifted uneasily. "Well."

His phone rang and she left him to his calls. Walking from the room, she found herself breathing a sigh of relief. She couldn't say why, but that little moment of agreement or understanding or whatever it had been between them seemed somehow more dangerous than all the sexual attraction in the world.

She shook the feeling off, however.

And headed back to the kitchen to call a concierge she knew at the Fairmont Olympic to see what kind of deal they could make her on a room.

CHAPTER ELEVEN

What a long, exhausting day. I'm just beat right into the ground. So whataya bet this will be one of those nights I can't sleep for beans?

TONY STOPPED in his tracks a stride past the mansion kitchen archway, his blood flash-freezing in his veins. Silently, he bent backward to get another look—then eased upright in almost the same heartbeat.

Shit. He had seen exactly what he'd thought he'd seen. What the hell was Tarrof doing here?

Oh, Christ. Had he come to *ID* him? Were the cops on their way, as well?

Dammit, he *knew* he shouldn't have made a play for the original Wolcott mansion blueprints. He wasn't a goddamn second story man. As if anyone would choose to be when it was just plain easier to romance lonely women out of their money.

It was a whole lot safer, too. Besides, what house in the upper income brackets wasn't wired for security to the *nth* degree these days?

And yet...

The opportunity had been too good to pass up. When he'd heard someone on the set telling somebody else that Tarrof's granddaddy had built this joint and—more importantly, from his point of view—that the original

blueprints were one of Stan the Man's prize posses-
sions, he'd known he'd found his solution to the trick
wall. So while everyone was busy shooting elsewhere,
he'd gone to the room Beks used as an office, stolen a
peek at Tarrof's information sheet and made a note of
his address.

The minute he'd turned his shift over to John last
night he'd headed straight to Tarrof's neighborhood.
He'd parked several blocks away, of course, then hoofed
it over to the right one.

It was sheer dumb luck that he'd been casing the joint
for less than ten minutes when the old guy's housekeeper had exited through the rear door. Tony couldn't
have timed it better if he'd tried, considering he'd just
let himself into the back yard. From his vantage point
around the ancient oak tree he'd dodged behind to keep
out of sight, he'd had an excellent view as she'd made
a beeline for an old-lady-mobile parked in the circular
driveway. It hadn't hurt his cause any that her attention
had been focused on the monster purse she'd been rum-
maging through.

And hadn't it just seemed like fucking kismet when
she'd all but snapped her fingers halfway to her car
and whirled to go back? Especially since she'd left the
kitchen door wide open behind her.

Grabbing opportunities that came his way was his
strong suit, but he had to admit that his heart had done
some serious tripping shit when he'd sidled up to the
door and peeked around its jamb. Because who was to
say the woman hadn't merely stepped into the kitchen
to boost a bottle of wine or a package of filet mignons
before hitting the road for the night?

She'd been nowhere in sight, however, so he'd slid

into the room slicker 'n snot. Working fast and silent, he'd found a walk-in pantry to close himself into.

When the housekeeper had come back through the kitchen a short while later, she hadn't acted as if anyone else was there. She'd neither walked particularly quietly nor called out to anyone. And while it might have been that she simply didn't have the kind of relationship that included calling goodbyes to her employer, he'd taken a wild shot and deduced the old man wasn't home. The housekeeper's car had been the only one in the drive, and the place had just felt empty when Tony had finally judged it safe to let himself out of the pantry.

He'd grabbed a pair of cleaning gloves from a box he'd found under the sink, pulled them on and yanked a paper towel from the roll on the counter, using it to wipe his prints from any surfaces he'd touched. Stuffing it in his back pocket to dispose of later, he'd gone in search of the old man's office.

While looking for it, he'd passed some spectacular *objets d'art*. But as he'd been on a mission that would net him a thousand times what those were worth, he'd left them untouched.

He'd finally found the room he was looking for upstairs, and was feeling pretty good when he'd pulled open the first in a series of cabinets with wide, shallow drawers.

Then things had turned to shit.

Jesus. There must have been five hundred blueprints in all those drawers—and the things weren't exactly easy reading.

He'd started out being real careful, since he'd fully expected to find what he was looking for and be out the door with no one the wiser.

But not only had Tarrof's grandfather been an architect, so had his daddy been, apparently. And between them they must have saved every fucking piece of paper they'd ever sketched on, never mind the fifty years worth of blueprints. It wasn't like he'd had the whole goddamn night to search either, so after a while he'd started just tossing the shit aside the instant he determined it wasn't what he was searching for, then moving on to the blueprint beneath it in hopes that this, *this,* would be the one he needed in order to grab the brass ring and get the hell outta drab, gray Seattle.

Midway through the third or fourth cabinet—who could keep track?—he'd wondered if maybe Tarrof had framed the damn thing and had it hanging in another room. He sure as hell hadn't heard anybody talking about all this other crap in here. So he'd searched room to room and in his mounting frustration had maybe thrown a few things around.

When he'd heard footsteps on the staircase, he'd damn near had a heart attack. Realizing he was probably in the old man's bedroom, he'd snatched up a nice hefty statuette and stepped behind the door. Then bashed the old man a good one as soon as he'd stepped into the room.

So here he was, hanging outside the mansion kitchen, wondering if he was about to get his ass hauled off to jail.

Jesus. This was supposed to be a gravy job.

But if not for the lousy luck he'd had since taking it on, he'd have no goddamn luck at all.

AVA HAD THOUGHT documentary-making was chaotic before. She discovered later that week that the interviewing portion was nothing compared to filming.

There was a mountain of additional equipment, and she didn't know if it was simply that—that there was so much more of it—or if the filming gear was larger than the digital equipment, as well. Either way, it seemed to suck up all the available space.

She did know that the noise levels before and after filming had ratcheted to new heights today. Which was hardly surprising considering how many more people were suddenly crowded into the mansion. Everyone's job appeared to be more task specific than during the interviews. Assistants had assistants.

Or so it looked to her. All she knew for sure was that the food service portion of this gig had suddenly gone from being a fun job to one that made her feel that there weren't enough hours in the day to pull together everything she needed to accomplish.

Not that she had any excuse for being caught by surprise. Cade had given her the new personnel list Beks had drawn up days ago, so it wasn't as if she hadn't known it was coming. Hell, she'd done the up-front preparations for it, had arranged the housing and transportation for the additional crew and actors. But that was work she could do in her sleep.

It was the logistics of feeding the larger group that was going to take a little longer to get straight in her head. And when she *used* her head, she knew it was too soon to panic. This was only the first day for cripes sake—of course she had to allow for some adjustments.

Her silly, emotional gut didn't feel quite so positive, however. She was accustomed to being good at what she did. And planning, buying and preparing everything in order to have it all table-ready, as well as keeping her platters stocked when the hordes tore through them like weevils through cotton, had eaten up way more time than she'd anticipated. She didn't have a handle yet on how much food was enough but not too much.

Where she'd had professional caterers to defray the work for the bigger events she'd put on in the past, she was now on her own. So, she'd give this one more day, then she would have to think hard if it looked like it was going to keep up this frenetic pace. If that were the case, she'd definitely have to come up with a different solution.

"Well, bitch, whine, complain." She hauled her second pineapple of the day to the counter and brought over the bowl of apples, a clamshell of kiwis and one of strawberries.

But before she started cutting everything up, she poured a bag of mandarin oranges into a bowl and slid it onto the service table. That and the decimated tray of deli meats would have to tide over anyone wandering in looking for something to nosh on while she refilled the platters. She'd added some odds and ends to her soup, and although it should stretch a little further, it was still reheating. Given how fast the newly enlarged group had gone through it, she had a feeling she might have to start making two pots full.

Great. That'd add another forty minutes to her evening schedule.

With a sigh, she pulled out a butcher-block cutting board, grabbed a knife…and worked on getting over herself.

The truth was, she could probably ask Cade for an assistant, as well. They could no doubt get a part-time prep cook for a negligible amount, given the overall budget for this production. So if stubborn pride prevented her from doing so—well, she could hardly blame it on him.

And didn't *that* just bite.

She tried keeping the facts rather than her reaction to them in mind as the day wore on. It was just tough luck that she was tired, frustrated and feeling increasingly cranky by the time the young woman with the suck-the-soul-right-out-of-your-body stare strolled into the kitchen.

She looked to be in her early twenties, a lanky brunette one latitude south of tall. Grabbing an orange out of the bowl, she came over to the working area, leaned her narrow hips back against the counter and locked her gaze on Ava. "Hi."

The avid intensity of her look made Ava feel almost claustrophobic. All the same, she gave the other woman a polite nod and said, "Hi, yourself." Then, stepping around her, she grabbed two containers of braided apple strudels. She had to move around the woman again to pluck a couple of cookie sheets from a lower cupboard and was starting to grit her teeth by the time she paused to fire up the oven. While it preheated, she placed the pastries on the pans. Things had gone quiet in the rest of the mansion, which meant they were probably filming or doing their test shots or whatever. And considering how late in the day it was getting to be, that meant people would likely be descending on her soon.

"I heard you knew Agnes Wolcott really well."

"Uh huh." Okay, she still had some of the fruit she'd cut up earlier. And there were crackers and—shit. She still needed to cube up some cheese. She headed for the fridge.

"I need to know everything there is to know about her."

Seriously? That pulled her attention away from the mental list she was running, and she glanced at the young woman over her shoulder. Who the hell *was* she?

She promptly shook the question aside, because it didn't matter. Ordinarily she would love talking about Miss A with someone involved in Agnes's documentary—which this woman must be or she wouldn't be here. But not when she felt not only hip-deep in preparations but a scant two steps ahead of getting buried in the avalanche of them. "Listen, I don't have time for this. Maybe after—"

The young woman whirled on her heel and stalked from the room.

"—I finish up here." The breath Ava blew upward contained enough gusty irritation to flutter her bangs. *Jeez, lady. Impatient much?*

As she suspected, the crew started pouring in a short while later. She was hot, sticky and starting to worry big-time about running out of food by the time the last person dished up and took a seat.

But she made it. By the skin of her teeth, but still. She recorded a few changes for tomorrow, then raced through the cleanup. Worn to a nub, all she could think of was how badly she needed to get away from here. *Now.* There was still a lot of prep work to do for tomorrow's spread when she got home, but at least she'd *be* home. Where it was blessedly quiet.

And where a bubble bath with her name on it waited down the hall as soon as she finished her chores.

Someone out in the hallway called Beks's name.

"Hold on," she heard the PA reply. "I need to tell Ava Cade wants to talk to her ASAP."

Oh, no. Grabbing her purse, she let herself out the back door. She knew her actions were less than professional, but she didn't care. She was seriously tapped out.

Besides, she assured herself as she climbed in her car, started it up and backed out of the driveway, she was doing them both a favor. No telling what she might say, given the frame of mind she was in at this moment. She'd be in a much more reasonable one first thing in the morning.

Walking into her condo a short while later, she didn't feel her tension immediately melt as she'd half expected. But she assured herself that was because she was still revving. She'd had to stop at Metropolitan Market on the way home, and it had been a madhouse of too many people crowding the aisles and long lines. That and the fact that even though she was finally home, she still had a ton of work to do.

She'd planned on sitting down and putting her feet up for ten minutes to catch her breath and decompress. But looking at the bags of groceries she'd dumped on the counter, she sighed.

Then kicked off her shoes and began pulling out items, separating them into two different groups for the dishes she needed to prepare for tomorrow.

She'd chopped red cabbage for the Thai chicken salad, had just begun on the head of green and was concluding her pissy factor probably had something to do with not taking the time to eat dinner, when someone started pounding on her door.

"Aw, *c'mon!*" Sliding off the stool onto her very tired

feet, she stalked over to the door and flung it open. *"What?"*

Then she blinked. "Oh, crap. It's you."

Cade bulled his way into her tiny foyer as if he owned the joint, slammed the door behind him—then had the nerve to lean down and shove his nose a fraction of an inch from hers. His eyes sparked gas-flame blue with temper. "Who the hell told you it was quitting time?" he demanded.

Her spine snapped ruler straight. "Ex*cuse* me?"

"I'm paying you a generous wage to be available when I need you, and you just go waltzing off without a word to anyone?"

"Seriously?" Fury surged through her veins. "I was there eleven hours!"

"And I was there fourteen!" he roared. "So—what?—you blew off your duties because you've got another hot date with your Brazilian stud, or something?"

"Argentinean," she snapped. "And do I *look* like I'm ready for a date? Do I look like I'm having any sort of fun at all?"

His insulting once-over was the final straw. With a glance at the tie he wore today—an article of apparel she hadn't seen on him since high school—she wrapped her fist around it, turned on her bare heel and marched for the kitchen. He could walk or he could choke. It made no difference to her.

Swearing a blue streak, he used one hot-skinned hand to unpeel her fingers from around the strip of patterned silk. But he followed in her wake when she kept walking. "Why the hell are you limping?"

"Because I've been on my feet for eleven freaking hours and they hurt!"

"Well, if you didn't wear those stupid heels all the time they'd probably feel a whole lot better."

She whirled to face him. "Screw you, Cade. I've still got a couple hours' worth of work before I can even *think* about putting my feet up and I'm in no mood to listen to your fashion advice or reprimands for not conforming to your fascist time clock. So if that's all you came to say, you can just march your butt out of my house."

"That's not why I'm here." Again he shoved his face aggressively close and said between perfect white teeth, "*That* would be to hear you tell me to my face why you blew off the actress who's going to play Agnes when I specifically sent her to you."

"Who?" Then her brain kicked in. "That girl with the soul-sucking stare and no social skills? *She's* going to play Miss A?"

She gave him a straight shot to his solar plexus with the heel of her hand, and, as he straightened, finally getting out of her face, she demanded, "And I was supposed to know this how? She came in while I was scrambling to get everything on the table for the postshoot rush. She didn't introduce herself, she didn't say you'd sent her—she just demanded I tell her everything I know about Agnes. When I said I didn't have the time she stormed out in a big huff without giving me a chance to finish my damn sentence, which would have been to tell her I'd be happy to talk to her after I got the food service ready." *Okay, "happy" might be pushing it.*

Still. Close enough.

But did Mr. High and Mighty say, Whoops, sorry for the misunderstanding, maybe I jumped to conclusions?

Hell, no.

"It's not like anyone on the crew is in imminent danger of starvation. It's a helluva lot more important to me that you help the actress portraying Agnes get some insight into her character than it is that you feed the crew," he informed her flatly.

"Then you should have told me that before I made myself crazy trying to keep up with doing just that! Next time I'll drop everything and *you* can deal with the cranky people wanting to know why they aren't getting anything to eat. And tell your precious actress to try communicating while you're at it!" About-facing, she headed back to the kitchen. "Now go away. I've still got a ton of stuff to do."

Cade knew he should probably do exactly that. They were both way too riled up, and pushing things now was just asking to escalate the situation into something he was sure to regret.

Yet still he tromped behind the angry twitch of her inverted-heart butt, reaching out to grasp her arm just as they rounded the end of the breakfast bar.

Turning on him, she jerked her arm free. "Don't. Touch me!"

I'll do more than touch you, baby. She was flushed and furious, and he wanted nothing more than to back her against the counter, lift her onto it, jerk her knees apart and step between them. He wanted to—

Jesus. Stepping back, he raised his hands in surrender. Sucked in a deep breath.

And blew it out. "No hands, see? Keeping 'em to myself here." He looked beyond her at the huge stainless bowl on the counter. It was half full of shredded cabbage, and piles of food spread from one end of the granite slab to the other. Looking back at her, he noticed for the first time that her usually pristine clothes were spotted with food stains. "What the hell?"

Delicate auburn brows drawing together, lush lips flattening and hands fisting, she crossed her arms beneath her breasts and tapped her foot.

"What are you doing here, Ava?"

"What does it *look* like I'm doing? Prepping food for tomorrow."

"You're *making* everything? By yourself?"

"Who do you think's been making it, the freaking food fairy?"

"I thought you were picking it up from a caterer." And you could've knocked him over with one of her long eyelashes to discover she'd been preparing it all.

She gave him a look that clearly said, *You're an idiot.* "Have you bothered to *look* at the bills I've submitted?"

This was the Ava he remembered. The Ava who from kindergarten to senior year had stood toe-to-toe with him and never hesitated to give him shit—or to call him on his own.

He much preferred dealing with this Ava over the woman who gave Miss Manners a run for her money. "I look at *all* the bills, babyface. I assumed you were scoring us one of your killer discounts like the ones you got for the housing."

She blew out a disgusted, "Pfft."

"Why the hell didn't you say something?"

"Why didn't *you*? Or have Beks tell me? I've never worked a documentary before. You said do the food service—I thought this was what you expected. Besides, it was fine until the number of people I was feeding started multiplying like rabbits. God." She shook her head. "Your communication skills rank right up there with your crappy actress's."

"Hire someone to either do it or help you do it."

She gave him a curt nod. "I'll get on that first thing in the morning. Meanwhile, I still have a Thai salad and a pot of soup to make." She flapped a dismissive hand at him. "So go away."

He found himself doing just that. A wry smile tugging one corner of his mouth, he closed her front door behind him.

Yep. No doubt about it. It sure rocked to be such a hotshot producer.

It was always a power rush to know you could command so much respect.

CHAPTER TWELVE

God, just when I think that maybe, MAYBE,
there's something there...

THE FOLLOWING morning, Ava contacted one of the caterers she used and hung up with a smile on her face,
knowing that her workload would drop dramatically
by this afternoon. In some respects it lessened immediately, since there was no need to prep all the replacement food for the stuff that got gobbled up this morning.
With the sudden wealth of time on her hands, she went
looking for the actress Cade had hired to play Miss A.

She found her pacing the upstairs hallway, mutter-
ing under her breath. Introducing herself, Ava learned
the actress's name was Heather McNulty. She led the
young woman to a guest bedroom, sat her down and
explained a little about her relationship with Miss A.
Then she invited her to ask whatever she wanted.

Two hours later, she still thought Heather's social
skills were lousy, and her reservations about the actress's ability to portray Agnes weren't exactly allayed.
She hoped she was wrong—but didn't have a wonderful
feeling about the chances. Heather could barely string
three or four words together when you talked to her
about anything other than Agnes. How on earth could

she convincingly portray the complexity of Miss A's personality?

The actress was intense about her craft, though. Ava would give her that. She must have insisted on practicing the deep timbre of Miss Agnes's voice close to a hundred times, trying to get it exactly right. It was admirable, Ava supposed—but tiring. Correcting the woman sure wore the hell out of *her*.

But she was willing to supply Heather with every scrap of information at her disposal if it would help her do Miss Agnes credit.

After the younger woman strode off, still mumbling to herself, Ava decided she needed to watch Cade film Heather's first segment, which was being shot today— if for no other reason than to reassure herself it wasn't as bad as she feared.

Surely that wasn't possible.

The grips had moved the hair and makeup gear out of Miss A's bedroom suite and moved the filming equipment in. When Ava slipped into the sitting room, she found it in the state of controlled chaos she'd come to expect. Grips were still moving gear around, the lighting engineer ran tests and the boom operator adjusted his microphones. Across the room, Cade and Louie discussed she-wasn't-sure-what in low voices, during which Cade leaned several times to look at something on a small screen.

Beks had told her the scene they were shooting this afternoon featured a disagreement between Agnes and Daddy Wolcott over Agnes's desire to take flying lessons. When Ava had asked why, the PA explained it would establish Miss A's take-charge-of-her-own-life personality faster and more interestingly than a voice-over would and recommended Ava imagine the brief dramatization followed by photos and an old newsreel snippet of Miss A with her plane, followed by Jane talking about how great it would've been to have known Miss Agnes then.

All of which sounded very cool—as long as the acting didn't blow.

Stomach uneasy, she leaned against a far wall as Cade left the director of photography doing his technical stuff and crossed to talk to the actors, who were dressed in clothing of a much earlier era. The longer she had to wait during the interval between discussion, positioning and shooting, the more her tension increased.

Finally they called for silence on the set. When they had it, Cade said, "Roll camera," then called for action after Louie let him know the cameras were up to speed and ready to roll.

The actors began their scene, and as Ava watched, the knots in her gut loosened one by one. The change in Heather once she was the focus of the camera was a revelation. One that made her remember what Poppy had said last November about Cade's reputation for discovering hot new talent destined for a meteoric rise to the top.

Maybe face-to-face Heather didn't display a discernible personality of her own, but she sure as hell came alive when the camera rolled. No. She did more than that. She promptly took it a step beyond and *became* her subject.

At least in this instance.

Ava could totally see her as a young Miss A. She had the mannerisms down cold, and her persistence in trying Agnes's voice over and over again, until Ava had finally agreed that that, *that* one, was about as close as it got, had paid off in spades. The longer Ava listened

to the actress speak her lines, the more she found herself grinning.

Yep. The woman had nailed it right on the prover-
bial head. She'd absorbed every detail Ava had given
her and used it to turn herself into Miss Agnes.

It was a little spooky.

But it was also pretty darn amazing. So much so
that Ava had the strongest urge to call Jane and Poppy
to tell them to get their fannies over here to see it for
themselves.

She doubted Cade would appreciate her inviting
people onto his set, however, so she would just have to
settle for calling them.

First she had to make sure the afternoon order, which
she'd asked the caterer to provide to round out what
she'd brought in this morning, had arrived. Then she
needed to take some time to catch up on her own business.

She headed back to the kitchen, where things were
temporarily quiet. And managed to check quite a few
items off both her concierge and her father's birthday
party lists before Beks found her there a while later.

"Hey," the PA said, breezing into the room.

Ava smiled at Beks's red lipstick, black Betty Blow-
torch T-shirt with its skull and crossed pistols, short
black skirt and clunky shoes. "Hey, yourself. Are you
the vanguard? I guess I'd better check my table to make
sure it's ready if the crew's on the way." Then she tilted
her head, listening. "Wait a minute. How come I don't
hear anything?"

Beks laughed. "They're still filming. My part up
there is done for a while."

"In that case, I've got some new stuff from a caterer

I'm going to be using from this point on if you wanna give it a try. They're taking over entirely tomorrow."

"No more homemade soup?"

"Nope. My evenings are mine, once again."

Beks gave her a crooked smile. "Cool for you, but bummer for us. I love your soups." Her expression brightened. "Still, now you'll have time to go dancing with me."

Ava perked up. "Really? I *love* to dance!"

"Yeah, I got that impression the day your friend had me bring music up to the makeup room for you. You bust some mad moves, too. So, whataya say? You know a place where we could go? I'll see if the crew I share the house with wants to join us and you can ask your friends." She made a face. "Not that I'm sure I can interest any of the guys in going. You know how a lot of men can be when it comes to dancing."

"I do, but if they don't wanna come, who needs them? We aren't our mamas—we don't need no stinkin' boys before we can get up and dance." For no good reason, that gave her a brief flash of Cade back in their cotillion days.

She promptly slammed a lid on it. "But I do know a couple of guys who like to dance."

"Yeah?" Beks was all interest. "They single?"

"One of them is. The other is married to Jane."

"One's all I need." She grinned. "Where do you think we should go?"

"The Alibi Room in Post Alley is, like, custom-made for you Hollywood types. A group of filmmakers own it and the club helps support independent films and their creators. Lotsa talking about filmmaking during the day. But the DJ rocks weekend nights—and sometimes they even get a live band."

"Sounds great. What do you think, Friday night?"

"Yeah. I'll talk to my friends, but I'm in even if they're busy."

"Ooh, this'll be fun. I'm pumped." Beks cocked her head. "Annnd, it sounds like we've either got elephants stampeding upstairs or filming has wrapped up. I'd better grab something to eat while the grabbing is good."

"YOU'RE A fucking masochist, you know that, Gallari?" Stuffing his hands in his pants pockets, Cade paused just steps inside the Alibi Room's downstairs dance club the following Friday night. "And talking to yourself isn't helping you sound real intelligent, either."

Not that anyone could hear. The thumping music being spun by a DJ no doubt drowned out his words for anyone standing less than a foot away.

But, Jesus. What was he doing here?

He'd been smart enough to say no when Beks had extended an invitation that included Ava and her friends. But the more he'd heard her and a couple of the grips talking about meeting up with them here tonight, the more he'd gotten a jones to dance with a certain Ms. Spencer.

So there she was across the room, sitting at a table with her usual posse—Poppy and Jane and some of the same guys he'd seen them with last year when he'd accosted her in that Columbia City bar. He knew better than to look for a welcome.

Nothing new there, of course. But did he really want his crew to see that in action? They respected him. He'd like to keep it that way, yet it likely wouldn't happen if he joined them and they learned what he'd done to her back in high school.

He turned to go.

"Hey, boss! Over here." Beks lurched out of the gloom and grabbed his arm. She gave him a big grin. "Glad you could make it."

Shit.

He looked down at her. "Yeah, look, I was just leaving," he yelled, then lowered his voice when the song wound to a close. "I realized I need to go over the dailies tonight while I've got the chance. We've got a full filming schedule tomorrow."

She wove her arm through his and tugged. "But you've got time for a beer, right? And a dance. There's never enough guys who like to dance at these things. I know Ava's right when she says we don't need no stinkin' boys to get out on the floor—but it sure is fun when you get a chance to dance with one."

Well, hell. Beks had a way about her that just made you hate to disappoint her. He'd feel as if he was kicking the world's friendliest puppy if he said no. "One drink, one dance."

"Deal!" She towed him across the room as the DJ spun a new tune.

To his relief, he saw Ava and company abandon the table, Ava already getting her groove on before she hit the dance floor. Maybe, just maybe, he could knock back a beer in record time, pull Beks to the opposite side of the floor for her dance and beat feet out of here with his working relationships still intact. It might not stop Ava's friends from assassinating his character after he left, but if that's what they were inclined to do, there wasn't a helluva lot he could do to prevent it. He'd just have to hope for the best.

His plan might have worked if there had been more than two waitresses working the packed club. As it was,

although one of them swung by to take his order, he
watched Ava dance three dances and still his beer didn't
arrive.

On the other hand, he got to watch Ava dance.

God, the woman could move. It was as if her body
were an instrument that knew every note, every beat
to whatever song was playing and flowed in sync with
it. Even as a girl, back in the god-awful cotillion class
days, she'd been the best dancer. But watching her hips
move like oiled ball bearings back then hadn't had him
shifting in his chair the way he was now.

"Jesus." He looked away.

When he looked back again a new song had started,
and she and her cronies were retiring from the floor.
Seeing them head back, he dropped a ten on the table in
front of his chair in case the waitress deigned to show
up and leaned over to interrupt Beks's conversation with
the new grip. "You ready for that dance?"

"Yes!" Excusing herself to the new guy, she surged
to her feet and danced away from their table with him
following in her wake.

By the time their number came to an end, Ava was
back on the floor and a draft sat sweating gently on the
table along with his change. Thinking this was turning out okay—if he didn't mind that he was acting
like a chickenshit and had yet to even say hello to the
woman—he sat and downed half his beer in one swallow. Leaving a couple bucks, he started gathering up
his change. He'd kill off his beer and do exactly what
he'd told Beks he was going to do: go back to the mansion and run the dailies.

Poppy dropped into the chair next to him. "Hello,
Gallari," she said under the music.

"Poppy." He nodded. "You're looking good. Did Ava

tell you how great you three turned out in your interview?"

"Yes." She studied him unsmilingly for a moment. "She also said we have to be civil to you tonight."

"She did?" Something inside him lightened, and a corner of his mouth crooked up in a small smile as he found himself searching the dance area for her again. "Huh."

"I could always ignore her instructions, of course," Poppy said, regaining his attention. "Janie and I put aside our differences for Miss A's documentary, but I'm on my own time now—I don't have to be all grown-up and professional. And I imagine I could make some trouble for you with your people here."

His smile turned cynical. "You think they'd care as long as I continue to employ them?"

"I think Beks would."

Shit. His blood chilled. Because Beks would. She'd never look at him the same way again.

If he were still the same boy who'd taken that bet back in high school, he probably wouldn't give a damn. But he hadn't been for a long time, and he did care about retaining her respect.

All the same, he shrugged. "I can't stop you," he said. "You're gonna do what you're gonna do. All I can say is I'm not that guy anymore. And I really regret what I did."

"I might even believe that. But I want you to know that if you hurt Ava again—"

"I'm not looking to hurt her!"

"Good. Because if you do, I will find a way to make you pay."

He was half bitter over her refusal to let him live down his age-old mistake and wholly envious over the women's relationship. Looking her in the eye, he told her the truth. "I wish I had a friend half as good as you."

She shrugged and climbed to her feet. "You reap what you sow."

"Yeah? Well, maybe if I'd had a friend like you I wouldn't have sowed in the first place."

She stilled for a minute. Studied him in silence. Then gave a brisk nod. "There is that possibility, I guess, if you come down on the nurture side of the old versus-nature debate." The music changed to a slow number, and she turned away to tap the shoulder of a tall, olive-skinned man whose teeth shone white in the dim light when he turned in his seat.

"C'mon, copper," she said. "They're playing our song."

"We have a song?" The guy unfolded his long body from the chair.

She ran a finger along his arm. "It's slow, isn't it?"

"Yeah, right." He grinned. "This is *definitely* our song."

It's slow, isn't it? Cade located Ava vacating the dance floor and rose to his feet to intercept her. This was the reason he'd come. For the potential to dance with her. He'd been thinking a fast number—if he was lucky. But what the hell, he might as well shoot the moon. Because slow trumped the hell out of fast any day.

It only remained to be seen whether he could convince her to dance with him, period.

Stopping in front of her, he gave her the formal bow as he'd been taught back in C.C. "Hello. My name is Buttface Gallari. May I have this dance?"

He saw her full mouth twitch and her dimples crease her cheeks before she compressed her lips in a severe line and gave him her haughtiest raised-brows look. "Well, I don't know," she said. "I generally make it a policy to avoid men named Buttface."

"It's a good policy," he agreed—then thrust out an authoritative hand. "Make an exception."

"Oh, what the hell." One shapely shoulder hitched toward her ear as she placed her hand in his. "Why not."

He grinned as she whirled with her hand still holding his over her shoulder and undulated back to the dance floor. Once there, she turned into his arms.

And the smile dropped from his face. Because he hadn't genuinely thought she would agree, had never truly believed, for all his outward bravado, that he would hold her tonight.

And, man, did she feel good. This was no bony, angular woman. She was round and ripe and plush in his arms, her body a cushiony furnace that sank heat into his bones everywhere she touched.

"You smell good," he said, breathing in her hair and her skin and the faintest exotic spice scent of some hot-mama perfume as he wrapped his arms around her and commenced a slow sway in place.

"Yes, I believe in regular bathing," she agreed dryly.

"It's working for you."

He felt her muffled snort against his collarbone and smiled into her hair.

He was nowhere near the dancer she was—but this he could do. He could handle the vertical rock-and-rub and appreciate every damn minute of the luscious give of her curvy body against the not-so-giving planes of his own.

The trick here was to avoid finding himself pressing a hard-on into her softly rounded stomach like some hormone driven, no-control eighteen-year-old. Stroking his cheek against her shiny hair, he visualized the chilly, damp evening outside to help him keep that from happening.

It only half succeeded. And the whole time he was thinking, *Play the long version, play the long version.*

The neediness of his thoughts made him uneasy. Because, really, how sappy could he get? He didn't *need* anyone. Hell, if he hadn't learned anything else, he'd at least learned not to place too much faith in others. Yeah, she was soft and warm and smelled like a million bucks. But he'd discovered the hard way that the only person he could depend on was himself.

It'd be smart to keep that in mind.

Which he did when the song ended and Ava raised her head from its resting place just beneath his collarbone and smiled up at him. It was such a pretty, *friendly* smile that he paused, thinking he'd somehow gotten off track.

Then he remembered that instant of helpless neediness and stepped back, reaching up to unclasp her hands from around his neck and gently pull them away. He released them. "Thanks for the dance," he said and gave her the cynically raised brow he'd perfected senior year. "So there's not really a Brazilian boyfriend, is there?"

When coolness ate up all the sweetness of her smile, he pretended he didn't feel faintly sick. Assured himself he hadn't just messed up, bollixed up, *sullied* a really nice moment between them.

"You danced with me just to find out if I—" Her face showed no expression.

But those eyes— God, it may have come and gone faster than heat lightning, but he recognized betrayal when he saw it. He should. He'd put it there before. "No!" He took a step forward.

She stepped back. "Well, you got me there, Gallari. I confess. I have no Brazilian lover."

Good, he thought as she whirled on her heel and walked away, her shapely hips ticking from side to side like a metronome. Not that it mattered to him, of course. But, still. Good.

Not the point, Ace. Going after her, he reached to turn her back to him. "Look, I didn't dance with you to—"

She pulled her arm out of his grasp and his defenses went on red alert at the smile she gave him. It was small and tight and glittered more sharply than a stiletto.

"You seem to have a hard time remembering this," she said, so softly he had to strain to hear over the new song. "But my lover boy? He's Argentinean."

Christ. *Was* the guy real? The way she'd been all loose and sort of snuggled up to him for that brief moment before he'd let his pride run his mouth…that hadn't struck him as the sort of thing a woman would do if she was getting it on with another guy.

Of course, it could simply be he didn't want to believe Ava was the kind of woman to juggle men in plurals.

He straightened. He *didn't* accept that as true. "Yeah? Prove it."

She looked at him as if he were an opportunistic panhandler on the street. "I don't have to prove anything to you. When Eduardo and I are together, you're not even a blip on my radar."

"I don't believe you."

"Of course you don't. Your ego's so overinflated, you probably have to turn your head sideways to get it through the door."

He shook his head. "No, I don't believe in your Latin lover."

"Well, gee. However will I sleep at night?" Her eyes went wide. "Oh, I know! In Eduardo's arms." And turning on her heel, she sauntered over to her friends.

He watched her go—and had to admire her exit. *Damn.* Clearly he wasn't the only one who knew how to play dirty.

"Fuck." He shook his head, disgusted with himself. Where the hell had that flash of insecurity that had started this whole thing come from? He'd had more style, girl smarts and definitely more sense in the sixth grade. "Good going there, Gallari."

But he stuck by one thing, by God. He doubted like hell there was an Eduardo.

CHAPTER THIRTEEN

Payback's...not as satisfying as I thought it would be.

"FREAKING BASTARD," Ava muttered in the ladies' a short while later as she repaired the makeup she'd sweated off on the dance floor.

Straightening from where she'd been leaning into the mirror to reapply her lipstick, Jane met her reflected gaze. "Who's a freaking— No. Wait. Cade?" Her eyes narrowed. "What'd the bastard do now?"

"Claimed Eduardo doesn't exist."

"That *ass*ho—" Jane's slender dark brows drew together, and her ready best-friend indignation faded. She turned to look at Ava directly. "Um, Av...Eduardo *doesn't* exist."

"I know that!" She shot her brunette friend an impatient frown. "It was the *way* he said it. All Mr. I'm-so-sardonically-amused-at-the-lengths-you'll-go-to-get-my-attention. As if, when I hadn't said a *word* about Eduardo! Then there's that stinking eyebrow lift thing he does. How the hell does anyone raise just one brow, anyhow?"

"Maybe he Botoxed the other."

A delighted laugh burbled out of her, and the dark cloud that had been hanging over her spirits since Cade had made her suspect she'd been suckered by that dirty-pool seductive slow dance finally lifted. "*Yes.* Yes, I bet he does. And you know what?" *About time you kicked in, brain.* "I know just how to make him eat his words over Eduardo, too."

Janie turned to rest her hips against the counter, crossing her arms beneath her petite breasts. "This oughtta be good. How are you going to do that when—at the risk of repeating myself—Eduardo isn't real?"

"I'm going to recruit Eddie. He was my inspiration, anyhow. And you know him, he'll love it."

A slow, evil smile curved Jane's lips. "Ava Spencer, you are such a nefarious chick. I don't know *why* you're going to so much trouble to prove something to some-one you don't give two figs about, but interesting so-lution." She shook her head. "And here people always think you're such a nice girl. Poppy and me, though? We know better. Because you are actually a wicked, wicked woman." Straightening away from the counter, she slung an arm around Ava's shoulders and, tipping her head until their temples touched, gave her a hug. "I've always admired that about you."

"WANNA TREAT yourself? You have *got* to go down to the kitchen when we're finished here."

Surprised at hearing Heather's voice sounding down-right conversational when the actress rarely said any-thing that wasn't directly related to her character, Cade paused outside the room where the grips had transferred the hair and makeup stations.

"Why?" he heard the makeup girl Molly ask. "Has Ava brought in a hot new dish?"

"I'll say. The guy is *smokin'!*"

No, Cade thought, his blood chilling.

"Huh?" Molly said.

"Her *friend,* Molly. Keep up. His name is—" Heather went silent for a second, then Cade could practically *hear* her shrug when she said, "Who the hell knows, I was too busy staring at him to take it in. He's like the most gorgeous guy I've ever seen! You gotta check him out for yourself, because words just fail."

Shit.

Shit, fuck...shit! Turning on his heel, he headed for the stairs.

As he approached the kitchen, he heard the murmur of voices, one definitely Ava's contralto and the other a deep masculine rumble. He was a scant step away from the archway when Ava let loose a deep belly laugh.

It drew his gaze straight to her as he stepped through the doorway.

Her hair blazed in a shaft of rare winter sunlight pouring through the back door window, and her cheeks held a pretty pink tinge as she howled at something the clown lounging against the counter was telling her. She faced the doorway but was oblivious to Cade's entrance. Her attention was all for the other man as she stood hip-shot in dark green heels, matching straight skirt and a prim cream-colored blouse that was rendered not so prim by the filminess of the material and the Maggie the Cat lace and satin slip visible beneath it.

It was hard to tell for sure from this vantage point, but if the angle of the guy was anything to go by, he appeared to be speaking directly to the shadowy cleavage that rose out of the lace.

Cade took an involuntary step closer. "Hey."

Looking reluctant to tear her attention away from her friend, Ava finally turned a cool-eyed gaze on him. "Hey," she said without enthusiasm.

He closed the gap between them and thrust his hand at the dark-haired, dark-eyed man. Now, men didn't rhapsodize over another dude's appearance the way a chick might; it violated some Y chromosome primal imprint or something. But he had to admit that Heather had a point—the guy was more than decent-looking. "I'm Cade Gallari."

Straightening from the counter, the man rose to his full height of six-four or so—an inch or two taller than *he* was at any rate—and took the proffered hand in a bruising grip. "It is good to meet you. I am Eduardo."

"Yeah, I guessed as much. Ava's Brazilian friend, right?"

"Argentinean!" Ava snapped.

"Sorry," he said insincerely. "That's what I meant."

"Not a problem." Eduardo shrugged. "I have learned that American men score much—how do you say it—below the curve when it comes to…geography."

Oh, I don't know. I know precisely where I'd like to send you—and it's a helluva lot farther south than your native country.

He flashed the other man a feral smile. "Your English is very good." Faultless, come to think of it. He studied Eduardo more closely. Maybe the guy wasn't actually Argentinean at all.

"Thank you!" Eduardo flashed a white smile. "I perfected it in American college. It's where I met Ava."

Cade's eyes narrowed suspiciously. "I thought Ava went to Scripps." A women's college.

She gave him a strange look, and he rolled his shoulders. What, he wasn't supposed to know what college she attended? He heard things.

But if she was curious about what he'd heard or from whom, it didn't show, for she merely said, "Scripps is part of the Claremont Consortium, which is actually five colleges. Eduardo went to Claremont McKenna."

"Huh." Then he got down to business. "I hate to bust up your reunion," he lied smoothly, "but I have to ask you to leave, Eduardo. We try to keep this a closed set."

"But of course." The tall Latino turned to Ava. "I will see you later at my hotel, yes?"

No, Cade thought.

"Yes," Ava agreed.

"It might be a late night," he said. "We're doing a complicated scene."

"Not a problem." Slinging a muscular arm around Ava's shoulders, Eduardo pulled her against his side and gave Cade a challenging look. "It will be worth the wait no matter how long it takes."

Not if I can keep her occupied all night.

AVA SHOULD have known better than to think Cade would slink away with his tail between his legs. Instead, he stood regarding them—*again* with that damn I'm-so-amused raised eyebrow. So she slipped out from beneath the heavy warmth of Eddie's arm, grabbed her coat from the pantry and walked her friend out to his car.

"Ooh, honey," he murmured sans the Latin accent as he dug his keys out of his pocket. He clicked the doors unlocked but didn't open the driver's side. Instead, he propped his butt against it and regarded her. "Why would you want to discourage *that* one? I'd do him in a heartbeat."

"Easy, boy," Ava advised dryly. "He doesn't play for your team."

Eddie sighed. "Too few do." Then he gave her a sardonic look. "Even without my gaydar, I could've told you that by the way he all but pissed circles around you to mark his territory. The guy wants you bad."

She refused to acknowledge the way her friend's words frissoned ghostly fingertips of gratification along her nerve endings. Or the fact that her shrug was perhaps a bit too elaborately casual. "Not interested."

Eddie made a rude noise. "Please. If you're gonna be such a liar, liar, pants on fire, at least try to be good at it." Smirking at her glare, he crossed his arms over his chest and settled deeper against the car. "So what the hell possessed you to make me Argentinean?"

"I don't know. It just sorta popped into my mind and then I was stuck with it."

"Good thing for both of us that the guy doesn't speak Spanish, huh? Considering my own grasp of it lets me order Mexican food with a halfway decent pronunciation and that's about it."

"He didn't when I knew him back when, so I figured it was probably a safe enough bet." Standing on her toes, she leaned in to give him a hug. "*Thank* you for doing this, Eddie."

"No problemo." Hugging her back, he offered her an insouciant smile then turned her loose. "You know I'll be giving you a call the next time some beautiful young stud stomps my heart to paste."

"I do," she agreed with a sigh. "And I sure wish, if you can't make better choices in the first place, that you'd let me teach you some tricks to at least make them work for your affection. Maybe if you played it a little aloof so they wouldn't cop right off the bat to what an easy touch you are, they'd value you more and wouldn't go breaking your heart so easily."

His wide shoulders twitched. "We can't all play hard to get like you, girly-girl." He gave her a knowing look.

"So when *are* you going to let Gallari off the hook and just do the boy?"

"N.E.V.E.R. *Never,*" she said with all the authority at her disposal, hoping to hell she wasn't blowing smoke. "Trust me."

"Uh-huh." Eddie tapped her nose with his fingertip, then pushed away from the car and turned to open his door. "You keep telling yourself that, sweetie."

IT WAS DAMN near midnight before Cade left the mansion. Between the level of difficulty in tonight's scene and Heather's perfectionism, which was proving to be even more compulsive than his own, filming had run late. But the end result had paid off big—he'd been more than satisfied by the time they'd wrapped things up.

Even so, he'd stayed long after everyone else went home. Well, he'd had a lot to do, hadn't he, what with the number of loose ends he'd left dangling for too long and going over the dailies. It had been well worth the extra time, considering how powerful the scene had turned out to be—exceeding even his already high expectations. There were a couple places that could stand to be trimmed, but when he thought about tackling them, he had to admit that maybe he wasn't in the best frame of mind to dive into work with such lasting consequences. He was too tired to do it justice.

That was when he packed up, found John to let the night watchman know he was taking off, then headed for home.

It wasn't until he stopped at the light at the bottom of Queen Anne Avenue, however, that he admitted the real problem—and it didn't have squat to do with fatigue.

He hadn't been able to—and hell, still couldn't—stop

thinking about what Ava might be doing right this minute. All night long he'd thought about it—even when she was still there. Then, when she'd left, he'd chewed on the possibilities of what she'd do even as he'd discussed scenes, talked to crew and directed his sometimes-pain-in-the-ass-but-always-talented actress. Because his big inner dialogue with Eduardo notwithstanding, he'd had no good reason to demand she stay when everyone else was going home.

He'd worried it so goddamn much, in fact, that he decided it might be a good idea to swing by the twenty-four-hour Metropolitan Market on his way home to get himself a six-pack. One way or the other, he planned on getting some sleep tonight—tomorrow was going to be too busy to burn energy tossing and turning all night. But the way he'd been brooding over the question of was she or wasn't she with Eduardo since she'd left, he had a feeling he could use some aid if he was going to get any shut-eye tonight.

The minute he entered his condo he got started on the let's-relax-enough-to-sleep project. After pulling two bottles of pale ale out of the carton, he put the rest in the fridge and hunted up a church key to remove the caps. Carrying his bottles in one hand, he crossed to a scaled-down overstuffed chair in the small space at the end of the bed and dropped down on it.

He set one bottle on the tiny table next to him and knocked back half of the other in one long swallow. And all the while he focused on not thinking.

Turned out beer drinking didn't facilitate that real well. Instead, it just made him wonder what hotel Hot Shit Latino Guy was staying at. Was it downtown, not far from here? Out by the airport?

Was she spending the night?

"What if she is, Gallari?" Using his thumbnail, he peeled the label off his second bottle as he slouched deeper into his seat. "You had your shot and used it to turn her into a laughingstock. The Argentinean Wonder made her laugh." He shook his head, and when the damn thing continued to shake even after he meant it to stop, dug his elbow into the arm of the chair and caught the side his jaw in his hand. "Man. That pretty, pretty laugh."

It was the first thing he remembered about her, that laugh. He'd first heard it back when they were—God— still little kids. That kind of wholehearted laughter was something there'd been damn little of in his life. He'd felt at the time that he spent every day chasing his father's attention, and it was such a fucking elusive objective. The old man didn't *smile* much, let alone laugh. Neither did his mother. Well, she did at those social events she was forever wrapped up in. But rarely at home.

So the first time he'd heard Ava cut loose, it had just stopped him in his tracks. He'd looked at her, seen a roly-poly little girl and tried to convince himself that fat people were supposed to be jolly. But something inside of him had both ached and felt inescapably drawn. To that joyful sound. To her.

So he'd done the only thing he could do. He'd found a spider to put on her shoulder. And except for those too brief, perfect weeks leading up to his betrayal in the high school cafeteria, he'd continued tormenting her with increasingly sophisticated degrees of the spider trick.

But dammit, he thought stubbornly, that was a long time ago, and they were adults now. Not those impossibly young kids they'd been then. He'd said it before but he'd say it again: "I am not that guy anymore." Hell, he'd worked his ass off *not* to be that guy. And he didn't know why it was important that she acknowledge that... but for some reason it was.

And yet—

For all the apologies he'd given her over the years, he realized blurrily as the day's events caught up with him and exhaustion hit like somebody had suddenly yanked his plug, he'd never once offered an explanation for why he'd done what he'd done to her. Not that there was a good excuse. But his reasons had seemed valid to him at the time.

Hell, he'd tell her now. As he reached for the phone, his sudden lean forward nearly shifted his balance right off the chair. And he realized he was a little drunk. He must be more played out than he'd thought if two brews could knock him out of gear like this.

He pulled himself to his feet and stumbled the two feet to the bed. Drinking after a couple days of too little sleep and on an empty stomach might not have been his brightest idea. "I'll tell her tomorrow."

Maybe, he amended as he fell face-first. Lifting his suddenly heavy head out of the pillow he'd landed on, he tried to focus on his thought. *What* was that again?

Oh, yeah. It was time to come clean. Tomorrow he'd finally tell her the truth.

CHAPTER FOURTEEN

If it wasn't one freaking thing today, it was another.

TO RUN AN effective con, you had to set up expectations. Tony had done just that the past several days by implementing patrols around the mansion grounds, one in the morning and another in the afternoon. So as he slipped out the front door into the sullen Seattle daylight, he felt confident no one would find it worth commenting on.

Supposing anyone noticed in the first place.

Fat, low clouds the color of wet concrete wept intermittent drizzle as he duplicated the route he'd used during his prior rounds. The only difference this morning was the titanium wire snips he'd slipped into his pockets.

Well, that and the fact that after a quick look around, he stepped off the path between two towering bushes denuded of foliage but clustered with red berries. He studied the utility meter as he pulled on a pair of latex gloves. It appeared to be as straightforward as the internet article he'd read had promised.

He slipped the snips from his pocket and opened them around the padlock's stainless hasp. Lining it up with the tool's cutting groove, he snipped the wire in two. Carefully, he opened the utility meter box. And blew out an impatient breath.

Well, shit. It had a freaking meter seal. Talk about overkill. He quickly dispatched that as well, but wished he had brought a replacement.

Not that it likely mattered, he acknowledged as he turned his head away and closed his eyes. Hell, if too much power was flowing through the meter from all the equipment being used upstairs, they'd find his crispy corpse in the bushes anyway—which would pretty much leave little doubt as to who had done the deed, if not the reasons why. Holding his breath, he yanked the utility meter out of its base.

There was an audible arc-snap and a simultaneous flash of light that flared red through his eyelids. But, cracking those lids open, he grinned like an idiot at the village fair.

Because it could have fried his ass—and it hadn't.

The mansion's power had gone down in concert with his own light show, and faintly, if he listened hard, he could hear the rise of disconcerted voices coming from the second floor. Quickly, he reshut the box, slid the cut end of the wire back through the lock loop and bent the hasp until he had it as close as he could get to looking as if it hadn't been messed with.

"There," he breathed with satisfaction. Then he looked closer. "Well, for God's sake." The padlock seal didn't actually have a seal on it.

Which he supposed explained the sealed wire inside. Christ. Maybe he really was the village idiot.

That elicited a silent laugh. Right. Like anyone outside of City Light would know or care.

Sliding the snips into his pocket, Tony peered through the thick branches to make sure no one inside had gotten it into his head to come check the power supply to the box. Happily, the coast was clear and he eased back onto the path and made his way around to the front of the mansion.

He felt like doing an end goal boogie when he let himself back into the deserted main foyer undetected, but managed to contain himself. He did grin at the noise coming from upstairs. The voices he'd heard through the exterior walls were a whole lot louder inside. It sounded as though everyone and their brother was racing around like monkeys at an all-you-can-eat banana buffet.

Good. The confusion might make Gallari take a bit longer before he realized he had no choice but to let everyone go until his crew could figure out why they'd lost power—provided they even could without calling the city.

Tony chuckled. If City Light was like most bureaucracies, having to call them in could add *days* to his search time.

So for now he was more than happy to wait. Because no doubt sooner rather than later Mr. High and Mighty Gallari would realize just how cost prohibitive it was to have all these people hanging around sucking his budget drier by the hour, when they couldn't do a damn thing until he got somebody out here to restore the power.

It would likely take the entire day just for a noncity professional to discover the problem. So let them spin their wheels down in the basement for as long as they wanted. If it gave him time to finally tackle that fancy-ass-wood wall in peace and quiet, he was all for it.

He'd been patient, but enough was enough. It was time to get proactive. Hell, it was *past* time he got his hands on the goddamn prize.

He had a tropical-paradise-driven future to kick into gear.

"WELL?" CADE DEMANDED as his lighting engineer/gaffer climbed to his feet. It wasn't exactly black as night in here, but the dreary day had sure as hell rendered it dim the minute the bright lights they'd been using had switched off. He had to strain in the room's gloom just to make out the other man's expression.

"Sorry, Cade," Jim Short said, straightening. "There's nothing wrong up here."

"Then let's go check the breaker box."

He started to turn away, but the gaffer's regretful voice stopped him.

"I can't."

Incredulous, he swung back.

The shorter man shrugged. "I'm really sorry, man, but while I can fix any problem that crops up in any room with the production's equipment, the union prohibits me from chasing the problem throughout the building. They consider it the city or the building owner's responsibility."

"Shit." He said it without heat. But where the hell did they go from here? Glancing over at Ava, he saw she was on the phone. She looked up suddenly to meet his gaze—then turned her back on him.

He frowned. Dammit, she better not be talking to the Latin Wonder. This production was on a tight schedule and—his unexplainable knee-jerk territorialism aside—it was *not* a good time for her to be wasting time playing footsie. "Now what?" he wondered aloud.

Jim shrugged again.

Ava turned back to him, rubbing her full bottom lip with the knuckles of the fingers wrapped around her cell phone. Then she dropped her hand to her side. "Finn Kavanagh is on his way."

"And Finn Kavanagh would be…?"

"You know, from the Kavanagh brothers?" She smacked a hand off her forehead. "I forgot—no one introduced you to the guys at the bar. The sheik-looking guy is Poppy's husband, Jason de Sanges, but the other two are part of the contractors. I told you about who restored the mansion. I just called Devlin—that's Janie's husband—and he said Finn's their electrical specialist. They're remodeling a place over on Magnolia so it shouldn't take him long to get— *Cade!*" Her voice went up so high on his name as he snatched her up off her feet, it was a miracle dogs didn't start barking throughout the neighborhood. He swung her in a fast, energetic circle.

"You are *incredible,* Spencer!" Setting her back on her fancy red heels, he brought his hands up to plunge his fingers into the cool depths of her hair, framing her satin-skinned temples with his thumbs. Finessing her head toward him in the same movement, he planted an exaggerated, "Mmmmm-wha!" smacking kiss on her forehead. Then he grinned down at her, finding her startled expression priceless. "Thank you!"

Setting her loose, he turned to the crew and cast who had quit milling around the room to gape at his antics. "All right, people. Go down and grab yourself something to eat while you have the chance. I'll let you know how we're gonna handle the rest of the day as soon as I find out what we're dealing with."

Finn showed up about fifteen minutes later, and Cade realized that the redhead he'd seen at the bar must be Jane's husband, because this was the guy who looked like an oversexed, defrocked cleric.

He shrugged. For all he cared, Finn could screw anyone he damn well pleased as long as he got Cade's production back up and running—

Well, okay, maybe not *anyone*. Ava was off-limits for a ton of reasons he had no intention of examining at the moment.

But beyond that, he sure as hell liked that the dark-haired man seemed competent at his job. After greeting Beks and giving Ava an affectionate one-armed hug as he passed her on his way through the room, Kavanagh crossed over to Cade. He introduced himself and with no-nonsense briskness asked how the power had gone down.

Cade explained the situation as far as he knew it, then introduced Jim Short, who filled Kavanagh in on the technical details he had tried to troubleshoot so far and explained why he couldn't pursue it.

"Not a problem." Turning back to Cade, he jerked his chin toward the door. "Let's go check the basement."

He followed him down two floors.

"I replaced most of the wiring when we did the renovation last year," Finn said as they loped down the last flight into a basement considerably darker than the floors above. He switched on a flashlight. "So in all likelihood it'll be a City Light problem. But you always want to check the breaker box first, because sometimes it really is the obvious. And it's clear you had a shitload of lights and equipment running upstairs." Stopping in front of the service box, he paused to look at Cade over his shoulder. "You may have simply overloaded the breaker for the room you were working in."

Turning back, he pulled the door's wire triangle, opening the box.

And whistled. "Damn. Every single breaker's thrown. That must have taken one helluva power surge." He gave his head a disgusted shake. "I'm not exactly a master wizard to have missed the fact that every light in the joint is off, am I?" He flipped the basement breakers back into place. "Hell. Nothing." The door made a tinny clang when he banged it shut.

Turning back to Cade, Finn gave him a wry, one-sided smile. "There's a raft of outdated underground lighting cables in this district and it does occasionally fail. So I'm thinking this's most likely a utilities problem. I'll give City Light a call and see what kind of reports they've been fielding from the neighborhood."

A few minutes later, his dark eyebrows furrowed, he slid his cell phone back into his jacket pocket and met Cade's gaze. "They haven't heard squat. Let's take a look at the meter."

Everyone stopped talking when Finn led him through the kitchen a moment later, but the contractor merely grabbed an apple off the service table as he passed by and kept going. Cade shrugged in response to his people's questioning looks and followed the other man out the back door. They strode around to the north side of the mansion, the only sound in the mist-shrouded property the crisp crunch of Finn taking big bites from his apple.

Then the other man stepped off the path between two winter-bare bushes with bright red berries. Bending his long legs, he half squatted to look at the utility meter, then blew out a breath.

"Nothing?" Cade demanded.

"No. The padlock's still secure. I'm sorry, man, I was hoping for a quick resolution for Ava's sake, but—wait a minute." He reached back and pulled his flashlight out of the belt he wore around his hips.

Leaning over, Cade watched the other man train the beam on the utility meter's glass bowl cover. "What is it?"

"The disk's not moving. If it's drawing power, it moves. And the padlock doesn't have a seal to show whether or not it's been tampered with. It's possible it never had one, in which case there might be a wire seal inside. Still, it's unusual—" Grabbing the one-inch padlock, he tugged.

One half of the hasp popped free. "Shit," Finn muttered, then surged back to his full height. Stepping out onto the path, he rammed a hand through his hair as he looked at Cade. "We've got a problem. That underground wiring I told you about? It means you don't go to the pole to turn the power back on—the city has to come out and do it. Let's go talk to Ava. If anyone can get us fast service from the utilities, it's that girl. She's got an uncle or godfather or some shit who golfs with the mayor." A rumble of laughter escaped him. "Ask de Sanges sometime how she got his ass put back on not one, but two separate jobs he had told the girls he wouldn't do." He smiled at the thought but shook his head as he started for the kitchen. "Damn kids," he growled. "They coulda fried their stupid asses where they stood."

Cade thought of the interview with Mr. Tarrof where he'd talked about how he and his brothers had dared each other to run up, ring the doorbell and run away. Did neighborhood kids still consider the Wolcott mansion spooky? Given the renovation and the age of video games they lived in, it seemed far-fetched that they'd entertain themselves in the same manner that boys had fifty or sixty years ago when it was a slower-paced, quieter world. But what did he know? "You really think it was kids?"

"Who the hell else would be dumb enough to mess with live electricity? Anybody with half a brain knows it's nothing to fuck around with. And now we've got the damn city to contend with."

His gut churned when he considered how long that might take. He had little choice but to practice patience as he sat in the dining room chair across from Ava's a few minutes later and watched her punch numbers into her iPhone.

"Hey, Uncle Robert," she said in a warm, affectionate voice an instant later. "It's me." She traded a few pleasantries, then said, "Listen, I'm calling to ask a favor. Did Mother tell you I'm working with a production company? Yeah, it is interesting. But this morning some idiot messed with the utility meter and the entire Wolcott mansion is without power. We need someone from City Light to come out here and turn off the primary disconnect at the neighborhood box long enough for our guy to put the meter back in, then turn the power back on again. Do you think the mayor would help expedite that? You know how much the film industry contributes to this town and we're only talking a matter of twenty minutes, tops. Yeah? Okay, give me a call. Love you, Unca." Her lips curving up at whatever her uncle had replied, she disconnected. "He'll get back to us soon as he has something."

Having dealt with bureaucracies in a city or two, Cade didn't hold out any great hope. But Ava's phone rang less than five minutes later.

"Hey," she said into it, "that was fast." As she listened, the creases in her cheeks dented deeper and deeper until a guy could dip a finger knuckle deep in her dimples. "You. Are. The best! Thank you, Uncle Robert. If you need help getting Aunt Jeanine something really sparkly for Valentine's Day at a rock-bottom price, I'm your girl." She listened for another moment, then murmured, "Yeah. Love you, too," and hung up. She looked at him and Finn. "Someone's on the way."

Cade just stared at her. Damn. Could she be cloned? Because he could sure use someone like her on all his jobs.

Eleven minutes later her phone rang, and after answering it she passed it to Finn. "It's the utility guy."

Finn talked for a minute, then hung up. "Power's disconnected at the source, so I'm in business." He turned to Cade. "You want to come give me a hand?"

He did, although that mostly meant holding the flashlight as, with a few economical moves, Finn put the meter back together, then calling back the City Light worker to have him restore the power.

Almost simultaneously to the latter, Finn craned around to look up at him. "Disk's moving again. You're good to go."

Ten minutes later Cade watched Finn stroll out the kitchen door with a check he'd had Beks cut him tucked in his back pocket. Euphoric, he looked at his cast and crew sitting around the kitchen.

And gave them a big grin. "All right, people. Let's get back to work."

TONY SCOWLED as he stalked along the upstairs hallway. He could not fucking believe it. How the hell had they managed to call the one contractor in town who could immediately figure out the problem was in the meter? He'd risked frying himself for nothing!

Seeing Beks headed his way, he forced a smile. "Hey," he said as she came abreast of him. "Good work getting everything up and running again."

"I know, isn't it great? That Ava is amazing."

"Ava?" He had to think a second, then said incredulously, "The *kitchen* gal?"

She laughed. "She's our concierge, Tony. The woman knows everyone in town."

"That's…handy." Not to mention goddamn inconvenient.

Beks gave him a sunny smile. "Isn't it, though? She's the best."

"Yeah, sure," he agreed, all but choking on the words. "The best."

"Hey, Ava! Hold up!"

With one hand still curled around the handle of the car door she'd just opened, Ava looked over the top of her Beemer to see Cade loping across the apron and down the driveway toward her. To her disgust, her heart kicked up a beat when she took in the oughtta-be-outlawed blue eyes, rumpled hair and the dark stubble shading his jaw, chin and upper lip.

"What's up?" she asked as he rocked to a halt on the other side of the car.

He shoveled his fingers through his hair as he met her gaze across the car's roof. "Beks used my rental to run an errand for me and she just called to let me know she's hung up on 520. So I told her to take the car home. Can you give me a ride? My place is on your way if you don't mind going through downtown."

"Sorry," she said, not sorry at all that she was legitimately headed in the other direction. "I'm not going home, but I'd be happy to call you a cab."

His eyes glinted between narrowed lashes. "Got a hot date with your Brazilian boy toy?"

"I'm not sure why you'd think that's any of your business, but if you must know, I'm on my way to my

parents' house to inventory their supplies for a party
I'm putting together for my father's birthday."

"Great." He opened the passenger door. "I'll go with
you. I haven't been back to the 'hood in a long time."

And before she could open her mouth to say, "No,
you won't," or recommend that he see the "'hood"—
good God, what a misnomer for Broadmoor—on his
own time, he'd climbed into her car and settled himself.
He looked relaxed…and unmovable.

Squaring her shoulders, she smoothed her hands
down her hips beneath her open coat from the red belt
bisecting her tobacco-colored, crocheted-silk tunic to
the garment's hem where it met a matching-hued pencil
skirt. Then, unhooking her purse from her shoulder, she
lobbed it into his lap and climbed in the driver's side.

A few minutes later she had to admit he was a hard
guy to resist in the euphoric mood he was rocking tonight. He laughed and joked and must have thanked her
four times for getting Finn there so quickly this morning.

"Swear to God," he said now, "you saved the day.
Without Kavanagh, we probably wouldn't have gotten
any filming done—so if you need someone to count the
crystal or whatever it is you're planning to do at your
folks, I'm your man."

"Don't think I won't hold you to that." She wheeled
into the entrance to Broadmoor and stopped at the gate-
house. Rolling down the window, she smiled up at the
guard. "Hi, Mr. Ziegler."

The white-haired man beamed down at her. "Well,
hello, Ava. I haven't seen you around for a while."

"I know. My parents have been in Chicago since right
after Christmas. I'm stopping by to check on the house
and take care of some things before they get back."

"I wish you well on that," he said and pushed the button that opened the gate.

She drove through the community, passing lush, green estates, some viewable from the streets, others hidden. Eventually she turned into a driveway and cruised up to the 1929 brick Tudor. Stopping in front of the garage, she turned off the engine.

"Home, sweet home," she murmured, conflicted as always when confronted with the elegant house in which she'd grown up.

Cade looked over at her. "Lemme guess. This is a George Stoddard design? On—what?—the ninth fairway?"

Remembering he'd never been here, she nodded.

His face went curiously blank. "My old man was forever hacked off because the only thing available when he bought here was one of the houses built in 1940."

"Ah," she said wisely. "Nouveau." She grimaced. "At least according to my mother. I think stuff like that matters a whole lot more to their generation."

"Oh, I don't know," he disagreed as he followed her up the stone path leading to the front door. "I know some old schoolmates who still consider the size of our wallets of paramount importance."

She hitched an indifferent shoulder. "So, screw 'em."

Cade looked startled for a nanosecond, then threw back his head and roared with laughter.

Her mouth dropped open as the sound rolled over her, and she had to make a concerted effort to close it. But, God. She hadn't seen that kind of unguarded humor from Cade since…man…back in high school before the fallout. It caused her to fumble at the front door lock.

She managed to open it about the same time he got control of himself, and when she stepped inside and held the door for him to enter, he gave her a decisive nod. "Yeah," he agreed, a small smile crooking up one corner of his mouth as he followed her inside. "Screw 'em."

Leading him into the expansive foyer, she was aware of him looking around while she entered the security code in the alarm system. She shrugged out of her coat and took Cade's leather jacket when he did the same, throwing them over the fir banister on the open stairway. "C'mon into the library. We're on the hunt for candles."

"This is really nice," he said as he followed her into the room one door over.

She nodded. "I like that my mother hasn't fallen prey to the jump-on-the-decorator-du-jour bandwagon that's rolling through her crowd. Not that the current designer doesn't do an excellent job. But there's just something so generic about having all your friends' houses done by the same person." She gave him a wry twist of her lips. "All those understated striped draperies, I suppose. *Anyway!*" She led him to the other end of the bookshelf-lined room and pulled open several low cupboards in the built-in unit alongside the corner fireplace. "We're looking for candles. You start here, and I'll look in the ones over there."

"What kind of candles?"

"Just pull out everything you see. I'm still working on my color scheme—so it will depend on what my mother seems to be favoring at the moment."

"Why not just ask her?"

She snorted. "Clearly you've never met my mother. She expects me to design the party without her input— as long as I read her mind and do it her way." *Annnd I probably shouldn't have shared that.*

Seeing with a glance that there was nothing in the cupboard she was searching, she closed it and rose to her feet. "Keep looking down here. I'm gonna run up to my old room. Mother said something about utilizing the storage space up there." Ava knew she was more likely to find what she was looking for in the dining room or kitchen, but she found herself in sudden need of a little breathing room.

As she suspected, her old closet and the antique high-boy and matching dresser held seasonal clothing and items. So she simply spent a moment practicing meditation breathing to get her head back where it belonged.

She didn't know why being here had her undies in such a twist, especially over something she thought she'd reconciled herself to a long time ago. But for some reason it did.

It wasn't as if her folks were bad parents. They simply loved her in their own way. Of the two, her father tended to be a little more affectionate, but he traveled a lot for work and was hardly ever home.

Neither was Mother, for that matter. As long as Ava could remember, Jacqueline had traveled with him as often as she could. When Ava thought of the people who had been there for all her triumphs and failures, it was always Poppy, Jane and Miss Agnes who came to mind.

"Well, hell," a deep voice behind her drawled. "I was hoping for pink and girly."

She whirled to find Cade leaning in the doorway, his hands in his pants pockets. "What?"

The real question should have been, *What the hell are you doing up here?*

"I spent a lot of hours once upon a time, imagining you in your bedroom. Dancing naked, mostly." He glanced around at the elegantly appointed, mostly beige room and missed seeing her jaw go slack.

She had it firmly back in place when he returned his attention to her. "But I always envisioned the place all pink and girly." He crooked a reminiscent smile at her. "Like those panties you wore when I looked up your skirt from beneath the bleachers back in the tenth grade."

For a second her blood chilled the way it had that day at the thought of him seeing her fat thighs and probably laughing about them with those assholes he called friends. But she shook it off as she realized she was reacting to far more than just that age-old embarrassment. Regaining her composure, she sent him a mocking smile. The sudden wariness in his eyes almost made her break into a genuine grin.

"Why, Cade Gallari," she drawled, strolling over to him. "Who knew a bad boy like you would have so much in common with my mother?"

CHAPTER FIFTEEN

Sometimes it just doesn't seem to matter that I know what I should be doing. I still do what I'm gonna do.

NO GUY APPRECIATED being compared to a chick's mother, but Cade flashed Ava the easy smile he'd perfected years ago to cover up his real feelings and arched a brow. "Your mama hung out under the bleachers, too?"

"Nope. But she sure had a cow when she came home to find Poppy and I had painted my namby-pamby pink room a purple so deep it was almost black and dyed my stupid frilly comforter to match."

He looked at her curiously. "You remember the exact day you painted a room?"

"Of course I do. It was the day Kurt Cobain died. I had to do something to honor his memory." Her dimples suddenly flashed. "And I must say, the new paint job sure made my collection of Nirvana posters pop."

He studied her. "How come I never knew you were a Cobain groupie?"

"Beats me. Probably because by the time we were assigned as science partners and had a few conversations that weren't all sniping and one-upmanship it was a nonissue." With a shrug, she turned away. "But this isn't getting my work done. The candles aren't up here. I'm going to try the kitchen and dining room."

He followed in her wake, trying without success to keep his gaze from the provocative swing of her curvy hips. When he did raise his eyes, it was to notice the way her milkmaid skin played peekaboo through the holey weave of her top above its matching camisole.

Not that he planned to beat himself up for noticing. Hey, he was a guy, and her shoulders were pretty, her back was long and her waist was little. And that ass. Man, that round bootylicious ass. If a man were a touch less cosmopolitan, his mouth might go dry over the way her straight skirt cupped it so faithfully.

He gave his head a little shake. Because it took more than a killer body to make *this* dude's tongue hang out. At least that was his story.

And he was sticking to it.

He strolled around the family room for a few minutes while she banged around in the kitchen, checking out the family photos gracing many of the surfaces. The longer he looked, however, the more his eyebrows inched together.

Ava was only in a fraction of the pictures—and a frigging small fraction at that. You'd think as an only child she'd have her likeness plastered all over the damn house. He leaned closer to look at the few that she was in and picked up one in particular that he found half hidden in the back of a grouping.

It was a picture of the two of them and another boy and girl practicing their box step during one of the interminable dance classes they'd been subjected to as kids. He and the other boy were clearly hamming it up for the camera, while the girl looked as if she were counting the dance's six-beat meter under her breath.

Ava had that fluid, relaxed look of someone who loves dancing—and is good at it. Or at least she did in the version with which he was familiar.

Because in this one… "Am I missing something here?" he called into the kitchen.

"Probably," she said, rising from behind the counter to look down the length of the family room at him. "But what specifically this time?"

"Why are the only photos of you basically head shots?" He hefted the framed photograph in his hand. "This was taken in cotillion when we were what, eleven? I remember some old dude who used to go around taking shots that our parents bought. My mother's got this exact same one—except in hers we're shown full-length. This one's practically all matting."

Color flowed up Ava's chest to her neck and onto her face until her skin competed with her hair for brilliance. If she was embarrassed, however, he couldn't tell it by her voice. That was contrastingly placid when she said, "You know my mother and her issues."

While her tone was light, there was a darkness in the back of her clear green eyes, and he narrowed his own to study her. "No, I don't. I've never met your mother."

"Oh. That's right, I guess you haven't." She essayed an insouciant shrug. "Well, what can I say? Mom finds my weight problems…distasteful." Raising her chin, she looked him in the eye. "You of all people should be able to appreciate that."

Aw, crap. Anger he could have shrugged off, because God knows he'd had enough practice over the years. But the slight wobble in her voice, the flash of vulnerability she tried to hide, *those* threatened to bring him to his knees. He opened his mouth to say something lighthearted to smooth over the moment.

As if he'd ingested some mad scientist's truth serum, however, he muttered, "I learned my father wasn't really my father."

She blinked. "What?"

Shit! Where the hell had that come from? Telling himself to start backpedaling *now,* he instead heard himself say, "Senior year. Three weeks before you and I—" His hips executed an involuntary none-too-subtle thrust and, unable to believe he'd made such a teen-stud gesture, he stuffed his hands into his jeans pockets and looked at the hardwood floor.

Only to lift his gaze to meet hers again. "That was when I found out the cold, distant sonuvabitch I called Dad wasn't my father at all—that my mom'd had an affair almost nineteen years before, and I was the result."

His well-developed survivor instincts howled at him to shut the hell up. It was good, sound advice, yet instead of heeding it, his mind circled back to the way Ava had opened herself up both downstairs and in this very room. It couldn't have been easy to admit her mother neither quite trusted her professional abilities, nor approved of her body.

He found both concepts difficult to wrap his head around, because regarding her abilities, they were just killer impressive. As for her body...well, anyone with eyes in their head knew her mother's assessment was insane.

And he decided if she could put herself out there without a safety net, then so could he. "I guess it kind of explained why the old man never liked me."

He saw Ava staring at him with a what-the-hell-is-this-guy-babbling-about look on her face and really, *really* wanted to shut up then. She already thought he was the scum of the earth. Did he truly want her to think he was an incoherent loser with daddy issues on top of it?

Yet still he admitted, "I was...blindsided by the revelation. I'd tried my entire life to please the old bastard, but despite agreeing to raise me as his own, apparently every time he looked at me he was reminded of my mom's infidelity."

She gazed at him for one second, two. Then she said, "So you were hurt when you discovered the truth."

"Yes," he agreed. "Although at the time I would have denied it with my last teenage macho breath. Because I was also furious—" with a cold, hard kernel of rage that he hadn't merely embraced, but had nurtured "—and that was a helluva lot easier to handle. It edged out the pain."

Yet Ava saw a shadow of that hurt in Cade's eyes now, and it pulled at her in a way she didn't like and would give much to deny. She didn't want to feel sympathetic to his long-ago plight. Not to mention that she wasn't sure what to do with the information. On the one hand, she was kind of fascinated. But if he thought it bought him a free pass when *she* had paid the price of his anger, he was dead wrong.

And yet—

Sympathy did tug at her. She knew what it was like to feel as if you never quite measured up.

Damned if she was obligated to own up to it, however. With a roll of her shoulders, she demanded flatly, "So you thought you'd share the wealth by throwing me to the wolves?"

"I don't know how to explain it, Ava, and I'm not trying to justify or excuse it." He looked her in the eyes. "I honest to God liked you. But I was like a feral dog

during that period, more willing to snap fingers off
than accept an extended hand. Everything I'd ever believed about my parents had been obliterated, and I felt
like the guys in my crowd were all I had left. So when
they came up with that bet, which I'd ignored before,
I...agreed to it. I'd wanted to sleep with you for a long
time, anyway, so I convinced myself I didn't care, that
if you became collateral damage, I could live with that.
Because, hey, I was a bastard, wasn't I? You only had
to ask my old man."

Dammit, she almost got that. She had a sudden vision
of him as he'd been at eighteen, and if she was honest
with herself, there had been moments when she'd felt
something was...off, seconds when he'd disappear into
himself or the chill stillness that would take over his
expression for just a moment before he reverted to the
laughing, sardonic Mister Cool she was familiar with.
He'd been such a high school hottie, though, that she
had simply dismissed it as a product of her own insecurity.

Yet even seeing things in hindsight and maybe understanding the reasons behind his actions a little better,
the end result still smarted—even as it filled her with an
edgy anger. Not wanting him to see either reaction—or
that she was more comfortable with the anger than her
unwilling sympathy—she gave him a polite smile.

And an equally polite bum's rush.

"It's been a long day," she said with distant courtesy, "and as I said upstairs, this isn't getting my work
done. So paw through those cupboards over there while
I finish up in the kitchen, will you? I'm more than ready
to go home."

She managed to mostly keep a room between them
after that, until she finally located her mother's candle

supply in a deep side drawer of the built-in desk in the kitchen. "*Here* they are."

Cade strolled across the room to peer over her shoulder into the drawer. "That is one helluva lot of candles." He turned his head to look at her, and his breath first grazed the outer curve of her ear then insinuated itself down its whorls like magical smoke when he demanded, "And this is supposed to help narrow down your choices how?"

As much to get out of range of the sudden sensory overload as from a desire to take a closer look, she bent over the drawer. "See these balsam fir ones?"

"Huh?"

"The dark green with a slight blue tone?"

She could almost feel his eyes burning holes in her back when he said, "Are you messing with me, Spencer?"

"No, look. I'm talking about these." Bending farther forward, she ran her fingertip across the top layer of a box of tapers and turned her head to glance up at him.

He was studying her butt, and she snapped her fingers. "Hey, up here."

When she had his unabashed attention, she said, "My mother's got a mess of this color, so I'm guessing it's her new favorite. Plus I remember my dad wearing a sweater this shade the last time I saw him." Her lips curled in a tiny smile. "The man never buys his own clothes. So we'll take the balsam and these metallics—" she selected some silver and gold pillars and grinned at him "—and we've got ourselves a color scheme."

He stared at her. "How do chicks *do* that?"

"We have uteruses—they give us magic color sense."

His nonplussed expression made her mood do a one-eighty, and, feeling downright companionable, she straightened and gave his forearm beneath his pushed-up sleeve a sisterly pat.

Its hair-roughened warmth didn't feel all that brotherly beneath her fingers, however, and she retracted them. Delicately, she cleared her throat, then directed briskly, "Pull out every candleholder you can find. I'll figure out which ones I can use and where I'll need to supplement when I come over to do the linen count."

He nodded. "I saw some in the library."

"Excellent. Gather up what you can in there and I'll go look in the dining room. Let's put everything we find on the counter in here."

Twenty minutes later they had quite a collection, and a design for the decorations was beginning to take shape in Ava's mind. But looking at the assembled hurricanes, candelabras, votive trees and floater bowls, she blew out a tired breath and decided she could work on the details at home. Taking a couple of photos on her phone to help refresh her memory later, she said, "What do you say we call it a day? I'm played out."

"Yeah, you and me both. Let's hit the road."

The moment the two of them were enclosed in what up until today she'd considered a generously proportioned car, she became highly conscious of him again. *Sexually* conscious, dammit. She refused his offer to buy her dinner on the way home, and cited the need to pay attention to the road in order to avoid conversation. But her awareness of him grew by the moment, and it was with relief that she finally pulled up to the curb in a loading zone in front of his building.

"Well," she said, turning to face him for the first time since they'd climbed in the car, "thanks for your help."

"Not a problem. I dug seeing your old bedroom—

I'll forever envision you in a dark purple room with Nirvana posters."

She pretended the sound that escaped her wasn't actually a snort. "Yeah, because '94 decor is so au courant."

"Hey, it suits you a helluva lot more than the bland beige your mother painted it." One broad shoulder hitched. "Anyhow, I'll see you in the morning." He reached for the door handle.

Yet instead of opening it, he turned back to her, his expression serious. "I really meant it when I said I used to fantasize about you in high school—and I hate that the way I fucked everything up probably makes it hard for you to trust that I'm telling the truth."

The idea of a teenaged Cade lusting for her tugged at something deep inside her. But it was the look in his eyes that started her heart tripping, tripping, tripping.

Before she could even open her mouth to say...she didn't know what...he reached across to lightly trace his fingertips over the thrust of her cheekbone and down her cheek. The edge of his thumb brushed the outer curve of her lips, dragging the lower lip open for a second before his hand continued on to her chin, which he lightly grasped. He merely gazed at her for an attenuated heartbeat, his eyes bluer than a tropical sky.

"If you believe nothing else," he commanded in a low, I'm-not-screwing-around-here voice, "believe this. You gotta be aware that you're a knockout now, but even then? Baby, you may not've measured up to your mama's standards, but I thought you were—*God,* Ava— so ripe and round and beautiful." His mouth quirked in that crooked smile. "And seeing you naked remains to this day one of the highlights of my life."

Turning her loose, he opened the door and climbed

from the car. One hand on the roof and the other holding the door ajar, he leaned back in. Gave her a look of sizzling intent. "Think about that."

Think? Who the heck could *think?* As she tried to process the words swirling and spinning inside her brain, he shut the door and strode away. She leaned to watch through the side window until he disappeared inside his condo, then turned back in her seat and sat staring blindly through the windshield until a UPS truck honked for her to get out of the loading zone.

She pulled away from the curb but got only as far as the nearest parking lot a block and a half away. Slowing down as she approached, she saw it had available space and pulled in.

Then once again sat there. She couldn't get over Cade's revelation. God, she'd known him since they were, like, eight years old. She thought she knew exactly who he was. It couldn't have been easy for him to admit how much he wanted her. And the thing about his father! That was almost harder to wrap her mind around. He'd always been good-looking, athletic and popular—it had never occurred to her to consider his relationship with his family. She'd simply assumed he was the same golden boy at home he was at school.

Even so. "This is stupid. Not to mention a *big* ass mistake."

She got out of her car anyhow, beeped it locked and strode back to Cade's condominium. Falling in with a group of laughing twentysomethings going through the had-to-be-buzzed-in-or-have-a-key entry, she slid through in their wake without anyone challenging her. A minute later she was outside Cade's door.

She tried again to talk herself out of this, but her

hand apparently had a mind of its own, for it rose to rap purposefully on the wooden door.

It took what felt like an age before the door swung back and Cade stood in its opening, looking at her in surprise. "Hey. You forget something?"

"Lost, more like it," she muttered.

"You lost something?"

"That's what I'm thinking."

His dark brows furrowed. "You're not making a whole lot of sense, Spencer. What did you lose?"

"My freaking mind," she said. And launched herself at him.

CHAPTER SIXTEEN

Oh. My. God. Was that woman really me?

CADE STAGGERED back a step, unprepared as he found himself the sudden recipient of a hundred and fifty pounds of hot-blooded, velvet-skinned, willing woman. But when Ava wrapped her arms around his neck and aligned all those gorgeous curves against him until they were welded together from chest to knees, he took it like a man.

Sliding his hands inside her coat to grip her hips, he stared down at her for a moment, enjoying the supple give of her warm body against the harder planes of his own. Her cheeks blazed with color, her eyes were frankly sexual, her mouth, with its pearlescent hint of teeth gleaming beneath her plush upper lip, was a moist and rosy siren call. And she was in his arms.

It was like holding the winning lottery ticket. He didn't know why she'd changed her mind and given him a second chance, but he didn't really care as long as she didn't change it back again. All he could think was *thank God.*

Just looking at her wasn't enough for him, however, so he did what he'd wanted to do every time she'd sashayed within touching distance. He slanted his mouth over hers and kissed her, his mind emptying as his mouth turned hot and rough against the pliant fullness of hers. Maybe her decision to be with him was set in stone. But it could also be that he only had seconds before she recanted it. He intended to make every instant count.

It was unnerving, though, how quickly his control slipped away. His heart tried to hammer its way through his rib cage, his breath went ragged and a proprietary sound rumbled low in his throat. But, God, he loved kissing her. He'd never kissed another with lips so luxuriant. Ava's were plump and moist, inciting thoughts of both combustible nights and day-in, day-out cushy-comfort. They also promptly opened beneath his unspoken demand, imbuing the noise in his throat with a rough note of approval. Slipping his tongue over her teeth's serrations, he stroked into the hot, wet interior of her mouth.

One of the things he admired about Ava was her emotional honesty. As long as he'd known her, she had never been one to play coy. And thank God she didn't start now. Her tongue, firm and agile, rose to counter the claim he was staking, and as it tangled with his, she made a low, gritty, purrlike sound that caused his cock to jump.

Holding her close, he backed deeper into his condo's tiny hallway, kicked the door shut and swiftly reversed his backward locomotion to crowd her against its wooden panels. His kiss rapidly grew wilder, and the force of it drove her head back as he tried to wrestle his leather coat off without relinquishing her mouth.

His unwillingness to turn her loose for the moment it would take to do the job properly led him to yank one of his sleeves inside out, and he had to shake the damn thing like a monkey with his fist in a jar to unlock its death grip from around his left wrist. Then it flung free, and he went to work on hers. Rapidly he worked the buttons free, reached up to disentangle her fingers from behind his neck and peeled her coat off her shoulders and down her arms. Seconds later, the only thing preventing gravity from doing its job was the pressure of her back pinning the garment to the door.

He splayed his hands against the wooden panels on either side of her shoulders, intending to return to that beckoning mouth. But the press of her breasts against his diaphragm distracted him, and he instead strung damp, openmouthed kisses down her neck as one hand raced, as if it had a mind of its own, ahead of him. His fingers brushed the hollow of her throat and poked beneath the holey weave of her tunic to explore where her smooth chest gave way to the liberal hint of cleavage rising above her lingerie. His palm cupped her breast's fascinatingly unstable weight.

He curled his fingers and pressed it upward to meet his descending mouth. More layers than he liked separated him from the close contact he craved, but even beneath her clothing he felt her nipple rise in search of more attention. Closing his teeth around it, he gave a tug. Ava's pelvis tilted, and she made another of those gritty happy-kitty sounds.

Cade doubled his efforts.

It might have been one minute later or ten when one of her legs tried to climb the outside of his thigh. The narrow cut of her skirt restricted the movement, and with a frustrated sound, she dropped her foot back to the floor.

Slowly he raised his mouth from her now thoroughly dampened top, straightened from the half squat he'd assumed and looked down at her. Her pretty mouth was swollen from his kisses. Bending his head to catch her lower lip between his teeth, he gently tugged on it as he reached behind her to smooth his palms down the curve of her ass. He scraped the edge of his teeth with glacial slowness over the slick inner membrane and outer plumpness as his fingers dexterously gathered the fabric of her skirt to the top of her thighs.

Ava promptly hooked a leg over his hip and gave a little hop. Grasping a full, firm, satin-covered cheek in each hand, Cade hiked her up, feeling her wrap her other leg around him to cross her ankles behind his back. She made a minute adjustment and his hard-on suddenly slid against plump folds that parted to caress its length. Simultaneously they stilled, eyes meeting, breaths sharply indrawn and held deep.

Then, her gaze still locked on his, Ava exhaled and dug her heels into his butt, those three-inch red stilettos mercifully pointing in the opposite direction. Her pelvis instigated a subtle undulation, and he thrust in shallow counterpart, his fly gathering moisture with each enthusiastic rub. He planted openmouthed kisses on her temple, her cheekbones, behind her ear. The tip of his tongue flicked the indentation of a dimple.

And with every taste he garnered, he rocked more emphatically.

He was ready and willing to blow off foreplay and skip straight to fucking her right where they stood. But as he was contemplating the logistics of getting her out of her clothes without actually letting her out of his arms, it flitted through his mind that the only other time he'd had with her he'd failed spectacularly to do her anything remotely smacking of justice. She deserved better than a quickie against the door.

So utilizing every drop of willpower at his command,

he forced his hips to stop moving. "I've got a bed," he said, his voice husky from forcing it through a tight throat.

She blinked heavy-lidded eyes at him. "What?"

"There's a bed right behind this wall."

"Oh." Her lips crooked up in a tiny smile. "A bed would be good. Although I gotta say, this ain't too shabby." She executed a small swivel that had him sucking for breath.

"Yeah, not shabby at all. But why stand when you can lie down, know what I mean?"

She narrowed her eyes at him. "You're not gonna go all lazy on me, are you? Because I gotta tell you, Gallari, I expect a lot better job from you tonight than the last time we did this."

A laugh stuck in his throat. "Couldn't do much worse," he agreed.

She nodded. "That was my thought."

Stepping back from the wall, he bounced her up, then caught her firm, round cheeks again in his hands. With a yelp, she tightened her arms around his neck and her legs around his waist and pinned him with a chastising look.

Grinning at her, he shrugged. "I love your ass," he admitted and about-faced to stride down the short hallway and around the wall that gave the queen-size bed its modicum of privacy, enjoying the feel of her sweet, full butt in his hands and the movement of her breasts against his chest with every step he took.

He set her on her feet at the end of the bed. "Let's lose some of these clothes."

"Yes," she agreed and reached out to slide her hands beneath the hem of his sweater.

Okay, not exactly what he had in mind, but his abs

tightened as her long fingers traced their definition up to his chest, the soft cashmere dragging upward in their wake. "I meant your top, Spencer," he said.

Then jerked like he'd been Tasered when she instead sank onto her fuck-me heels and pressed an open-mouthed kiss just below his navel before releasing his sweater and going for the metal button on his waistband.

"Whoa, whoa, whoa!" Squatting down to face her, he took her hands, which had fallen away with his movement, and held them between his own, trying his best to keep his gaze off the stripper spread of her legs and that little slice of damp mocha satin peeping between her creamy thighs thanks to the skirt rucked up around her hips. "This time's gonna be even shorter than the last if you don't cut me a little slack here. C'mon, Ava. Give me a chance to get you as primed as I am so we can at least start on a level playing field, okay?"

She licked her lips. Clamped her thighs together and wriggled in place. "What makes you think I'm not?"

"Aw, God, girl, you're killing me here." He rose to his feet, pulling her along with him. "Raise your arms," he commanded.

She rolled her eyes, but did as she was bade.

He pulled her peekaboo tunic over her head and tossed it aside. "Keep 'em up there so I can get this whatayacallit off, too," he said, his fingers gathering the fragile undergarment and sliding it up her diaphragm. He nodded toward her skirt. "Then you can lose that."

"Well, aren't you Mr. Forceful." But she allowed him to strip the tank/chemise thing over her head and, without further prompting, tugged her skirt back in place and reached behind her for the zipper.

Cade felt his Adam's apple take a slow slide up the length of his throat and back down again at the sight of the generous freckled cleavage her action thrust forward. But when she raised her eyes to look at him, he slapped his best badass expression in place and responded to her crack. "You don't have to call me Mister. But I am in charge here, baby."

She snorted. "You just keep telling yourself that." She unhooked her waistband and pulled down the zipper, then pushed the fabric past her curvy hips. Clearing them, it slid down her legs to pool around her feet. Daintily, she stepped out of the circle of silk-lined fabric.

And he was suddenly staring at sixty-nine inches of a creamy skinned, flame-haired woman clad only in a shimmery chocolate-colored panty-and-bra set and red stilettos.

"Now you." She pointed an imperious finger at his jeans. "Drop 'em."

"On the bed, on your back," he counter-ordered with a jerk of his chin toward the mattress.

"Fine." She kicked off her heels and flopped down upon the bed, lounging on her elbows. "But I expect a show." She looked him up and down, her gaze lingering for a moment on his erection where it attempted to push through the tough denim of his fly. Pink tinged her cheeks, but she gave him her Ice Princess Meets the Peon expression and said haughtily, "And make it good."

"How 'bout we go for speed instead?" Reaching over his shoulders, he grabbed two fistfuls of the back of his sweater, hauled it off over his head and tossed it aside.

"Um…that works, too." Ava could barely push the words out of her throat, it had gone so dry. But, holy freakin' hell. Cade's shoulders had gotten wider, his biceps more muscled, his forearms more corded, than the last time she'd seen him without a shirt.

Which, okay, was more than a decade ago. Still, there was no denying he was more powerfully built these days. The boy had grown up *fine*. His chest was not only more strapping, but where he'd only had a patch of hair between his pecs back in the day, he now sported a fan of black from his collarbones to the bottom of his pectorals before it arrowed down an impressive six-pack, widened fractionally around his belly button, then narrowed again to disappear beneath the low-slung waistband of his jeans.

She watched as his lean fingers popped the metal button free of its waistband buttonhole and grasped the zipper tab. He pulled it down, exposing more firm skin in the widening V until a pair of navy-banded, silver-gray knit boxers interfered with the view. Burrowing his hands beneath the gaping denim, he started pushing both jeans and boxers down.

Then he stopped. Looked at her breasts rising from the demi cups of her bra. And licked his lips. "Take that off."

She'd half expected to be nervous at the thought of exposing her body to Cade again, but his eyes were a blue blaze of raw, determined hunger, and without a qualm she sat up on the mattress and reached behind her to unclasp her bra. Its straps slid down and its cups fell away. She peeled it down her arms and dropped it over the side of the bed.

"Panties, too," Cade said and pushed his clothes past his hips. His sex sprang free, and he stepped out of the puddle of denim and cotton around his ankles. Not taking his gaze off her, he stood on first one foot, then the other to pull off his socks.

"Holy shit," she whispered, staring at his penis as it stood at rigid attention, removing her own undies on

automatic pilot. That bad boy was…beautiful, all long
and hard, except for the soft standing veins twisting up
its length. It bobbed as he walked toward her, and she
rolled onto her hands and knees to prowl to the end of
the mattress to meet him.

She wanted to touch it, taste it. Badly.

"Look at you," Cade crooned, and she pulled her
gaze away to find him doing just that: making a slow,
thorough perusal of her naked body. "God. You're my
fantasy woman come to life." Squatting in front of her,
he reached out to cup her chin. "I just want to lick you
all over." The corner of his mouth quirked up. "But I'll
settle for this." And leaning in, he opened his mouth
over hers.

Ava ignited. Scratching her nails across his scalp as
she plunged her fingers into his hair, framing his temples with her thumbs, she held him to her as if he might
make a break for it at any moment.

It wasn't enough, however, and surging up onto her
knees, she responded to his mobile mouth with avid lips
and insistent tongue.

He reached around to grip her butt and yank her
closer and finally—*finally*—she felt his bare skin,
rough here, heartbreakingly smooth there, everywhere
it touched hers. His hard-on pressed insistently against
her stomach.

She'd barely registered the fact before he hiked her
a little higher and rose to his feet, lifting her as effort-
lessly as she might a child. Once again she wrapped
her legs around him, but found it gained a whole new
dimension with no clothing between them. His chest
hair abraded her tight nipples as he climbed onto the
bed and knee-walked a short way up the mattress. She
was wedging one hand between them, frantic to get it

on his penis, when he tipped her onto her back on the comforter and came down on top of her.

"I'm sorry," he said hoarsely. "I really want to make this good for you, but I don't think I can hold out for long."

She spread her legs. "So don't—I don't need you to. You have condoms?"

"Shit. Yeah. Hang on." Rolling off her, he dove for the nightstand, yanking its drawer open so vigorously it pulled clear out. He swore as its contents dumped on the floor, and he slid his upper body over the side of the bed. "Pretty suave, huh?"

"Oh, very," she agreed, but in all honesty, she wasn't paying strict attention. He had a really great butt, all round and firm, with those sucked-in hips that only men ever seem to achieve—and it called to her. So she shifted around a bit.

Scooted closer.

And took a little bite.

"Jesus!" He shot up, the accordion of condoms in his fist unpleating from the floor, and flipped around to sit on the spot she'd nipped. The condoms whipped around in his wake.

The view was firmly covered, but there was an upside—that luscious penis pointed straight at her was equally firm—and mere inches from her face. "Oooh."

"No!" he barked, and she glanced up at him. He was breathing like he'd run a marathon, and his eyes were hot and wild as he stared down at her lips.

"God," he panted. "I want it. I want to see that mouth on me so bad."

"Cool." Licking her lips, she reached for him.

His hand came out of nowhere to snatch her wrist and pull it away. When she sighed and looked up once again, it was to see a pained expression crossing his face.

"But you're gonna keeps those lips off my dick," he said flatly. "I promised I'd make this better for you than the last time. You put your mouth on me and it's all over."

Okay, she did not want that. "Maybe another time, then," she said and reached for the end condom on the conga line of them and ripped it free. She thrust it out at him. "Here. Suit up."

He took it from her hand but said, "Let's get something straight, buttercup. You are not in charge here."

She looked at his penis. Opened her mouth and ran her tongue in a slow circle around its inner membranes.

He swore. "Okay, maybe you're partly in charge. But I'm taking over for now."

Since she was having a tough time pulling her gaze away from watching him apply the condom, she decided she could live with that. But, holy Krakow. There was just something about seeing a man handle his own sex. And Cade's jutted up between his hands as he unrolled the rubber down its length.

He looked up to see her watching and gave himself a rough stroke, stretching his hard-on at the apex of the pull. "You like that?"

Squeezing her thighs together, clutching her breasts and trapping her nipples between the sides of her thumbs and index fingers, she nodded.

"Damn!" he said, tackling her and driving her down onto the mattress. He scowled. "I don't know how you do it. I've got experience on my side, you know? Quite a bit of it."

"Big deal," she said coolly, "I have some, myself."

Then honesty compelled her to admit, "But, okay, maybe not what anyone would call quite a bit."

He blew out a disgusted breath. "Like mine's doing me a damn bit of good. Because I look at you and it's as if I'm that horny kid all over again—the one who wants you so fucking bad he loses control before he can do you right."

"No kidding?" Tickled, she flashed him a big smile. "That's actually sort of…flattering."

He stilled, looking at her. Then he cleared his throat. Dipped his fingertip into one of her dimples. "Yeah?" he said huskily. "Well, my ego's feeling a little battered, so let's see if we can't do something to push you out of control, too."

And he set about doing precisely that. It was as if he suddenly had more than the usual complement of hands, for his touch seemed to be everywhere, scorching her, sparking fires, making her burn. He pinned her hands over her head and held her down with hard thighs spread over her own as his teeth nipped her neck, her collarbone, her nipples. He licked her underarms, which she'd never dreamed could be so erogenous. He rocked that wicked penis between her legs but didn't enter her.

Then he slid down her body. Shouldering her legs apart, he reached to cup her butt in splayed hands, his fingers curling in its division to separate her cheeks. His breath feathered the curls between her legs.

"Redheads rock," he murmured and kissed her abdomen above the curls. He brushed the tip of his finger across a spot she didn't expect and she jumped. No man had ever—

He looked up at her and brushed it again. Rubbed a tiny, gentle circle around it.

Ava shot up onto her elbows. "Cade! You can't—"

Holding her gaze, he lapped his tongue up the swollen, split tissues between her legs. He grazed his teeth over her clitoris. Surrounded it with his lips and sucked.

And her elbows melted out from under her. Oh, God, who was she fooling? He could do whatever he wanted.

And he did. Wicked wonderful things with his tongue, his lips, his fingers, that made her writhe and moan and beg. Until, just as she was finally on the brink of what she *knew* was going to be the climax of her life, he suddenly pulled back.

"Nooooo!"

He dropped over her with a force that lifted her head off the comforter when his elbow drove into the mattress next to it. His hand speared into her hair, and his mouth rocked over hers. Then the knuckles of his other hand brushed down her slippery furrow a second before the broad head of his penis pushed past the ring of muscle guarding her opening. He plunged his tongue into her mouth even as he sank into her body with an emphatic thrust.

And Ava's world turned scarlet as the tension that had been steadily tightening inside her detonated. Sensation exploded in wave after ever-expanding concentric wave. And somewhere in the room a woman emitted a drawn-out, muffled scream.

Cade ripped his mouth free and stared down at Ava as he thrust in and out of her with edge-of-control ferocity. Her eyes blazed green, her teeth sank deep into her full lower lip and her breasts, those beautiful, beautiful breasts, jiggled against his pecs with every forceful thrust of his hips, her nipples punching through his chest hair like diamond drill bits.

"God, Ava, God," he said through a sandpaper throat. Because he was so close, so fucking close, balanced on the edge of heaven as her hot, muscular sheath contracted up and down the length of his cock. "You are so—"

His balls drew up.

"—damn—"

Thrusting deep, he ground into the slick clasp of her. "Beautif—aww, *Jeeeeeeeezus!*" Stiff-arming himself up on his palms, he pressed as deep as he could go and gritted his teeth as he began to come in pulsation after heaven-sent, hell-hot pulsation.

He had no idea how much time passed before his cock quit jerking and his head dropped forward on a suddenly weak neck. But the position left him gazing at where they were joined and his dick gave a final pulse at the sight of her red curls meshing with his black. He dragged his gaze up to meet hers. "Damn," he said hoarsely. "That was…"

"Amazing," Ava breathed, lolling beneath him in a boneless sprawl.

"Freakin' A. You totaled me six ways from Sunday, Av. I can't feel my hands." And his arms were starting to tremble. But he could still raise one eyebrow. "You gotta admit, though, it was better than the last time."

Then his strength gave way completely, and he crashed down on top of her.

CHAPTER SEVENTEEN

Holy crap. Was there an emotion I didn't feel today? They were are all over the damn place!

CADE TURNED out to be a cover hog.

Ava awoke with a toasty back at the same time chilly air poked sly, frigid fingers down her front beneath the only bedding still covering her, a high thread count, wholly inadequate Egyptian cotton sheet. Pushing up on one forearm, she rubbed sleep from her eyes and felt the heavy weight of Cade's arm slide away from her waist. Grumbling in his sleep, he rolled onto his back, taking his body heat with him. She shivered and turned to reach for the blanket and comforter he'd commandeered. Straightening them out, she pulled her newly reclaimed share up around her neck.

Then she faced him fully for the first time and simply stared for a moment, a small smile tugging at her lips.

A romance book hero he wasn't. He had a serious case of bed head, his mouth hung slack, and he snored.

But after last night she had to admit he did have *one* thing in common with that larger-than-life species. Her gaze drifted down his torso. His body might be bundled beneath blankets, but the vision of him buck-naked was burned into her brain.

For all time, she feared.

Then her eyebrows drew together. Because speaking of brains, what had she been thinking to even start this with him? Well, sure, *thinking* hadn't had a whole lot to do with it. But even a half-baked attempt to look beyond her sudden itch to climb in his pants would have been a nice idea.

Not that she could bring herself to regret scratching that itch, exactly.

Or, okay, at all; neither the first time nor their second round, either. Hell, she was an adult—she'd known what she was getting into.

But great as the sex had been, it was sort of a dead-end relationship, wasn't it? Cade had built a life for himself in L.A., or wherever he lived, while she'd built hers here. So even if they managed to cobble something together, it hardly seemed like an association destined to prosper.

She wasn't even sure she wanted a relationship with him. Their history was loaded with so much baggage they could open their own storefront—if only their luggage weren't so freaking shopworn. She liked to believe she had the maturity to move beyond that history, but in her heart of hearts she wasn't at all confident that she did.

Of course, this even was supposing *he* was interested, which was a mega-big "if" indeed.

"You're thinking way too hard."

She started, having failed to notice the sudden lack of snoring. She'd been too busy looking inward. Now she focused on Cade.

He smiled at her, his eyes still sleepy beneath their heavy fringe of dark lashes. There was something in their rich blue depths, however, an indefinable emotion or intent she couldn't quite put a finger on.

But it made her heart pound.

Then he distracted her by saying dryly, "I can practically smell the circuits frying. You are so transparent, Spencer."

"I am not!"

"No? Then tell me you weren't lying there wondering what the hell you'd gotten yourself into."

"Of course I wasn't," she said with great dignity—then shrugged. "So, maybe I was. But you have to admit—"

Snaking out a hand, he hooked the back of her neck and leaned close to lay a soft, lazy kiss on her. A kiss that made her melt. When he finally drew back, it was only far enough to rest his forehead against hers. "Mornin'," he said in a gravelly voice.

"Good morning, yourself," she replied. But her brain was sputtering like a combustible engine running on fumes, rendering her more confused than ever. Because that hadn't been one of the hot, let's-get-it-on kisses they'd shared last night. This one had been sweeter, more tender, almost like the kiss of a guy in lov—

Cade's cell phone rang, chopping the unlikely thought in half.

"Crap," he muttered, then rolled to pick it up off the nightstand. He looked at the screen, then glanced at her. "I'm sorry, it's Beks. I've got to get this."

"Of course," she murmured, unsure whether she felt relieved or disappointed.

Before she could decide, the incredulousness in Cade's voice caught her attention. Climbing to his feet, he said something about John, and, from what she could glean from his end of the conversation, it sounded as if the night watchman might have been hurt. She could be misinterpreting, but whatever it was, it wasn't good. Cade looked upset.

Without stopping to ask herself why, she scooted closer.

He disconnected a moment later, thrust a hand all the way though his train-wreck hair until he stood gripping the back of his neck. He stared at the floor in front of him. "Well, that wasn't news I've been holding my breath to hear." Then he turned to stare at her. "I don't suppose your contacts extend to a night watchman, do they?"

TONY STUCK his head into the room Gallari used as an office. "Beks said you wanted to see me?"

The producer/director looked up from whatever he was working on. It was hard to say, considering all the junk, from paperwork to props, piled atop the desk. "Yeah, have a seat."

Tony dropped into the one indicated.

"Beks tells me you're a student."

It caught him by surprise, but he was a professional; he allowed the fact that the PA had passed along his lie to neither show nor rattle him. "Yeah."

"And that you wouldn't mind taking over the night shift?"

Mind? Hell, hadn't he been turning himself inside out trying to figure out a way to do precisely that? He wanted to laugh like an asylum escapee but slapped on a slightly puzzled expression instead. "That would be great, actually. Not only could I get my homework done in the downtime, but it would free me up to take more classes during the day."

"Then the job is yours, if you don't mind pulling a double shift today and—worst-case scenario—tomorrow as well. But Ava's working on a replacement and we're hoping to have one in place by tomorrow."

"Sure. But what about John?"

"He had to fly to Phoenix. Apparently his mother fell down her basement stairs and busted her leg all to hell."

"That sucks."

A corner of Gallari's mouth tipped up. "To say the least."

They talked a few minutes longer, then Tony left Gallari to go back to his messy desk. He maintained an everyday normal expression as he nodded and exchanged greetings with the crew members he passed, then took the stairs two at a time up the sweeping central staircase. He strode down the hallway past the Wolcott broad's sitting room, catching a snatch of conversation between the makeup chick and someone. A moment later he reached a deserted room, stepped inside and eased the door shut.

Where, erupting into laughter, he broke into a victory boogie.

He didn't allow himself to carry on for long. But damned if his luck hadn't finally taken a turn for the better! It had seemed like one fucking thing after another on this gig, but where he'd run different scenarios through his head for getting John out of the way long enough to give him time to search the sitting room without fear of somebody catching him doing so, the night man's old lady had done the job for him.

He had considered hitting John with his car to put him out of commission, but balked at the inability to guarantee the evening security guard wouldn't recognize his vehicle. He'd thought of putting Visine in John's coffee but didn't know how much would just make the guy sick and how much might kill him. Not that he was morally against killing, necessarily. But a death would likely mean an autopsy—and he was sure as hell against setting off any alarms that might make anyone look more closely at his credentials.

Sometimes life was just one big crapshoot—but with this throw he'd rolled himself a pretty little eleven. Damn, he oughtta send John's mama some flowers.

He didn't know how much time he'd have before the older man returned. But, hell, the night watchman must be somewhere in his fifties—and probably late fifties, at that. The guy's mother really had to be up there in years. It would likely take several days to see a woman that old through hospitalization and probably some rehab as well, right? So it should be plenty long enough. And if it wasn't?

Well, Mother John's fall had presented him with a third option. He could always string some nice transparent fishing wire from railing spindle to railing spindle halfway up that fancy stair case and help John have a few fractures of his own. So, the guy had better hope his mother's recovery took a while.

Or his old lady wouldn't be the only one to take a tumble.

UP ON THE third floor Ava picked her way across the ballroom. They hadn't started filming up here yet, but it was crowded with furnishings, props and the usual complement of crew busy performing their specialized jobs. She wove through the bustle, stepping over cables and dodging grips moving ladders and furniture, to make her way to where Cade stood deep in conversation with Jim Short. Reaching them, she politely halted a few feet away to wait until they were finished.

It took almost ten minutes, but eventually the gaffer turned to her and grinned. "He's all yours, doll," he said, and raising his voice bellowed, "Ryan! Get over here, boy. We've got work to do."

He strode off, leaving her facing Cade, unasked-for visions of last night playing through her mind. The emergency with John this morning had knocked personal considerations aside. She'd driven home for a quick change while Cade had headed straight to the mansion to talk to Tony about switching over to the night security position. Since then, he'd been doing his thing while she'd done hers, and any communication between them had been filtered through Beks.

Taking a deep breath, she buried the unexpected frisson of nerves she experienced coming face-to-face with him again. "I found you a day security guard," she said. "She can't start until the day after tomorrow, but she came highly recommended so I think it might be worth the wait. I told her, however, that I'd have to call her back."

"That'll work," he said. "The odds of someone waltzing in and trying to liberate hundreds of thousands of dollars worth of production equipment are a helluva lot lower during the day with all the people swarming around here than at night when the place is empty. Thanks, Ava."

"Not a problem. I'll call her back to let her know." She turned away.

"Hold up."

When she turned back, she found Cade had closed the distance between them. Those damn visions popped front and center once more, making her heart trip over itself.

He looked down at her. "Have dinner with me tonight."

"What?" Not that she hadn't heard him perfectly well, but being caught by surprise made her a little slow on the uptake.

"You and I have screwed our brains out," he said in a low, rough voice, "but we've never been on a date. Not back in the day and not as adults. Let me buy you dinner."

She should say no, of course, but, when she opened her mouth, what came out was, "Okay."

His eyes lit up. "Really? Okay?"

"Yes." A dinner date sounded so normal, and she could use some normal. It was something that had been in short supply in their relationship.

"Excellent. I'll make a reservation somewhere nice for—what?—say, around seven-thirty?"

"Seven-thirty sounds good." She took a tiny step away. "Well, I'd better get back to work."

"Doing what?" He followed her retreat, looking down at her with those cerulean eyes. "I thought things were slow for you around here right now."

"They are, but I've got a few things to cross off my own business list."

"What kind of things? No, wait, I've got to get back to it, too, if we're gonna have any chance of getting out of here on time. Tell me over dinner." He looked at her as if he wanted to kiss her, and for a second she held her breath thinking he was going to do just that. Then, with a roll of his shoulders, he turned away.

She blew out the breath she hadn't realized she'd been holding. "Hoo, boy," she whispered and turned away. She'd go talk to the caterer about tomorrow's menu, then dive into her own stuff.

SHORTLY AFTER seven that evening, she and Cade met in the kitchen. "I had Beks do a little research on restaurants," he said, as she buttoned her coat and wrapped a scarf around her neck. "And one that kept coming up is Spring Hill. I understand it's even in your neighborhood, so I made a reservation there."

"Oh, that's a great choice!"

"I thought I could follow you home and drive us from there, so you don't have to come back for your car."

"That would be nice. Feed me a good meal and the last thing I want to do afterward is have to head across town and then drive back again. I usually just wanna go to bed." *Crap!* That had *not* been an invitation. God, did he think it was an invitation?

She couldn't tell, for he merely gave her a ghost of a smile and walked her out to her car. He saw her inside, got in his own vehicle, then did as he'd said and followed her to her condo, where he waited out on the street while she pushed the garage door opener to the secured parking beneath her building and put her car away. When she emerged a few minutes later, she found him leaning against his fender waiting for her.

A scant ten minutes after that, they were being seated in Spring Hill Restaurant and Bar. After ordering wine, looking at the menu and agreeing on selections to share, Cade leaned into the table. "So, I gotta ask. Are you still dating the Argentinean Wonder?"

"Oh. No." She gave him a sheepish smile, which she should have known he'd pick right up on.

His gaze turned sharp, and he leaned toward her even more. "What? What aren't you telling me?"

"Oh, there are a lot of things I don't tell you, Gallari."

"Okay, what aren't you telling me about Mr. Argentina?"

Crap. "That maybe he's my friend Eddie." She offered him another smile. "And that he thought you were *real* cute."

"The guy's gay?"

She nodded, hoping that wouldn't be a problem for him, because Eddie was a good friend.

But Cade merely grinned. "*Ex*-cellent."

Over an appetizer of Manila clams, Dinah's cheese and wheat crackers, it was her turn to lean across the table. "You said you were taking off right behind me this morning. So how did you tame your morning bed head? It looked like nothing short of a whip and a chair would do the trick."

He laughed. "Yeah, and I wasn't about to show up at the mansion looking like that. I stuck my head beneath the kitchen faucet."

As they started their main course, mushroom risotto for him, sautéed halibut for her, Cade said, "So tell me about the jobs you've been working on for your own business."

"I arranged a house and pet sitter for one client today—that was quick and easy." She licked a dribble of buttered clam nectar off the side of her hand. "But I have new clients who are relocating to the area and that's more complex. The husband has a job waiting at Microsoft and he doesn't want to have to commute across the bridge. So I set them up with a good Realtor on the east side a few weeks back. They've been out here twice and it looks as if they're leaning toward a place in Kirkland. So now I'm polling my contacts in that area, which frankly aren't nearly as extensive as my Seattle network. But I'm trying to find my clients good doctors, dentists, lawyers, etc.

"Once they pick a house I'll arrange a reputable mover to get their stuff here. Then I'll stock the kitchen and buy the usual paper products to get them through until they unpack all their boxes." She shrugged and took a sip of her wine. "Or, who knows, that might become my job, as well." She held up her goblet. "This is an excellent Roussanne."

Then she gave him a serious look. "Can I ask you something about your dad?"

If his eyes went the slightest bit remote, he nevertheless nodded. "All right."

"You never really said how you found out about him not being your father."

He blew out a quiet breath. "He was angry with me about…I don't even remember what, since he was always mad at me. I'm sure I was mouthing off, because that was during my damned-if-I'd-continue-seeking-his-approval stage. Then out of the blue he said, in that fucking icy, superior voice he always used with me, 'I am through taking this disrespect from a child who is not even my own.' And told me exactly how that had come to be."

She jerked, hurting for him, and reached out to touch his balled fingers. "Oh, my God. I can see where you'd feel blindsided."

"And angry. God, I didn't know what true rage was before then."

She drew in a deep breath and quietly let it go. "Is that when you made the bet?"

"Yes." He gave a curt tip of his chin. Ava wished she'd never started this topic. It wasn't exactly fun-night-out date conversation.

"It was about three days earlier," he said. "The guys had brought it up before, but I'd blown it off. And I promise you, Ava, I wasn't thinking of that when I slept with you. But, God, I was wicked furious, so when they brought it up again I said, 'Sure.' I guess I thought why not kill two birds with one stone. But I didn't know they'd ambush you in the cafeteria—"

"Cade? *Cade Gallari?*"

They looked up at a tallish man with sandy-brown hair that was beginning to thin.

"It is you!" the man exclaimed. "It's me—Dylan Vanderkamp."

Ava's gut iced over and, feeling a déjà vu moment of betrayal, she stared at Cade. "If this is another bet," she said in a low voice, "you are a dead man."

Cursing inwardly, Cade reached across the table to grip her hand. "No. I swear to you." Damn, could the timing *be* any worse? She'd been so sweet, so empathetic and nonaggressive for once about the bet and—

"Huh?" Dylan said, then gave her a closer perusal. "Ho-ly—*Ava Spencer?* Jesus, when did you get so hot?"

Thinking he'd kill the guy himself if Vanderkamp screwed up the progress he'd finally managed to make with her, Cade watched Ava give Dylan a level look.

Color flowed up the other man's neck. "Uh, that didn't come out right. What I meant to say is nice to see you, you're lookin' good." Then he blew out a breath, squared his shoulders and looked her directly in the eye. "Look, I'm sorry about that crappy bet, but I swear to you I'm not the same asshole I was back in high school. And if it's any comfort, the bad karma from my actions came back to kick my family's ass."

She clearly didn't have a clue what the latter part of his comment meant, but she gave him a regal nod.

You would have thought the unamused Queen of Hearts had rescinded her "Off with his head!" decree, so palpable was the relief with which Dylan turned to Cade. "How come you escaped the karmic payback?"

"Who says I did?"

"Well, look what you've done! You've sure made a name for yourself. Jesus, Gallari, my wife and I have seen every one of your films. She doesn't believe me when I tell her I used to know you. I wish she were here, but we live in St. Paul now—I'm just in town for a quick business trip. What are the odds we'd run into each other? But the scientist I've been trying to wine and dine away from Amgen to come work for the biotech my partner and I own heard about this place and wanted to come."

He glanced over his shoulder. "Which reminds me, I better get back to my table. I've been head-hunting this guy for our R and D department for two solid months now. He's about seven-eighths ready to sign but is still hesitating because of our winters. I sure as hell don't want to lose him due to neglect." He looked from Cade to Ava and shook his head. "So you two are together, huh?" he murmured. "Funny how things work out."

With a shrug, he turned and walked to a table across from the bar at the back of the room.

Cade gave Ava a wry smile. "Well, he hasn't changed. He's just as big a motormouth as ever—and it's still all about him. What *are* the odds?"

She tilted her head to one side. "You took that bet to sleep with me in order to keep your friends. So how is it you lost touch with Vanderkamp?"

"I know, ironic, isn't it?" He grimaced. "At the time I thought they were the only constant in my life. But maybe a week after we graduated, Dunn's older sister

ODed on tequila and cocaine and damn near died. They got her into rehab in a small private place in Bremerton and the rest of the family stayed at their place on the canal to be closer. A few weeks after that Dylan's dad's company went belly-up. They sold everything they owned and moved away. Things were tenser than ever at home so I left and just trucked around the country until college started."

He studied her curiously. "I get you not hearing about Serena Dunn, but I'm surprised you didn't know about Vanderkamp's family, given the role he played in that fucking bet—and how plugged in you are in this town."

"Mother sent me to a 'fat' camp in Paris right after graduation."

He snapped upright. "She did *what?* I thought you and Jane and Poppy were going to San Francisco for a couple of weeks. Didn't you tell me they'd been saving for that trip all year?"

"Mother thought this was more important."

"I don't think I like your mother much." He wanted to ask why Poppy or Jane hadn't told her about his friends when she'd come back. But it didn't take a genius to figure out they probably hadn't wanted to make her revisit the pain of that day all over again.

They went back to more general conversation, but Cade was aware of a slight reserve beneath Ava's surface sociability. So when dinner was over and he'd taken her home, after he kissed her at her door, then lifted his head and said, "Let me come in, Av," he held his breath, fully expecting a cool refusal. He was surprised when she instead wordlessly took his hand in both of hers, pulled him inside and shut the door.

"I thought you were gonna say no," he admitted, reaching for the buttons on her cashmere coat.

"Don't think I didn't consider it." She pinned him with solemn eyes as she stood quietly while he divested her of her outerwear. "I keep wondering if I'm giving in too easily, if I shouldn't make you pay more—"

"Are you kidding me? I *have* paid. Every damn time I've seen you for the past thirteen years, I've paid."

"Then I considered that," she agreed with a minute nod and her lips curled up in a tiny smile. "Why do you think you made it past my door?"

CHAPTER EIGHTEEN

How am I supposed to know how I feel? Things have been moving at warp speed. What I feel is wicked crazy.

AVA'S IPHONE chimed the next day as she started down the stairs to tell Beks she was taking off for the evening. Pulling the device from her purse, she glanced at the screen and smiled when she saw she had a text from Poppy.

Girlz Nite, it read. My place @ 7:30. Bring chocolate. Or something salty. Or both. No excuses. C U then.

"Yes!" She tossed her phone back in her purse. Girls' night was exactly what she needed; it had been too long since she'd spent any face-to-face time with her friends—at least any that included an actual opportunity for conversation.

Of course that was her own fault. To say she was torn when it came to Cade was an understatement. Yet she must not be *that* conflicted. Not when it suddenly occurred to her that she had mostly been avoiding Jane and Poppy for fear they would reinforce her own arguments on the negative side of the pro and con ledger. The damn thing seemed to stream like a continual stock ticker in her head as it was. The last thing she needed was opinions she might not like adding to her confusion.

Still, while her motives might be murky, the bottom line was she'd gone too long without her BFFs' company and was ready for some quality girlfriend time.

A couple hours later found her knocking on the door of the little Craftsman bungalow Poppy and Jase had bought in Fremont a couple of months back. The reverberation of the first rap of her knuckles had barely been followed up by the second when the entry whipped open. She jerked back her fist. "Jeez! Were you standing on the other side? I damn near bopped you in the nose!"

"But you didn't. Come in, c'min!" Poppy danced back into the narrow entryway. "You're right on time—fifteen minutes late."

"Whoa!" Ava ignored the dig, since it was hard to argue with the truth. "What's got you so wired? You sell another greeting card to Shoe Box or something?"

"I wish. So, what did you bring? Chocolate or salty?"

"I'm a pro, baby." She fumbled in her oversized bag and pulled out a charcoal-colored box tied with a gold satin ribbon. "I brought both."

"Omigawd, *Fran's!* Janie, Ava brought salted caramels!"

"Gray or smoked?" Jane demanded from the living room on the other side of the wall.

Poppy removed the ribbon from the box, lifted a corner and peeked inside. She shot Ava a smile.

"You *are* a pro." Raising her voice, she answered their friend. "Both. Dark chocolate for you, milk for me, and either for Miss I'm-not-picky here." She turned back to Ava and gave her a one-armed squeeze. "You de woo-mon! Here, you take 'em into the living room. I'll go put on the tea water." Sliding the candy box's satin ribbon beneath her hair, she fashioned the ends into a bowtied headband as she danced into the kitchen.

Ava went to join Jane, who was lounging on the de Sanges couch in front of a crackling fire. She gave her friend the once-over.

"Well, look at you, all colorful and all," she said, admiring Jane's pale green, long-sleeved girl-T and the emerald velvet lounging pants it was tucked into. A flowing jacket that matched the pants was tossed atop the back of the davenport.

Jane looked down at her outfit. "Isn't it pretty? Dev bought it for me." She grinned. "I'm starting to get downright comfortable with colorful clothes."

"As you should be." She dropped down on the far end of the couch. "You look really good in them." Opening the caramel box, she offered one to Jane, then took one for herself. "So has Poppy been this manic since you've been here?"

"I heard that!" their friend called from the kitchen.

"Yep," Jane agreed. "Pretty much." She raised her voice. "She's not saying why."

Their friend swept into the room bearing a tray that held a teapot and three colorful mugs. "Ava, this is just perfect," she said, coming to a halt in front of the coffee table in a swirl of red fabric. Setting the tray down, she poured the tea and handed her a cup. "Here, you get first pour. I don't know how you do it, but you always bring exactly the right thing." She handed a mug to Jane next, then took the last one for herself and sat in the chair facing them.

"Jase at work?" Ava asked as she took a sip of the Earl Grey and reached for another caramel.

"Yes. He's been working a case this week that's kept

him busy till all hours. He hopes to wrap it up tonight, but you know how that can go." She took a bite of one of the milk chocolate and smoked salt caramels and closed her eyes as she chewed. Swallowing a moment later, she looked at Ava and Jane. "*Damn,* these are good. Anyhow, I thought it was the perfect opportunity to get us together. It's been way too long."

"Precisely my thought when I got your text."

"Plus, I have something I've been dying to share with you."

Jane and Ava exchanged glances, and Poppy laughed. "Yeah, I know, I suck at secrets. But I promised Jason I'd wait until we were sure." She reached for another caramel but merely held it as she gave her friends a blinding smile. "I'm pregnant."

"What?" they demanded in nearly one voice.

Then all three women laughed and leapt to their feet. Jane said, "Oh my God," at the same time Ava demanded, "We're going to be aunties?"

"Yes!"

She screamed her enthusiasm over the idea, then demanded, "When?"

"Late October, near as I can tell."

"You haven't been to a doctor yet?" Jane asked.

"I have, but only to make sure the three home pregnancy tests I took weren't messing with me. I have an appointment with her next week for the full workup, so I should know more after that. But isn't it *cool?*"

Ava was suddenly too choked up to do anything but nod her agreement, but Janie echoed what she was thinking when she said, "The coolest!"

Poppy tipped her head to peer at Ava. "Are you crying?" she said.

"I know, it's dumb." She wiped some tears away.

"But this is just so fabulous—you're gonna be a mama. God, Poppy. It makes you seem so grown-up."

The blonde laughed. "I know! I'm so excited. But another part of me is scared spitless. Because it is mega grown-up. And so, I don't know—responsible or something."

Ava hugged her friend. "Aw, you'll be a natural. Look how good you are with all your at-risk art kids."

"Yeah," Jane agreed. "Not to mention you've got Detective Sheik, whose picture is probably in the dictionary right next to Responsible."

"Yes." She gave them a radiant smile. "There is that. He is *so* psyched over the whole thing."

"I bet your folks are gonna flip. Have you told them yet?"

"Tomorrow. We're supposed to have dinner at their house—and I'm going even if Jason can't make it, because I cannot keep this to myself one more day. But he thinks they're really close to wrapping things up, so here's hoping."

"How about Murphy?" Ava asked, referring to the man who had turned Jase from the life of crime he'd been heading toward as a teen to the cop he was now.

"We're going to invite Murph to go with us—my folks always love to see him and he's family. It's important to Jase to be there when we tell Murphy, though, so if he can't leave work, we'll tell him the next day before Jason heads back to the precinct."

They hashed over boys versus girls and possible names for the next hour, then debated whether it was best to throw a baby shower in August or September. Finally, Poppy waved a dismissive hand.

"As much as I love that it's been all about me tonight," she said with a grin, "what have you been up to, Av? Jane and I talk all the time, but you have been one elusive girl recently."

Ava inhaled a quick breath, blew it out—and braced herself. "I've been working at the shoot, fitting my own work in where I can…and seeing Cade."

Jane cocked her head. "Define seeing."

"Hanging out. Going to dinner. Having sex."

There was a moment of silence, then, "Told you," Jane said to Poppy.

Blowing out a short, sharp breath, the blonde stretched over the side of her chair, then sat back up holding her purse. She pulled out her wallet and handed Jane a five-dollar bill.

"Seriously?" Ava stared from one to the other. "You've been making bets on my sex life? You don't find that a little tasteless, considering?"

"Nah," Janie said calmly, tucking the fiver in her pants pocket. "I saw the way you looked at each other at the mansion the day I came to talk to him about the collections and on the dance floor at the Alibi Room and it just seemed like a good way to get rid of the bad bet karma." She shot Ava a crooked smile. "Plus this is Cade we're talking about. You've had strong feelings about him one way or the other since—what?—we were ten, twelve years old?"

"Now, me, I didn't think you'd ever get past the bet," Poppy said.

"I sometimes worry I never will, completely," she admitted, then looked back at Jane, who was tucking her shiny brown hair behind her ears and observing her with a slight smile. "What made you think I would?" She really wanted to know, because she didn't want to be stuck in a high school moment for the rest of her life. But remembering her knee-jerk reaction to Dylan

Vanderkamp's sudden appearance practically on the heels of her and Cade making love, she did fear an inability to completely let that day in the cafeteria go.

Jane shrugged. "We're not eighteen anymore. And like the rest of us, Cade seems to have grown up. Actually, he seems to have grown up pretty good." She studied Ava's expression. "The real question is, what made you change your mind?"

"Well, lust played a part, for sure."

Poppy gave her a wry smile. "I take it he's improved then?"

Just the memory of their times together had heat pooling low in her body. "And then some. But it's not only that. It's a number of things I've been discovering—about him and about myself."

"Like?"

"Like his mindset when he took that bet." She told them about the way he'd discovered his father wasn't really his father and how it had made him cling more tightly to his friends. "Not that he got much comfort from that association," she said and related what she'd found out last night. "Did you guys know about this?"

"I heard about Vanderkamp's family," Poppy said, "but I never heard anything about Dunn's sister."

"Same here," Jane agreed. "Then again, why would we? I was the scholarship kid in that school and everyone knew Poppy's folks were hippies and her grandmother had paid her tuition. We weren't as plugged into that social set as you were and only heard about Vanderkamp because of the role he'd played in the bet."

"Why didn't you ever say anything to me about it?"

"You were gone most of that summer and by the time you got back you were doing better emotionally than you'd been when your mom shipped you off to Paris.

So we debated whether knowing would make you feel better or just bring back all the pain. It was Miss A who finally said it was probably better to let sleeping dogs lie."

Ava braced an elbow on the arm of the couch and propped her head on her fist. "It's funny, you know? That damn bet turned into much too large a part of my life. It's colored my thoughts for years. Hell, it used to shape every damn minute of every damn day—and occasionally I feel as if I still allow it to do that. But then last night—"

She blew out a breath. Looked at her friends. "I was so wrapped up in my own misery that summer I never once wondered how anybody else's life was going— especially not Cade's crowd of idiots. I just assumed they were merrily trucking along and it was all blue skies and honey for them. But it turns out they weren't immune to bad times either. I guess no one is.

"Vanderkamp looked me in the eye last night and apologized. When he first showed up at the table I expected him to be the same braying ass he'd been back when. But his world had fallen apart after that day as well and, like me, he'd had to put it back together again. He seems to have turned into…an okay guy." She sat a little straighter. "And it doesn't pain me near as much to say that as I thought it would."

Poppy studied her for a moment. "Are you in love with Gallari, Av?"

"No!" Her heart pounded with instant panic. *God,* no! Falling in love with Cade Gallari was a fast track to heartache. "I'm not an idiot."

"No one would ever suggest you were." Her friend gave her a puzzled look. "But you aren't exactly Little Miss Let's-jump-in-the-sack. You're pretty darn…

cautious. So if you're diving headfirst into sex with him when you've done so with maybe a handful of guys, it seems reasonable to assume—"

"That I'm enjoying myself. Period. Okay, sure, maybe more than I expected. Still. Cade and me? That's a relationship with a finite shelf life. He's got his life in Los Angeles. Mine's here."

The panic receded beneath her own logic and she gave her friends a wry smile. "This is about sex—and I guess a growing friendship. But I can tell you categorically—

"Whatever we have, it isn't about love."

So, is this what love feels like? Cade slumped behind the wheel of his car in front of Ava's condo, pondering the question even as he wondered where the hell she was and when she'd be home. All he knew was what Beks had told him: that Ava had left the mansion around seven. Well, that and the fact that he was sitting here like some lovelorn chump, freezing his ass off and letting jealousy chew a hole in his gut. Because what if she was out with another guy?

He assured himself that he was just suffering a weird case of temporary possessiveness. But deep down he feared his idiocy came from having fallen face-first in love. And if this was what it felt like, it sucked.

Yet when he was with her, it just felt so...*man.*
Amazing.

Like a dog shedding water, he gave himself a shake and smacked the heel of his hand against the steering wheel. Hell, what did he know about love? It wasn't as if his life had been overburdened with the emotion.

Not that he hadn't come a long way in his dealings with women. Well, he'd be an idiot not to, wouldn't

he? He'd learned the hard way of the long-term consequences that could come from a single bad move.

So he took more care with women's feelings these
days. But he'd sure never fancied himself in love.

And yet…

He felt…happy…around Ava. When he could make
her flash those dimples or—even better—laugh, something inside of him just lit up. She had a way about her,
as if the simplest little thing delighted her, and a kindness that nurtured. He'd never known anyone like her.

He looked at her and wished he had some artistic
ability, because that coloring, that body, deserved to
be commemorated.

And it wasn't simply that she had pretty breasts or
a stunning ass. The other night, he'd spent a solid ten
minutes caught up in admiration of the taut, satin sheen
of the skin covering her damn collarbones.

Which, added to wanting to *immortalize* her on
canvas, for God's sake—given he couldn't draw a stick
figure with a ruler—pretty much indicated he had it
bad.

Sitting here until she came home, however, was not
only pathetic, it was stupid. He had work he should be
doing back at his place, and, reaching for the key, he
fired up the car. After allowing himself an additional
couple of minutes to get the heater pumping out some
warmth, he put the rental in gear and pulled away from
the curb.

He was headed down the beach when he thought he
recognized the shape of her headlights in his rearview.
Pulling over, he watched in the mirror as the car drew
closer, then blew out a quiet breath when it turned into
her condo garage.

Pulling a Uie, he drove back and parked across the

street. He'd barely had time to turn off his headlights before lights started coming on in her apartment. He watched her cross back and forth in front of the window a couple times.

Then, feeling lighter knowing that she was home safe and sound, and thinking, since they'd had no plans, that it was probably better not to show up on her doorstep like some stalker, he put the car in gear and drove away.

CHAPTER NINETEEN

I'll be glad when Dad's party is behind me. Right now I have too much other stuff on my plate to get everything done.

"I MISSED YOU last night."

At the sound of Cade's voice, Ava looked up from the notes she'd been keying in her iPhone. She hadn't heard him approach over the muted thumps, bumps and scrapes of the production crew working in the ballroom overhead. But there he was, leaning against the door-jamb of the second-floor room she had taken over for a couple minutes of alone time.

A flash of pleasure suffused her and she rose to her feet, smiling at him. This might not be true love, but she couldn't deny she enjoyed his company. "I had a girls' night with Jane and Poppy that came up at the last minute." She hesitated, then added, "I'm sorry, I probably should have told you. I guess I'm not quite sure how involved we're supposed to be."

His dark eyebrows drew together. "This isn't just about the sex, Ava."

"No, I realize that. We're friends."

Those brows stayed knitted. "Friends," he said, almost as if he'd never heard the word before.

She laughed. "I know, it sounds weird, doesn't

it? Given all our history, who'da thought *that* would happen?"

His face softening, he pushed away from the doorway and sauntered over to her with that easy walk of his. "I love it when you laugh. It punches those pretty dimples right here…and here." He wiggled the tips of his forefingers into the twin indentations under discussion.

It was a purely platonic gesture, yet heat pooled deep and low. She took a step closer.

Cade's cerulean eyes turned to midnight.

"There you are!" Gripping the doorjambs in either hand, Beks leaned into the room, the bouncy fans of her high, short pigtails—streaked with blue today—still shimmying after the rest of her had stilled. With a clear case of tunnel vision, she locked in on Ava. "Any chance you got those chandelier candles I asked you about the other day?"

"Yes. There are four boxes in the pantry. But I thought night filming wasn't scheduled until the day after—"

She found herself talking to an empty doorway. Beks had pushed back as abruptly as she'd appeared, the clomp of her boots down the hallway the only thing to mark that she'd been there.

"—tomorrow," Ava finished dryly and turned raised eyebrows on Cade.

"That was the other thing I came in to talk to you about," he said with his crooked smile. "We had to switch up the night shoot schedule and I wondered if you could come in late the next few days, then work part of the evenings."

"Sure. Spencer's Specialties has had a rash of calls

the last couple days, so it will actually give me time to take care of some of my own work."

"Excellent."

"It is," she agreed, then shot him a smile of her own. "You're probably talking about my ability to adapt to your schedule, but I'm really pleased that my business is picking up. But what does any of this have to do with the chandelier candles and changing the night schedule?"

"I don't know if you knew that Heather—you know, who plays Agnes?—attends the U-Dub. She scored the lead in their drama department's new production and they start evening rehearsals on Monday. So we're changing some things around."

And just like that, she melted. This was one of the reasons she found herself liking Cade so much. Great sex was…well, great. Her lips curled up. Okay, more than great. But how many other producers in Cade's position would have switched things around to accommodate an unknown actress's schedule so she could star in a university drama production? Ava wanted to plunge her hands in his hair, hold him firmly in place and plant the hottest kiss on him the world had ever seen.

Instead she straightened and found herself blurting, "My folks are going to be back Saturday morning for my father's birthday party that evening. If your night filming is finished by then, would you like to be my date?" She stilled. *Okay, freaking out a bit here.* Because where had that come from?

But she pushed the question aside and merely raised her eyebrows at him. Because it felt right.

He took a step that brought him so close she had to tip her head back. "Yeah," he said, looking down at her. "I would like that. Hell, I'd like a whole lot more than—"

He cut himself off. Rolling his shoulders, he took a step back. "Sorry. This isn't the time or place and it sure isn't getting my work done. And if I'm gonna finish up in time for our date night, I'd better get my ass in gear."

A laugh erupted from his throat. "Jesus." Self-deprecating humor laced his tone as he turned and strode for the door. "Date night. Now there're two words I never expected to hear coming out of my mouth."

Sonovabitch! C'mon, move it, move it, move it!

Trying to clamp down on the frustration that threatened to obliterate his self-control, Tony recited multiplication tables in his head as he watched the crew mosey from the mansion in a slower-than-a-possum lazy-ass trickle. But his concentration kept slipping, and it took more effort than he'd ever before had to expend just to slap a lid on his growing temper. As quickly as he stuffed one mental imprecation down, another popped up to take its place.

Goddamn, motherfu—

He held himself very still. Tried to make his mind go blank.

Failed. Curses screamed through his head as he mentally urged the crew to get a fricking *move* on. It seemed to take forever before he finally locked the door behind Beks, who was the last to leave. Through the kitchen door window, he eyed her retreating, as usual black-clad butt, then punched in the security code and listened to the sound of car engines firing up on the back drive and out on the street. Not until the last one had finally faded into the distance did he relax his rigid posture.

"I'm taking off now, too."

Shit! How had he forgotten about Selena, his day shift replacement? "Okay." Clearing his throat, he looked over at her as she pulled her mousy brown hair out from beneath her coat collar. "Have a good night."

He let her out the back and reset the alarm once more.

Then rammed his fingers through his hair. Jesus. He was so wired, so hacked off, he could barely see straight.

He knew better than to let anger get the better of him, knew that he had to get past it, to let it go.

Even so, he couldn't seem to stop himself from lashing out and kicking a kitchen chair across the floor so hard it bounced off a cupboard, leaving a chip behind. "Goddamn, flaming shit, son of a syphilitic *bitch!*"

Dropping his hands to his sides, he blew out a final emphatic breath and squared his shoulders. Now, *that* had felt good. A helluva lot better than any of that pansy-ass zen breathing shit. Because, Christ on a cracker, he couldn't frigging *believe* his rotten luck!

This job was supposed to have been so easy. Hell, for the first time since he'd pulled his initial con at nineteen, he didn't need to slap on the charm every damn second of the day. Didn't need to play nice and lie through his teeth to get some stupid old broad to fork over her money. All he'd had to do—hypothetically anyway—was waltz in, liberate himself a fortune in jewels and waltz right back out again, then head for the nearest airport to jump a plane for the destination of his choice.

Yet not one goddamn thing had gone right and he was good and pissed.

Pissed at Uncle Mike, who'd gotten him all excited about the Wolcott Suite diamonds, only to go and die on him before he'd gotten around to handing out better advice than that fucking useless, "Look behind the ornate woodwork."

Pissed at all the stupid people crawling all over this stupid pile of bricks.

Pissed at having his plans dicked up every time he thought he'd finally get a chance at the damn woodwork.

Most of all, though, he was pissed at himself. He'd had two entire nights to find the stinking secret compartment, but had he done so?

He had not. Hell, he hadn't even made it to the midpoint of the wall yet. He'd blown too much of the first night when he'd fallen asleep halfway into his shift. Sure, he'd worked two back-to-backs that day, but he should have knocked back a pot of coffee, slipped out to buy some No-Doz, done *something* to keep his sorry ass awake.

Instead, he'd leaned back against the sitting room wall to rest his eyes for just a few minutes—and hadn't woken up again until he'd heard the first crew members stomping up the stairs nearly five hours later.

Last night he'd picked up inspecting the fancy woodwork from the point where he'd left off. But given the necessity of going over it inch by meticulous inch, he'd only managed to examine maybe a third of it.

And had come up empty on what he *had* managed to go over. It didn't help that he didn't have a clue exactly what it was he was looking for—although he imagined it was some sort of pressure release switch he would recognize when he felt it.

But if he didn't find the damn thing tonight, he didn't know when he'd get another opportunity. Because, starting tomorrow, they were changing to goddamn *night* filming.

How the hell could one guy's luck be so bad? Here he'd thought that John returning before he could accomplish his mission was his biggest problem. But it turned out he'd been worrying in the wrong direction.

It didn't help that he'd painted himself into a damn corner by rhapsodizing over the benefits the night shift would have on his nonexistent college career.

He might appreciate the irony that a two-bit actress's real college career was responsible for the change in plans—if it hadn't screwed him in the process. Without the K-Y.

Who the hell had thought it would be this hard? He'd never carried a gun in his life until the security firm had issued him one. His M.O. had always been to finesse someone out of a fortune, not to strong-arm them out of it.

If he had the slightest belief, however, that it would somehow help his cause, he'd shoot that Heather bitch right between the eyes.

Instead, he'd probably be wiser to get his ass in gear and make use of whatever time he had left.

Then hope like hell that sometime between now and when Selena arrived to relieve him in the morning, his stinking luck took a turn for the better.

CHAPTER TWENTY

Once it's been said, it's impossible to pretend you didn't hear it.

WITH A MUCH more critical eye than usual, Ava inspected the fit of the dress she'd donned for her father's birthday party. A smart woman would no doubt focus on the fact that she'd maintained her weight for more than a decade. But the sad reality was she still had moments, like now, when she looked in the mirror and saw her "fat" self instead of the perfectly fit size twelve/fourteen body she had today.

Most of the time she cut herself some slack. She was never going to be runway model slender, but she had worked like the devil to both achieve and maintain her current weight. And, overall, she thought she looked pretty damn good.

Not everyone was as enamored of her accomplishment, of course. There would always be people who thought she could do better, diet herself thinner. She tried not to let their opinions matter. Men, bless their hearts, tended to be less critical than women. Not all of them, of course—some still looked at her and saw chunky. But she'd discovered over the past dozen years that more guys than not actually *liked* women with a generous booty and boobs.

Her issues tonight, however, had nothing to do with men's opinions. Rather, they stemmed from knowing that her mother was CEO of the Ava-could-do-so-much-better-if-she-only-*tried* contingent. And it did no good telling herself not to let it bother her. Anytime she knew she'd be seeing her mother, it just seemed to color her view of herself—with or without a mirror.

So she checked her image front, back and sideways to make sure her silk Ralph Lauren cocktail dress skimmed her body as she remembered it doing the last time she'd worn it. She loved this dress; with its simple sleeveless sheath cut, it was an updated version of something Audrey Hepburn might have worn. Its neckline was high and gently rounded in front and sported a wide V in the back. The knee-length skirt flared slightly from the pleated knot detail at the waist. It was subtle and elegant—the perfect little black dress—except that this was a deep elderberry purple. She usually felt like a princess in it.

So why was she pretty sure her abundant curves were just wrong, wrong, wrong for it tonight?

"Well, if they are, it's too damn late to do anything about it now," she muttered. Cade would be here in ten minutes to pick her up; she didn't have time to change yet again.

Shaking her misgivings aside, she went into the bathroom to put the finishing touches on her makeup, then rummaged through her closet for the right shoes. Locating a pair that were little more than four-inch heels, a narrow alligator-embossed leather ankle strap and a few matching straps that crisscrossed her toes, she sat on the side of her bed to put them on.

She had just plucked a small pair of gold, silver and bronze twisted wire hoop earrings from her jewelry box when her doorbell rang. She took one final look at herself in the mirror, blew out a breath and went to answer it.

"Hey," she said a moment later as she opened the door to Cade. "Come on in. I'm just finishing up." Her head tipped to one side, she slipped the remaining hoop's wire through her ear and snapped it into its back closure.

"There!" She gave him her full attention. "Don't you look spiff." *And then some,* she thought, checking out his elegant gray Italian suit and an Ed Hardy tie her mother would hate.

She grinned at him over the latter. But her smile faltered when she found him simply staring at her silently in return. Oh, crap. The dress *was* all wrong.

"And you," he said slowly as if unsure what to say. He cleared his throat. "You look…beautiful. God. Incredible."

But she'd caught the hesitation. She tried not to let it hurt, but it reinforced every insecurity she'd been struggling with tonight.

Still, she forced a wry, who-cares smile. "Um-hmm," she agreed lightly. "Not bad for a Reubenesque woman, huh?" She turned away to get her coat.

"What?" Wrapping a hand around her forearm, Cade turned her back to him. "No, wait, *no.*" He gave her a little shake. "For *any* woman. You look beautiful—full stop, period." He stepped closer, and she stared, mesmerized, as his gaze drilled into hers with a blue-hot intensity.

Because she saw in it a no-bullshit sincerity that caused her heart to trip all over itself.

"Jesus, Av," he said in a low voice, "you have got to know by now that I love your curves. I've *always* loved your curves."

Now that was going too far. "Uh-huh."

His fingers tightened slightly on her arm. "Yes, dammit, I acted like an ass in high school—are you *ever* going to let me get past that? Because I've said it before, but I'll say it again. Even then you knocked me on my butt. Your skin, your hair, those dimples. And that's before I even got to the killer tits and ass."

"Why, you romantic silver-tongued devil, you." Still. It might not have been the way she'd have phrased it, but she felt much better.

"Fine, breasts and…no, I flat-out refuse to say buttocks—it's too *Forrest Gump.* You've got killer breasts and ass. Or butt, if you prefer." He shook his head. "That's not the point. I would have said you were a Botticelli woman, myself. Not his Madonnas, though. More *Birth of Venus. Reubenesque,*" he said with a snort. "Where the hell did that come from?" His eyes narrowed. "Oh. Wait. Let me guess. Your mother, am I right?"

"I'm sorry. It was dumb." She shrugged, unable to admit he was smack-dab on the money, and turned away once more to get her coat from the closet. "I still suffer an occasional 'fat' moment."

"Well, knock it off," he ordered and took the wrap from her. He held it for her to slip her arms into, then curled his hands over her shoulders. Holding her in place, he stepped close, his breath feathering the hair next to her ear. "You look too amazing, you *are* too amazing, for that shit. Don't let anybody make you doubt that." His fingers tightened. "Not your mother, not me, not even you. Because you are so goddamn beautiful, Ava, inside and out."

She felt the warmth of his words surge through her, but all she could do was murmur, "If you say so."

"I do say so. And you damn well better remember it."

CADE STOOD in Ava's parents' living room forty-five minutes later, chatting with a group of people she had introduced him to. He sipped from the glass of champagne in his hand and shouldered his share of the conversation. But most of his attention was focused on Ava.

She was buzzing around, chatting here and there with the guests while unobtrusively directing the production of her father's sixtieth birthday party.

And a production was exactly what it was. Those candles he'd helped her look for a while back glowed from myriad surfaces in myriad holders, casting a warm shimmer on everything they touched. A string quartet played by the fireplace, and flowers brightened a table here and an étagère shelf there. A minibouquet sat on the open bar in the library.

He accepted a stuffed mushroom cap from a circulating waiter and looked through the archway to the dining room to admire the dessert table with its champagne fountains, arrays of works-of-art desserts and its centerpiece multitiered cake that Ava had called a mad hattor, presumably because each layer was a slightly tipsy-looking irregular shape decorated with fancy frostings of varying patterns in a palette of pale gold and white. Flowers topped it, with a few scattered on a layer here or there and along a portion of its bottom edge.

As he watched, she stopped to tweak the arrangement of alternating metallic silver and gold cocktail napkins at one end of the table, used a crumpled one to discreetly blot up a spill, then swept what he supposed were some scattered crumbs into her hand—all the while showing every indication of paying attention to a woman chattering in her ear. She interrupted the other woman for a moment to catch a server's attention. She spoke to him briefly as she lifted the table's cloth to dispose of the used napkin and crumbs in a wastebasket hidden beneath, then went back to her conversation with the guest. The server disappeared, only to return a moment later with a platter of chocolate-dipped strawberries to replenish the half empty one on the table. Ava gestured for the woman to try one and reached out to touch the arm of a gentleman who had come over to peruse the offerings, somehow getting him involved in conversation with her companion.

This was the woman who had to be convinced she was beautiful? Who thought she was *fat?* How could someone so accomplished, so deft at reading people and nuances be so clueless as to her own desirability? A slight rueful smile tugging up his mouth, he shook his head.

"You don't agree?"

"What?" The question jerked his attention back to the stylish sixtysomething woman with whom he'd been discussing the latest crop of films. "I'm sorry, Mrs. Bueller. My attention wandered to my date for a moment."

"Please, call me Beth. And who's your date, dear?" Then, obviously tracking the direction in which he'd been looking, her eyes lit up. "Ava? Oh, how lovely! I didn't realize when she introduced us that you were here with her. She is such a sweetheart—and this 'do simply has her stamp all over it, doesn't it? She puts on the most amazing parties."

"Yeah. She's pretty amazing, period."

She laughed in delight, then turned to her husband, who was standing on her other side talking golf with a couple other men. "David, did you know that Cade here is dating Ava?"

The man leaned around his wife. "You are, huh? You're that big Hollywood director, right?"

"The jury's still out on the big part, but I am a director," Cade agreed.

The older man gave him a brisk nod. "Well, you're a lucky man, sir. Ava is a *fine* young woman."

He grinned. "I couldn't agree more."

AVA FOUND Cade an hour or so later shooting pool with her father and a group of his cronies down in the billiards room. She watched him sink several of the solid color balls. "May I steal my date away for a few minutes?" she asked when the blue two-ball his cue sent rolling toward a side pocket rimmed it instead of dropping in.

"If you must," her father said. "But don't keep him long. He's the main reason we're ahead."

She gave her father a kiss on the cheek. "I'll try to be brief," she promised and led Cade away.

When they reached a relatively private corner, she turned to him, placing a conciliatory hand on his jacket lapel. "I am so sorry," she said guiltily. "My intention when I invited you to come with me tonight truly wasn't to drop you in a house full of strangers and leave you to fend for yourself."

He shrugged a wide shoulder. "I'm a big boy—I can entertain myself. Besides, I've had fun watching you do your thing." Cupping warm-skinned fingers around her nape, he bent his head to press a soft kiss on her lips. Straightening, he swept his thumb down her cheek. "You are something else, Ms. Spencer. Not only are you universally revered around here for your event skills, I've been warned by more than one party that I'd better not do you wrong."

She laughed. "I'd be happy to tell them you've been doing me right quite regularly if you'd like."

"Tempting." Shooting her a smile, he shook his head. "But maybe not. I'm afraid that might be too much information where most of them are concerned." He leaned in. Lowered his voice. "But I'd be happy to do you right again as soon as you can shake loose from here."

"Ooh. Give me half an hour. I'll go tell my mother she's on her own after we cut the cake."

"Deal." Then he sobered. "Hey, before you go, though, I didn't get the chance to tell you that I nearly finished up today. I've only got about two hours worth of filming left to do tomorrow, then I should be done—at least with that part. I know this is short notice, but could I get you to organize the food and drinks for a wrap party tomorrow night? Or Monday, if that works better for you."

"Your documentary's done?" She'd known it was

coming, of course. She simply hadn't expected it to be so soon.

"I've still got a good week or two of post-production work, but the filming portion is the next best thing to finished." He grinned at her. "Looks like we're going to be either a little ahead or right on schedule. Bonuses for both of us."

It was exactly what she'd wanted when she had agreed to this job. Her balloon payment was secure—that was the important thing, right? She could quit worrying about losing her condo. That was definitely good news. As she left Cade to go looking for her mother, she told herself she'd be happy to get back to her real life.

And she would.

As soon as this low-grade churning in her stomach eased up.

She tracked down her mother in the library, where she was chatting with some of her bridge group. Ava strode across the room to the small group and leaned in. "I hope everyone's enjoying themselves?"

There was a chorus of "Wonderful, magnificent, fabulous party!" and she flashed them a delighted smile. "I'm so glad you're pleased with it. And I hate to interrupt, but may I borrow my mother for a moment?"

Jacqueline glanced forcefully at a friend as she allowed Ava to lead her away. "Not a word until I return, Nance."

Then she focused on Ava. "What is it, dear?" she asked as she followed her daughter out of the room and into a much quieter alcove at the end of the hall. "Rumors have been circulating recently that the Wilsons are getting a divorce and Nancy—who is Susan Wilson's sister-in-law, you'll recall—was just about to

give us the…what do you children call it these days—
the lowdown? I don't want to miss that."

"This will only take a minute. I need to know when
you'd like to cut Dad's cake. I'm leaving after that, but
the caterers are beautifully trained, so there shouldn't
be much for you to do. The quartet is scheduled until
eleven and the bar will stay open as long as you want it
to, but the bartender's rate goes up considerably after
midnight. So if people are still here at that time you
might consider switching strictly to the champagne
fountains. There are an extra half dozen magnums in
the pantry just in case."

Her mother consulted her diamond wristwatch.
"Let's make it in fifteen minutes." She reached out and
briefly touched Ava's cheek. "This is a fabulous party,
darling. Simply everyone has raved about it."

The praise warmed her all over. "Thanks, Mom."

"Mother," Jacqueline corrected.

She sighed.

Her mother smiled. "Very well. Mom. But just for tonight." She looked Ava over. "Your dress is truly lovely.
I don't believe I could have chosen better myself."

Holy crap. Pigs really could fly!

"Now if you were just a few pounds lighter."

"For God's sake, Mom!" Usually a weight reference from Jacqueline made her doubt herself, made
her feel…less. Less than attractive, less than worthy.
But Cade's *I love your curves* and *You're beautiful—full
stop, period* echoed in her head. And perhaps because
for a second there she had basked in her mother's ap-
probation, what she felt now was furious betrayal. "I'm
not doing this anymore. I am just tired to *death* of feel-

ing that unless I fit in your mold I'm never going to be good enough for you."

Her mother stared at her in shock. "I have *never* said that!"

"Not in so many words, maybe. But every time you tell me I did something well but it would be better if I would just lose however many pounds it is you deem acceptable, that's exactly what you're saying. That, yes, I'm accomplished—just not accomplished enough to make up for my physical shortcomings. And I'm through listening to it.

"Look at me, Mom. See *me*. I have Grandmother Spencer's big bones. I am *never* going to be fine-boned like you, am never going to wear a size four. So you can accept that, or you can keep doing this soul-destroying you-could-do-better crap. I'm telling you right now, though, that the latter will drive me away. Because I am not going to let you make me feel bad about myself, make me feel inadequate, ever again." She focused a level look on her mother. "Are you hearing me?"

"Yes," Jacqueline said through stiff lips.

"Good." Even though her heart pounded in distress over the confrontation, she felt immeasurably lighter for having finally said what she should have said years ago.

She turned and walked away.

CADE HAD NEVER seen Ava quite like this. She'd talked nonstop all the way back to her place, hammering him with questions about what a wrap party entailed, throwing detailed idea after detailed idea at him for his consideration. Then the minute they cleared her front door, she grabbed him by his tie and strode straight for her bedroom, making it necessary for him to hunch over and pick up his pace to keep from being strangled. Nobody's fool, he decided to save his breath until she no longer had her hot little fist around the tie-turned-garrote circling his neck.

Even after they entered her bedroom and she turned him loose, however, she remained the aggressor. It was that, in a nutshell, that constituted the difference in her behavior. It wasn't the rapid-fire party talk. That he got—he hadn't given her any real time to prepare. No, this had to do with the fact that up until now the aggressor role in their sex life had been primarily his job description.

He liked that she'd switched things up.

She suddenly gave him a shove and, like some old Three Stooges routine, the mattress behind him caught him off balance and tumbled him on his back on her bed. "Whoa!" He pushed up on his elbows and watched as she kicked off her heels, hiked up the skirt of her dress and climbed onto the bed to knee-walk over to him. She threw a thigh over his hips and settled astride him.

Gripping her hips, he bumped his ready erection against the damp satin-covered sex she'd aligned with it. "What's gotten into you? Not that I'm complaining, mind you, but did something happen after you left me in your dad's pool room? Because something's got you all fired up."

"My mother started in on my weight again."

He went still under her. "Dammit, Av!"

She gave his chest a placating pat. "The key word here is started. I didn't really give her a chance to say much before I went off all over her and told her what I should have made clear years ago—that I'm not okay with her making me feel bad about my body."

Her beautiful, beautiful body that not only her mother but he had helped to make an issue for her. He rubbed his thumbs over the silk dress that had ridden up to bunch around the full curve of her hips. "Are you okay?"

"Yeah. There's a part of me that feels a little sick over the whole business, but you know what? Mostly I feel empowered. God, Cade, I finally told her once and for all that her constant criticism is *not* all right. Whether or not she listened, of course—" She hitched a shoulder. "Well, I have no control over that."

She undid his tie, slid it out from beneath his collar and tossed it on the nightstand. Then she went to work on his buttons, unfastening his shirt with the same efficiency she gave everything she turned her mind to. "What I *do* have control over is what I choose to put in my body. And right now, Gallari—" she wiggled atop the hard-on still pressed between her thighs "—that would be this bad boy."

He had an urge to roll her over, hold her down and demonstrate just how fast he could help make that happen. But this was her show tonight. So he sucked in a breath and kept his hands where they were as she began stripping him of his shirt. When she slid off him and climbed from the bed to remove his shoes and socks, then reached for his pants, however, he had to transfer his grip to the comforter to keep from wresting control from her.

Once she had him buck-naked, his cock taking aim at the ceiling, she reached behind her to unzip her dress. The garment loosened, and she pushed it over her hips and down her legs to pool in a purple spill around her feet. Then she unfastened the front hook of her black bra and slid it off.

Leaving her in the skimpiest pair of black panties he had ever had the pleasure of viewing, a nude-pink-and-black-striped garter belt and sheer thigh-high hose the color of smoke. She shimmied her shoulders at him, making her breasts jiggle. "Do *you* think I could stand to lose more weight?"

"*God,* no."

"Good answer. Neither do I. And for the record, that was the last time I ask that question. My days of letting anyone but me weigh in on the matter—no pun intended—are over." She climbed back on the bed and crawled over to him. Stretching out on her stomach between his splayed thighs, she spread her fingers on his abs and pressed those lush tits—*breasts*—against his dick.

He sucked in a breath and made an adjustment to drive his cock into the channel of her cleavage.

"Ooh." Lifting onto her elbows, she pressed her arms to the sides of her breasts to intensify their pressure around him.

"God!" He raised his hips off the bed, retracted them, then thrust again, all the while watching Ava watch the head of his sex appear from and disappear into the hot hollow between her breasts. She glanced up at him and licked her lips, and his cock jumped. "This is not the time to mess with me," he warned. Not when his control was hanging by a thread.

She sent him a guileless smile. "I have no idea what you're talking about."

He had the impression she hadn't been messing with

him with the lip lick—but that she was now. "The hell you don't."

With a shrug, she bent her head until her breath wafted over him, and he froze with his hips thrust high. "Kiss it," he growled. "God, Ava, I want you to kiss it. Lick it. *Suck* it."

Her eyes widened, and her cheeks went pink. But she lowered her head and pressed a prim, closed-mouth kiss on the tip of his cock. He made a sound, and she opened her full, pillowy lips just the slightest bit and sipped it.

The groan that escaped him this time was a wordless *You're killing me.* She smiled demurely.

And lapped him with her tongue.

His hips thrust higher yet, pushing him into the warm, wet cavern of her mouth. And finally—finally!—she quit toying with him and set about doing her best to flat-out destroy him.

He hung on as long as he could, standing on the edge of hell, one elusive tongue stroke, a slick pull of her lips and cheeks, from achieving heaven. When he truly feared he was about to go the distance without so much as having even kissed her, he pulled back, rolled her over and came down on his knees between her sprawled legs. After swiftly donning a condom, he stripped her of her panties, hooked the bend of his elbows in the bend of her knees and, pressing her knees toward her chest, sank into her.

Where he discovered that for someone who'd given all of and received none of the foreplay, she was beautifully, liquidly primed. A moan purled out of her chest, and hot, strong tissues clamped around him like a wet velvet fist. He pumped into her, finessing his position in order to bump her clit at the apex of each stroke.

And as he felt her winding mind-bendingly tighter and tighter, as he sensed her drawing closer by the second to her climax, words began crowding his throat.

Words he tried to bite back.

Then she screamed beneath him, and the kiln-hot vise surrounding him clamped down in blistering, undulating contractions. As his own climax boiled and built, he gritted his teeth. "Christ, oh, Christ, I'm gonna—"

It broke over him, roaring up and out in strong, hot pulsations, making him thrust deep and grind against her in mindless oscillations. And as he came he heard himself chant, "I love you, Ava.

"God, Spencer, I love you, love you, love you so damn much."

CHAPTER TWENTY-ONE

If you keep pushing people away, eventually you're bound to accomplish what you thought you wanted.

I LOVE YOU SO DAMN MUCH.

Ava lay very still beneath Cade's weight for a long moment, her pulse racing even faster from his words than it had from the screaming orgasm he'd just given her. The only sound in her bedroom was that of their harsh breathing slowly mellowing out. She knew she should probably say something. No, there was no probably about it. She knew she should.

But what?

Nothing. Trust me, sister, he probably didn't mean love *you love you, anyway, and brilliant or stupid, once words have left your mouth, you can't take them back.* Silence was better than talking merely to fill the void. She knew from personal experience how well *that* usually worked out.

And really. When had she ever found impulsive talk to be brilliant?

So it was decided then. She'd follow her own advice and keep her trap shut.

Which made it doubly appalling to hear herself promptly blurt, "Thank you."

Crap!

He stilled, then slowly pushed up on his palms. His penis might not be as rampant as it'd been a moment ago, but it was plenty sturdy enough to push a little deeper with his motion, to rasp against her still sensitive clitoris.

She swallowed a little moan.

Brows furrowing, he stared down at her. "Thank you? I tell you I love you and you say *thank you?* What the hell kind of response is that?"

"You mean you meant it?"

"Jesus, Ava. Yes, I meant it!"

"Oh." Now, as when she'd first heard the raspy-voiced words, her heart lurched against the wall of her chest. And, yes, for a moment she once again hugged the rush of warmth of his words to her breast.

But only for a moment because, face it, it would never work. Having understood that the first time he'd said it, she had assumed— "I thought it was, you know, sex talk." Even though the lazy way he'd been sprawled atop her, plus the soft, tender postcoital kisses he'd pressed to her throat, her chin, her shoulders, had suggested that he just might mean it.

"Jesus," he said again.

"I'm sorry, I'm sorry, I'm screwing this all up. But I really wish you hadn't said that."

"You want to tell me why?"

Not while she was naked, she didn't. Which was probably absurd, considering how bold she'd been just a little while ago.

But that was then. This was now.

And now she was feeling a little panicky.

No. She straightened as much as a bare-naked, sprawled-across-the-mattress woman with a man still inside of her, for cri'sake, could do. She wasn't panicky. She was cautious. Big difference.

She gestured for him to get off her.

Pulling out, he climbed to his feet and strode without a hint of self-consciousness toward the bathroom, although he did pause long enough to sweep his slacks up off the floor. He disappeared inside but was back before she had a chance to locate her discarded clothing, let alone put anything on. He'd donned his pants and had her Spa Collection bathrobe gripped in one hand. He tossed it to her.

Mentally blessing him for his sensitivity, she rolled out of bed, wrapped herself in the robe's long, plush folds and tied the belt. She opened her mouth to say something—*anything*—then considered how swell that had worked for her so far.

Still. She stared at him, stubbornly not wanting to admit that when it came to a place to begin, her mind kept drawing one big, embarrassing blank after another.

Cade stepped forward and said, "I do love you, you know. And I think you love me, too."

The panic she wasn't feeling beat harder in her pulse points, and raising her eyebrows, she gave him a look she hoped to hell came across as a lot more amused than she felt. "Nothing wrong with your ego."

He brushed a strand of hair out of her eyes. "Ego's got nothing to do with it, Ava. I know you. And I know you wouldn't be sleeping with me at every opportunity the way we've been doing if you didn't have strong feelings for me."

The nonpanic was nudging into the real deal, but she made a rude noise and forced herself to meet his eyes. "Please. It's a new millennium, Gallari. Women have great sex strictly *for* the sex all the time."

"Yeah. A lot of women do. Maybe even most." He stepped closer. "But the first time you slept with me this go-round, great sex wasn't exactly something you had any real expectation of getting, was it?"

She glommed onto the opening he'd provided. "Because you sucked large our first time out of the gate, you mean?" Hey, when in doubt, lay the burden on the other guy. That was her shiny new motto from the school of The Best Defense is a Good Offense.

"I wouldn't have put it quite like that, but basically, yeah." He crossed his arms over his chest and pinned her in place with a gimlet-eyed gaze. He was shirtless and shoeless, for heaven's sake; he shouldn't make her think of some hard-nosed cop from an old film noir movie. "So if expecting great sex wasn't the reason you slept with me the first time, what was?"

"Because—" Her mind shut down. She looked at the ceiling for inspiration and didn't find it. Looked for it on the floor—with the same result.

Finally, she crossed her own arms under her breasts and looked him in the eye. "Fine. I care about you, okay?"

"You *love*—"

"I *care*." God, why was her heart trying to pound its way out of her chest? "But you know as well as I do that we've got nil long-term potential."

"Do I?" Stepping away, he braced his shoulders against the wall and lounged back, his crossed arms now matched by negligently crossed ankles. He quirked an eyebrow. "And how did I reach this conclusion?"

"C'mon! You're based in L.A. My friends, my family—" benignly neglectful as the latter might be "—and my work are all here. It's not like I could just pick up and go, even if I wanted to. Which—" she looked him in the eye "—contrary to your assumption, I do not."

"So I guess we do the long-distance thing."

She felt her anxiety lessen slightly. "Oh, sure—that being so all-fired successful and all." She'd been feeling uneasy over nothing. This was a no-brainer. Cade could be stubborn, but even he would have to admit that a relationship between them was destined to fail.

But not quite yet, apparently. "Hey," he said easily, "it's a two and a half hour plane ride. That's not much longer than bucking rush-hour traffic."

She made a rude noise. "Until you factor in the time it takes to get to the terminal, be at the airport two hours early to get through security, and how long it takes to get to your or my place at the other end. Face it, traveling these days is an all-day ordeal."

"We live on the same coast," he said with a shrug. "It'd only be a half day ordeal."

"And yet *ordeal* remains the operative word. It wouldn't work, Cade. I don't know anyone who's been successful with a long-distance relationship. I'll admit the people I know who tried one seemed to start out great guns. But it's almost as if there's a written-in-stone shelf date on the damn things. Because the couples I know all broke up around the six month point from sheer attrition, caused—I don't doubt for a minute—by the stress of all that backing and forthing." Her shoulders hitched. "Well, that or never being able to do a damn thing together that didn't have to be planned to death first. Or both."

"Okay, so long-distance is out. We'll just have to go to plan B."

"Which is?" Why couldn't he just give up?

"You joining Scorched Earth Productions."

She literally felt her jaw drop. "Are you serious?"

"As a sailor on shore leave looking to score." He flashed her the smile she'd privately labeled The Panty Charmer-Offer back in the day. She'd rarely seen it since signing up for this job. "You've been fantastic to work with on this project, and I can promise you a shitload of variety—not to mention the occasional exotic location."

She felt downright relaxed now, and, spotting her panties, she disentangled them from the knob of the nightstand drawer, then sat on the side of the bed to don them. It was probably silly considering it was late and she'd undoubtedly be taking them back off to go to bed soon. But she just felt better armored with them on.

She looked over at Cade as she wiggled into them. "The reason I'm so effective in Seattle is largely due to the roster of contacts I've compiled over the past decade. Heck, some of them—like my Uncle Robert who's a golfing buddy of the mayor's and a few of my folks' more clout-heavy friends—I've known since birth. I don't have anything even close to that anywhere but here. If we'd had that blown utility meter problem in L.A., it likely would have taken me two or three days to get the city crew out to fix it. Anybody can make the calls, Cade. It's who the caller knows that moves their problem to the top of the fix-it schedule."

"I could introduce you to all sorts of people in L.A.," he said easily. "With your way with people, you'd have contacts in no time."

The unease snuck back. Why did he have to be so damn persistent? "You don't get it. I'm not giving up a business I spent the past nine years building to be your—or anybody else's—employee."

"Okay," he agreed without any apparent regret, and she blew out a little sigh of relief. Only to be immediately alarmed when he added, "I guess I'll just have to move my home base to Seattle."

"What?" No two ways about it—this wasn't simple unease or anything so namby-pamby as disquiet, and she quit trying to fool herself that it was. This was flat-out panic. "No!"

He raised a brow at her. "No?"

"You can't just disrupt your entire life—hell, *my* life!—this way! We've been having a relationship, if you can even *call* it that, for—what?—ten minutes in the overall scheme of things?"

"We've been having a relationship—and make no mistake, baby, we damn well *can* call it that—since we were eight years old. I love you." He gave her a level look. "And you love me."

"Stop saying that!"

"Why?" He shrugged. "We both know it's true."

"No, we both know I *care* about you. *Care,* Cade. You're a smart man, you oughtta know there's a big difference between that and the freaking L word. Which, by the way, I have never, not once, mentioned."

"That only proves my point. I clearly need to be up here where I can help you learn to do that."

She clutched her hair and screamed.

Pushing away from the wall, he came over and rubbed a soothing hand down her hair from the crown of her head to her nape. When she looked up at him, he gave her a faint smile. "Okay, I'll concede to 'care about me.'"

"Well, it's a start. Thank you."

"Not a problem. So, you care for me." He looked at her expectantly. "And?"

"And what? That's it. That's all I've got." She could barely swallow around her heart, which seemed to be lodged high in her throat. The condition, of course, had nada to do with the fact that maybe she was prevaricating a little. That maybe she feared he might be right and she did love him.

He merely raised that damn brow at her. Repeated patiently, "And?"

She rolled her shoulders. "Oh, all right. I know you're a good man, okay?" But what if she said she loved him back, and a week, a month or a year from now, after she'd let her guard down because he'd gotten her addicted to him, he changed his mind?

He merely stood there, silently looking at her, and she sighed. "I know you've evolved worlds from the boy you were in high school."

"And?"

She could not say the words. She simply couldn't. The last time she'd even *thought* of telling him she loved him she had ended up standing emotionally naked in a high school cafeteria, the butt of everyone's joke.

She knew she wasn't being fair, but she couldn't seem to catch her breath, and her heart kept beating faster and faster, until she wondered if it would simply explode. At least that would put her out of her misery once and for all. Because—

"What if I get *fat?*"

Oh, God. It was as if the world stilled.

She froze. Cade froze.

Only her mind seemed to keep spinning. Had she really said that out loud?

What the hell is your problem? her barely functioning rational side demanded. *You* know *that's just wrong.*

For God's sake, this evening she had declared her

independence from this exact kind of unproductive thinking. Yet, here she stood, a small part of her clearly still rubbed raw from years of being made to feel as if she simply didn't quite measure up.

A small part that clearly felt she still didn't.

But that's not Cade, her conscience howled. *My mother might be like that, but...*

That's.

Not.

Cade.

He thinks I'm wonderful just the way I am. He thinks—

"That's what you think?" he demanded. "That I'm so…shallow…that ten pounds or a hundred would matter to me? That it's your body I love and not the whole package?"

"No. But…you don't know. I mean, the whole package might not hold up and your feelings might change." She trailed off as his eyes went blank and distant.

It shocked her into realizing that she had virtually just told him she had zero trust in his feelings. She reached out.

He stepped away before she could touch him. "So this is what it comes down to," he said levelly, no anger or sorrow or expression of any kind that she could discern in his voice. He picked his shirt up off the floor and pulled it on. "No matter what I say, what I do, we're never going to get past my one fuckup."

"No—" Her voice cracked, and she cleared her throat. It was so damn devoid of moisture, every word felt as if she were forcing ground glass through the eye of a needle. But force it through she would, because she needed to let him know she'd been wrong to doubt him.

"No, I'm *sorry*. That was my insecurities talking, not my intellect—"

"You know, tomorrow's going to be a really busy day," he said, cutting her off. "I'd better shove off." He thrust his feet into his shoes.

"Cade," she pleaded.

"You'll arrange for the wrap party, right?"

"Of course."

"Good. If you could make it for tomorrow night that would be great."

She swallowed again. "Sure. As long as you don't mind that it's a Sunday so we might have to compromise on the cake. Still, I'll do my best. But Cade—"

"I know you will. Just grab a Costco cake. That'll work fine—you've spoiled the crew with your fare, but when it comes right down to it they don't give a shit if it's from Safeway or a fancy bakery—as long as there's plenty of it."

He took another step back. "Let Beks know what time you can have everything ready so she can pass the info along to the cast and crew." He retreated another subtle step away, and Ava stilled, knowing stalking him across the room did neither of them any favors.

"Hey, go ahead and sleep in, though," he said. "None of the arrangements need to be done first thing in the morning."

"Cade, please."

"Goodnight, Ava," he said firmly. And a second later he was gone.

Leaving her with the realization that she hadn't had the first idea of what real panic felt like until now.

CHAPTER TWENTY-TWO

It doesn't pay to think things can't get worse. Because they really can.

WHEN AVA'S doorbell chimed as she was about to grab her purse and head for the mansion the next morning, it could have been a chorus of angels singing Cade's name, so brightly did hope flare in her heart. She sent gratitude winging heavenward as she raced to the door. *Thanks for giving me a second chance, God. I appreciate the do-over.* Intending to do a better job this time—even if her heart had begun to beat with renewed anxiety—she pulled the door open.

Only to find her mother on the other side. "Oh," she said, deflated. "It's you."

"Not precisely the greeting I might have hoped for," Jacqueline said coolly, stepping past her into the condominium. "It's lovely to see you, too, darling."

Ava was *so* not in the mood for her mother's company. If it hadn't been for years of being made to feel that her weight was her one defining attribute, she might not have been such an idiot last night.

Then she straightened her shoulders and stepped back from the door. "I'm sorry, Mother, where are my manners? Please. Come in." Last night was on her and her alone. Her mother might have assisted her insecurities, but it was she who had allowed them to become a handicap at the worst possible moment. "Can I make you a cup of tea?"

"Do you have time?" Jacqueline nodded at Ava's coat draped over the back of one of her red chairs and her purse on the seat beneath it.

It was so out of character for her mother to even notice such a thing—let alone care if her unexpected visit might inconvenience her daughter—that Ava found her insides going all mushy. Reaching out, she stroked her fingers along the back of Jacqueline's hand, noticing for the first time how thin the skin there had become, making the veins on the back of her mom's hand more noticeable. "I have to leave for the mansion soon, but I've got time for a quick cup if you do."

"That would be lovely, dear. Thank you." The older woman took a stool at the breakfast bar while Ava went around it to the kitchen side.

She turned on her Capresso electric kettle and got out the Moroccan inlaid tray. After grabbing the half-and-half that her mother liked from the fridge, she poured some into a little china creamer and set it aside to select a tea. Opening the cupboard, she glanced over her shoulder and caught her mother's eye. "Is Monkey Picked oolong okay? Or would you prefer the Dragonwell green?"

"Oolong sounds lovely."

Yes, everything's lovely, lovely, Ava thought sardonically. Except for the parts that totally sucked.

No. She struggled for an attitude adjustment. *It's not her fault I'm not going to feel right until I get the chance to make Cade believe I didn't mean to throw his love back in his face in such an undeserving way.*

A moment later she had the tray assembled with

a steaming, fragrant pot of tea, the creamer and two dainty tea cups from one of Miss A's collections. The eclectic set had been one of her first choices when she, Jane and Poppy were selecting personal mementos of their time with their mentor.

God, she missed Miss Agnes right now. The older woman had always known just what to say when Ava was confused or anxious or hurt. She was the first person Ava had gone to that day back in high school. Agnes couldn't fix it, but Ava had taken comfort in the fact that Miss A had seen she was hurting, that she had opened her arms before Ava had even said a word. And she felt residual warmth now at the remembered affection that had woven through Miss A's deep voice as she'd murmured to her, even if she couldn't recall the actual words.

It was beyond sad that her own mother sat only a few feet away, yet Ava didn't have the first idea how to broach the subject with her.

And likely wouldn't even if she did.

"Shall we sit in the living room?" she asked and followed Jacqueline over to the couch. After setting the tray on the coffee table, she poured the tea, added cream to her mother's and handed the cup and saucer to her. Picking up her own, she took a seat on the opposite end of the sofa.

For a few moments, as they sipped their oolong in silence, Ava let her mind wander to the best way to apologize to Cade, ways in which she could make him understand how sorry she was for botching the moment, to make him see she in no way disregarded his declaration—even if it still gave her a crazy surge of residual anxiety right alongside a definite hug-to-your-heart warmth. When her mother suddenly set her cup in its

saucer and placed both on the tray on the table, she
started.

Sitting back, Jacqueline turned on the couch to face
her more fully. "Last night's party was a rousing success," she said.

"Yes, I thought it turned out quite well."

"Oh, much more than that, dear. My friends couldn't
stop raving about the food, the decorations, the service."
She offered a smile that was more tentative than usual.
"You really are amazing. And so very talented. I don't
think I've told you that enough."

I'm not sure you've told me that, ever. Still, a kernel
of warmth unfurled in her breast. "Thank you."

"And I never dreamed—" Jacqueline cut herself off
and cleared her throat. "That is, I'm sorry I made you
feel as if you weren't good enough."

Shock zapped like high-voltage electricity through
her system, leaving nerve endings tingling in its wake.
She was so surprised, so…gratified by the apology that
she almost, nearly, just about, said, "That's all right."

But the truth was, it wasn't all right, and she set her
own cup and saucer on the tray. "Why is it so important
to you that I conform to the popular idea of a perfect
body, when it's clear to anyone who looks at me that
I'm simply not built for it?"

Her mother studied her impeccable, buffed nails for
a moment, but finally looked up at Ava. "It's learned
behavior, I suppose. That was how my mother got me
to lose weight when I was a teen."

Ava's posture snapped erect on the couch cushions.
"*You* were fat?" Whoa. *That* had certainly never made
the rounds in the Spencer household.

"Yes. And my mother kept at me and kept at me
until I lost the weight. I thought about this quite a bit

last night," she said slowly. "And I must admit I wasn't all that keen on her methods.

"But, darling." She leaned forward eagerly. "In the end, I felt so much better for it. So, I suppose I thought if I kept at you, you'd feel better for it, as well." She studied her daughter. "But I was blind not to see until now that you *have* gotten down to a good weight for you, and that you did so a long while ago. And you are right, of course. You do have Donald's mother's bone structure." Her small smile had a wry tilt. "All of which is a long way of saying I *don't* want to drive you away, and I won't hound you about it again."

It didn't really address why all her photographs had been cut off beneath her collarbones, yet still it soothed a hurt she hadn't realized she'd been carrying around for most of her life. Scooting across to close the space between them on the couch, she leaned in to kiss her mother's cheek. "That means a lot to me, Mom. Thanks."

"Mother," Jacqueline corrected.

"Mother," she agreed, biting back a sigh. Yet inwardly she smiled. Because, what the hell. She'd won the big war today.

She'd worry about the smaller battles another time.

Tony left Cade getting ready to shoot the final scene in one of the downstairs rooms and headed up to the now deserted ballroom. Thinking about the talk he'd just had with the director, he closed the ornate double doors behind him and looked around the bare room to make sure he had it to himself.

He resisted breaking into the end-zone dance, however. Face it, he'd done that before, only to have the don't-count-your-chickens fairy kick his teeth in.

And this was, after all, his final night, since the first

thing Gallari had given him when he'd called him in was his walking papers. But the good news was that after everybody finally left the wrap party tonight, he'd have the joint to himself.

All. Night. Long.

And a good part of tomorrow, too, if he had anything to say about it. The crew would be back to pack up their gear in the morning, but Cade had told him he was letting the new day guard go, as well. Once the grips removed the expensive equipment, Scorched Earth Productions' responsibility was at an end, and liability reverted to the mansion owners' insurance company. And since the crew would be busy doing exactly that— packing their gear—Tony planned to offer to stay on until they were through. Just from the goodness of his heart.

He permitted himself a laugh. Because he was sly like a fox, man. All the production gear was now on the first floor—leaving the upstairs free and him with even more time to search the sitting room.

He cautioned himself not be over optimistic about his chances of finding the hiding place. But a *little* optimism couldn't hurt. Even if he didn't find it tonight, he'd bet the bank it would be a while before it occurred to anyone to change the security codes.

And by one means or another, he planned to walk out of here a rich, rich man.

"Cade."

Torn from an internal debate that ping-ponged between whether the RED camera digital style or filming would best suit the final scene, he stiffened at the sound of his name. He didn't need to look around to know who was speaking. He'd be able to identify that voice in his dotage.

He really didn't want to talk to Ava right now. And it had zilch to do with the fact he was trying to make a decision on something that should have—and ordinarily would have—been decided well before he'd reached this point.

From the moment he and Ava had started working together on this project, he'd busted his butt to make up for the humiliation he'd caused her back in high school. But he should have saved his energy, because it hadn't made a goddamn bit of difference. She clearly believed he was still the same jerk he'd been thirteen years ago. She thought her damn *body*—and whether or not she regained the fucking weight she'd lost an eon ago—would be the deal-breaker for him. He was pissed as hell that she didn't know him any better than that.

Worse—and unlike his eighteen-year-old self, he could admit this—he was hurt.

Not that he was about to let her know. He was through putting himself on the line for her—at least until he could scratch a couple minutes together to figure out what was and was not worth doing to save their relationship.

Or, hell, maybe he'd just shit-can the whole damn thing and head back to L.A. tomorrow with the rest of his crew. He could do his editing there as well as he could up here. Better, really—he had connections up the wazoo that could get him any equipment he needed damn near as fast as he could put in a request.

For now, however, he relaxed his shoulders, composed his expression into polite, noncommittal inquiry and turned to face her. "Hey," he said with remote amiability. "Is there something I can do for you?"

But, dammit, one look at her standing before him with determined eyes but a slight, vulnerable slant to her mouth and he knew both leaving for L.A. and that dumping their relationship thing were not gonna happen.

Shit.

It didn't negate the fact he was still seriously hacked off, however, so he was more than happy to turn away and discuss the RED camera/filming dilemma with Louie when his DP tapped him to ask which piece of equipment to set up.

Hoping while he did so that Ava would get tired of waiting and go back to her own chores. Leaving him to complete his.

She was still there, however, when he decided filming was his best option, and Louie strode off to get his cameras in place and up to speed. Squaring his shoulders, Cade turned back to her. And raised an eyebrow.

Stepping closer, she lowered her voice so it traveled no farther than the two of them beneath the bustle of grips moving props and Heather, who stood a short distance away murmuring her lines and making broad, Miss Agnes–type gestures. "Can I talk to you for a minute?"

No. Not a good idea, given his temper every time he thought about last night. But he gave her a courteous smile. "I'm up to my eyeballs right now. Maybe later."

"When, later?"

When I damn well say so. "I have no way of knowing at this point. I'll catch up with you." And before Ava could say another word—if, in actuality, she even wanted to—he gave her a cordial nod and strode away.

Everyone was having a rocking time at the wrap party. Everyone except Ava.

Cade had made it real clear he wasn't going to forgive her anytime soon for not handling his declaration well. She'd tried a couple of times to grab a minute alone with him. And she got it, she really did, that when she'd interrupted him when he was up to his neck first preparing for the final scene, then shooting it, it hadn't been fabulous timing on her part. Not to mention less than her shiniest display of professionalism. So she'd backed off and waited for him to "catch up with her."

But when he'd finished shooting, he hadn't even attempted to catch up. And while he'd been oh, so polite as she'd attempted one final time to get a moment alone with him, she may as well have been talking to him from the far shore of Puget Sound, so emotionally distant had he been.

She watched him now as he stood across the room. The cast and crew were clearly ready to party, and Cade smiled and acted as though he was, as well. But, God. Those blue, blue eyes of his, usually so warm and engaged, were one hundred percent aloof. At least the few times they touched on her.

Well, to hell with him. Calling on years of social training, she made the rounds, chatting with everyone but Cade as she made sure the trays of hors d'oeuvres, crudités, meats, cheeses and breads that she'd had to call in some favors to score on a Sunday were replenished when they ran low. That the beer, wine and pop were plentiful.

"Because, you know, I'm sorry if I didn't handle things as well as I might've last night," she muttered when she found herself alone in the kitchen a few moments later. "Damned if I plan to *beg* him to listen, though."

Frankly, she had to wonder how deep his love could be, if he found it that easy to blow her off. If he couldn't even spare her five stinking minutes to try to explain the panic that had led to her idiocy.

And she would give him that—he had gone out of his way to shore up her up-and-down body image far too many times for her to pretend she hadn't been a complete ass with that whole but-what-if-I-get-fat question.

Jeez Marie. Trust issues with Cade aside, she was embarrassed for *herself.* She was smart, skilled and capable. And although she might not be in Poppy's league, she was attractive, as well. So what the hell was she doing? Her days as an eighteen-year-old were far behind her, so why was she flip-flopping all over the place, thinking she was pretty darn hot one minute, only to turn around the next and allow her old shopworn insecurities to regress her right back to the maturity level of her high school self? It said reams more about her than it did about Cade that she had to keep relearning the same lessons over and over again.

That she had the same damn issues with trust.

For the second time in less than twelve hours, missing Miss Agnes was a wrenching pang in her heart. The older woman had always known how to make her *think,* had had ways of helping her cut through the bullshit to the heart of whatever was dragging her down.

Well, she couldn't have Miss A, but maybe she could at least grab herself a few minutes of peace and quiet. The party was finally starting to wind down, but she was so tired of pretending to share the euphoria everyone else felt that she doubted her ability to last until then. So, slipping away, she went upstairs to Agnes's sitting room, where she tried to recall the specifics of how the older woman had talked her through her problems. Flopping down in a slipper chair, she stared moodily at the ornate paneling on the wall.

And heard her mentor's foghorn voice whisper through her mind as clearly as if they'd sat side by side. *So how do you feel about your young man's anger with you?*

Her automatic shrug was every bit as sulky as her habitual go-to response had been back in her tween-and-teenaged years.

But Miss A had never let her get away with that, and, sitting straighter in her chair, Ava knew that neither could she let herself wiggle off the hook. For as much as she'd rather stick bamboo shoots under her finger-nails than conduct a soul search, it was a valid question.

What *did* she feel, knowing the tables were turned and Cade was mad at her?

Well, resentful, for starters.

As if she were on shaky ground.

Suspicious that she may have finally taken things a step too far, have played the guilt card one time too many.

Scared.

God, she hated that last one, hated recognizing that she was petrified she had driven Cade away once and for all because she'd been too damn chickenshit to admit—to him, to herself—that she would give her left boob to have him, and the love he offered, in her life.

She hated it even more that, after acknowledging the truth of that, she still had jittery, jumpy, afraid-to-depend-on-him feelings. That, even knowing what she risked losing, she honestly didn't know if she would do anything differently.

Crap. She was seriously screwed up. There came a time when you had to have some faith or get off the pot, so to speak.

She couldn't say why she wasn't quite there yet.

"There you are."

Startled, Ava swiveled in her seat to look toward the door as Beks breezed into the room carrying the boom box in one hand and a magnum of champagne in the other, two fingers anchoring plastic cups to its side.

It sank in then that the mansion had grown quiet.

More than willing to be diverted from thoughts that kept circling and circling without resolving a damn thing, she smiled at the younger woman, whose hair was purple and black today and looked as though it had been styled at the Finger In The Light Socket Salon. "Are you and I the only ones left?" *Has Cade gone?*

"I assume the night guy is around somewhere, but other than him, it's just you and me. Cade was the last to leave and he took off about ten minutes ago. I had a little paperwork to finish up, then decided to see if you were still around." She shrugged. "When I saw your car out back, I came looking."

Crossing to where Ava sat, Beks extended the boom box. "Here, you look like you could use some dance therapy. Hook this up and I'll pour us some bubbly."

Ava rose to her feet and went behind the grouping of the little table and two slipper chairs, but couldn't find a nearby outlet. Locating one all but hidden in the beautifully carved wainscoting, she squatted to plug in the CD player.

Then she glanced over at Beks, who had taken the companion chair to the one she'd just abandoned. "Will you be around for a while or are you heading back to L.A. right away?" *Is Cade?* "If you get a little time between projects I hope you stick around. Because I'm going to miss you when you're gone."

Directing her attention back to the boom box, she turned it on and selected a song off Beks's preloaded disk. She rose to her feet to the beat of Rihanna's "Only Girl."

But for once in her life she didn't feel them automatically move in rhythm to a dance beat. Nor did her hips. And her shoulders and arms remained stubbornly stationary, as well.

"I'm gonna miss you too," Beks said. "But as for when we're leaving, I don't have a clue. The boss hasn't told me a damn thing—he's been in one helluva mood today."

"Tell me about it," Ava muttered.

Beks popped the cork and grabbed a cup to catch the wine foaming up and over the neck of the bottle. Once she'd poured one for both of them, she looked over at Ava. "Yeah, I had a feeling you'd know more about that than I do."

"Hey, don't look at me," she said. "He's barely said two words to me. Everything he's wanted me to know or do has come through you."

"Exactly, so don't play stupid. He hasn't had eyes for anyone *but* you since we came to town—and suddenly he's refusing to even look at you?" The younger woman scowled. "What the hell did you do?"

Had a little panic attack when he said he loved me. Guilt drove her back to the small table to snatch up her cup. She drained the drink in one long swallow. "Nothing I want to talk about." Seeing the stubborn look in Beks's eyes, however, she whirled back to the boom box. Maybe she could find Al Green. Al always made her want to dance.

But she turned too fast and without a shred of her usual grace, found her upper body lurching forward when the thick nap of the throw rug caught at her foot. Staggering on tiptoes, she flung out her arms to prevent a collision with the ornate wooden wall.

Her right hand made contact first, skittering over the panel's whorls and grooves before it caught in the dip of an elaborate pattern. Gripping the rich, carved paneling, she came to a panting halt, her heart pounding and her lungs heaving for the breath that had been startled right out of her.

And could have sworn she felt the solid wood shift beneath her fingertip.

CHAPTER TWENTY-THREE

Nothing like a good near-death experience to drive home what's really important in life.

BEKS RUSHED over. "Are you okay?" She reached out to help Ava from her uncomfortable, bent position.

"Wait, wait!" Ava waved the younger woman away with her free hand, afraid of the time it would take to relocate the piece she was almost certain had moved beneath her fingers if she took them off of it. "This might be a secret compartment."

Beks froze. "Are you serious?"

"I'm not positive what I've got here, but I swear I felt something move. Give me a second."

Okay, it was going to take a little longer than that, she conceded after a couple of minutes. Bending was awkward—not to mention hard on the back—but when she tried squatting she found herself too low to see what she was doing. She looked at Beks, who was hovering a scant foot away. "Drag that slipper chair over here, will you?"

Beks thunked the chair down next to her a moment later and she slid her rear onto its seat. "Oh, that's better," she said in relief. Stretching out her back, she smiled up into the production assistant's gray-blue eyes, rounded now with excitement. "Okay, let me see if this is anything like the other one in here."

Beks's eyes grew wider yet. "There's *another* secret hidey-hole in here?"

"There's an entire secret closet. Jane kept Miss A's couture collection in it while she prepared the show she put on at the Metropolitan Museum last year."

"You and your friends are so interesting," Beks murmured.

Ava grinned at her, then turned back to the woodwork puzzle. Her fingers had developed a fine tremor from all the possibilities—including the one where she had just *imagined* she'd felt the wood shift beneath them. Still, she kept at it for what seemed like forever.

The thing was obstinately, sturdily immobile, and she was about to concede defeat when she suddenly felt something trip. The next thing she knew, a piece of the wall recessed, sliding out of sight to the left.

She gawked at the hole it left. The opening was roughly twelve by eight inches but had been so skillfully cut around the elaborate pattern of the wood that it was virtually undetectable if one didn't know it was there.

Hell, she'd been pretty certain this was what had lain beneath her fingertips when she thought she'd felt it move, but even then she hadn't been able to discern its outlines in the wall. She glanced up at Beks in wonder. "We're in."

Beks made a squeaky sound behind lips pressed together as if to keep from screaming out loud. Her hands performed a frenzied little wave.

Ava blew out a breath, turned back to the opening and reached inside. Feeling several leather boxes, stacked one upon the other, she made a squeaky noise of her own.

Pulling them out, she sat them in her lap and turned slightly in her chair so Beks could also see as she extracted the largest—a flat, almost square, affair of faded black leather—from the bottom of the pile. She opened it, then for a moment simply stared in stunned silence at its contents. Diamonds glistened against black velvet beneath the overhead lights.

"Omigawd," she finally breathed as she reached in to remove an intricate twenties-era necklace from its velvet bed. "Oh. My. God. I've seen it in a couple of pictures, but this—*this* is magnificent."

It was all platinum and diamonds, diamonds, diamonds in an art deco design whose short chain alternated lacy links with round diamond-set triangles, before changing to square cut diamonds. Those anchored interconnected diamond-studded triangular links, which in turn widened into a sparkling V-shaped centerpiece, crowned by a large round center diamond and a matching pear-shaped diamond suspended below.

Tearing her eyes away, she stared up at Beks. "I didn't actually believe I'd find the Wolcott Suite. Even when the wall opened and I felt the boxes, I suspected what it might be but I didn't truly believe it."

The excitement of the discovery belatedly kicking in, she laughed. And fastened the necklace around her neck. "How do I look?" Without awaiting an answer, she thrust a medium-sized box at Beks. "Here. You open this one. I bet it's the bracelet. Or maybe the hair clips." She hefted the smallest box. "I bet these are the earrings."

She'd called the bracelet correctly, and, urging the younger woman to try it on, she clipped the earrings on her own earlobes, then had Beks fasten a section of her purple-and-black hair back with the diamond hair clips.

Laughing, she grabbed her purse and pulled out her iPhone. "I have *got* to tell Jane and Poppy about this."

"I'll call Cade," Beks said, her eyes alight with excitement. "This is gonna put the documentary right over the top!"

Ava's first instinct was to protest, but she knew Beks was right. The discovery of the Wolcott Suite during the actual shooting of the documentary would add a whole new dimension to the film, not to mention hand deliver a promotional campaign better than anything even the greatest ad company in the world could invent.

She simply nodded and made her calls.

She tried Jane first, but nobody was home. She dialed Poppy next, and almost whooped when her friend answered right away. But Ava only got as far as, "You are *not*—" when her friend interrupted.

"Oh, good timing!" she said. "Jane's here. Why don't you come by, too?"

"Have her grab the other phone," she said excitedly. "Because you guys are *not* gonna believe what I found!"

The second she told them about the Wolcott diamonds they insisted on coming over. And since the Fremont neighborhood where Poppy and Jason lived was just over the hill from Queen Anne, the women burst through the sitting room door less than ten minutes later.

Poppy skidded to a halt, staring at the dazzling bling adorning both women. "Holy shitskis," she breathed. "You really did find it." She shook her head. "I mean, I know you said you did. I'm just having a hard time wrapping my mind around it."

Ava nodded in fervent agreement. "I *so* know the feeling."

"I wonder why Miss A didn't know about this compartment," Jane said. "She did the closet."

Ava just shrugged, for she didn't have the first idea.

"Would *you* suspect there'd be two of them in the same room?" Poppy said, then turned to Ava. "How did you find it?"

"By pure happenstance. I got up to dance and tripped instead."

"*You* tripped? Miss Honest-to-gawd-we're-not-being-ironic-she-really-*is*-poetry-in-motion?"

Yeah, well, for the first time in my life I didn't feel like dancing and got tripped up by this fat rug. But she couldn't say that, because her BFFs would want to know why. And she didn't want to—couldn't—talk about it. Not right now.

God. She had to figure out what to do about her and Cade. But not, thank God, at this precise moment. Because, much to her relief, Jane interrupted.

"Give me summa that!" she demanded, thrusting out a hand.

Beks started to remove the bracelet from around her wrist, but Ava wagged a staying hand. "No, keep it on—you were in on the find. Except for her wedding ring, Poppy isn't all that into jewelry, but give her the hair clips—she has to try something on and they aren't really your style anyhow.

"And, here, Janie." She unclipped the drop earrings, which were miniatures of the necklace's centerpiece. "You wear these. My lobes are too fat for clip-ons." She rubbed some relief into her ears. "I don't know how anyone can wear these things."

"You do realize," Jane said to Beks as she clipped on

the earrings, "that Av's just saving face because she's always been jealous of my skinny lobes." Hooking her shiny brown hair behind her ears, she looked around. "Where's a mirror when a girl needs one? What are we doing in the sitting room, anyhow, when all the reflective surfaces are in the bedroom?"

"Good point." Ava surged up out of the chair, stooped long enough to unplug and snatch the boom box, then headed for the other room. "Let's go. Beks, grab that bottle."

"We only have the two glasses. Want me to run downstairs for more?"

"Nah. We don't need no stinkin' glasses. We'll pass the bottle around." She gave them all a brilliant smile. "Look at us! We're decked out in famous diamonds. Only thing we need besides that is a celebratory swig or two and a dance."

CADE HAD BEEN restless before Beks called. After they hung up, he felt as if he were jumping out of his skin.

It didn't help that sometime before his assistant had called, he'd decided that maybe he hadn't handled Ava's response to his declaration of love as well as he could have.

That maybe, in fact, he'd handled it with all the suaveness of a sulky high school Romeo shot down by the recipient of his lust and affection.

Except, what he felt for Ava was a helluva lot more than a simple case of lust and so far beyond your basic vanilla affection it wasn't even funny. Having her toss his love back in his face had hurt—he wouldn't deny it. But when he'd gotten back to his condo and couldn't find a damn thing needing his immediate attention—which would have at least helped divert his single-minded focus—he had been forced to admit that if Ava lacked faith…well, he was one of the main reasons why.

And, yeah, yeah, it had been a long time ago.

That didn't negate the fact that he'd turned her into the public butt of a joke.

It was hypocritical to complain that she oughtta get the hell over it. Not when he himself had ignored his mother's pleas for forgiveness up until—what?—three years ago?

No one knew better than he how impossible it had been to live with Allan Gallari's cold perfectionism. Yet still he'd blamed his mother for the sense of worthlessness that had come from dealing with his old man. It had been tough enough when the reasons behind it were incomprehensible. But a good part of his rage had stemmed from knowing that she'd known perfectly well why his father had treated him the way he had, yet instead of telling *him* why the old man had hated his guts, she'd kept it a secret and made him work his way through it blind.

He had taken his own sweet time getting over that mad-on. So maybe he ought to man up and tell Ava he'd give her all the time she needed to get past her issues with him, as well.

Which he knew she eventually would. She interacted with him, made love with him, as if she loved him. He just had to give her a little space—and shoot for supportive instead of impatient when her insecurities hit.

That wasn't what bothered him most right now, anyway. Ever since Delco had called to say Ava had found the Wolcott diamonds, something had been niggling at the back of his brain. He paced from the condo's bed to the minuscule kitchenette to the front door, then reversed the unsatisfactorily short route. He couldn't put his finger on exactly why, but unease itched like a bad rash.

Which didn't make sense. Hell, this was *good* news. Not only was it beyond cool for Ava and her friends, it was the crowning touch for what he already felt in his gut was going to be a kick-ass documentary. And you couldn't *buy* the kind of publicity this discovery would generate. There was no downside.

He stilled midstep. Yes. There was. Ava and Beks were alone in a big old mansion with a fortune in recovered diamonds. It admittedly had low problem potential, but his gut still didn't like it.

"Shit. You're overreacting." His gut was wrong. The night guard was there; it was the man's job to see that no one got in.

On the other hand, the gods hadn't exactly been on Cade's side today. So who could swear this wouldn't be the night Tony got clubbed over the head as he made his rounds outside the house?

Extreme reach, dude.

Still. He'd learned a long time ago to listen to his gut. And his gut was screaming that Ava and Beks were alone with a night guard who maybe did, maybe didn't, know about their find. And if he didn't, how the hell was the guy supposed to take extra measures?

Coming to a decision, Cade pulled out his cell phone and dialed 411 for information.

A moment later, he placed a call.

MUSIC DRIFTED down the staircase, and it took everything Tony had not to howl his impatience as he raced up it. All that time he'd counted on having to finally discover the wall's secret was ticking away while a couple of idiot women whooped it up in the very room he needed to be in. And he couldn't even run them off— not when he'd recently learned that one half of the duo, the redhead he'd blown off as kitchen help, was not only the production company's concierge—she *owned* the goddamn mansion.

Hell, if he'd had that knowledge from the beginning, he might have forgotten the damn jewels and just romanced a smart chunk of change out of Spencer. He liked big girls, and they were usually sooo grateful for the attention. Plus, face it, conning lonely women was what he did best. It might not add up to retirement in a tropical paradise, but it probably would've gotten him eight months to a year of damn fine living.

And he really did like a woman with a rack and an ass that a man could get a solid grip on.

Well, it was too late for that, and he was bristling with irritation as he approached the sitting room doorway. That, however, was an attitude that would not do, so he breathed his exasperation away and plastered a pleasant smile on his face before poking his head into the room. Hell, charming women was his stock-in-trade. He oughtta be able to come up with a reasonable ploy to move them along. He'd take their measure and do what he always did: just open up his mind and let it connect to the right thing to say.

It was a method that worked for him nine times out of ten.

It likely would have worked now as well, except the room was empty. Brows furrowing, he hesitated for an instant before it sunk in that the music he'd heard from halfway down the stairs was coming from the bedroom. Even as he made the connection, he heard an eruption of female laughter, and, squaring his shoulders, he walked into the sitting room, casting a covetous glance at the carved wood wall as he crossed the plush rug.

He stopped dead. "No."

FucknofucknofucknofuckNO!

He executed a sharp, military-worthy left face and strode over to the wall.

He didn't, however, have to be close to see the fucking hole in it. *His* fucking hole, the one that *he* was supposed to have found!

How the hell had they? He peered inside and found it empty.

And the suave manner that had gotten him into dozens of women's bank accounts dissolved; his ability to think on the fly died a cold, bleak death. All that was left was a screaming sense of unfairness and a raging white-hot temper. Whirling on one heel, he whipped his gun from its holster as he stalked over to the inner doorway.

Where he stopped, one foot inside the bedroom. There were *four* women, not just the two he'd expected.

Four. Women.

And every last one of them had a fortune in diamonds adorning them.

His diamonds, dammit. He'd been busting his hump for those babies and damned if he planned to leave here without them. He pointed his gun at Ava, who stopped dancing, took one look at him...and screamed.

The other women looked at her, looked at him—and his gun—and screamed along with her.

Christ! The strip-the-paint-off-a-Caddie screeching was so piercing they were damn lucky he didn't start shooting up the joint. It wasn't like he'd had this damn gun long enough to get used to it himself. *"Shut up!"* he roared.

Mercifully, they did.

"Hoo!" Ava slapped a hand against her tits, which continued to shift gently even though the rest of her had stilled. The woman had some seriously fine jiggle.

He gave himself a mental head slap. *That is so not the point.*

"You scared the crap out of me," she said. But she gave him an apologetic smile. "I'm sorry. Did you think we were burglars?"

It's a good excuse—grab it and finesse the situation. Hell, maybe he could get them to give him the diamonds for safekeeping. Opening his mouth to do exactly that, he instead heard himself demand, "Hand over the necklace."

Shit! Even beyond his runaway mouth, something bothered him, tried to tell him…he didn't know what. So, he shrugged it aside and gestured impatiently with the gun.

But Ava didn't hurry to remove that gorgeous blinder of a necklace. She simply blinked big, green eyes at him. "Excuse me?"

"Take off the necklace and fork it over."

"You're *stealing* it?"

"Liberating it," he corrected. Jesus. He wasn't a common thief.

"No, Ava's right," Beks said, and he half turned to look at her. "It would be stealing. Liberating is more along the lines of Che Guevara."

"Do you think so?" a brunette on the other side of the room demanded skeptically. "I mean, Che had good intentions, but that world revolution thing was a little extreme—I'd consider him more of an insurgent. If you're talking liberators, I'd think more along the lines of Simón Bolívar and José de San Martín."

"I have to go with Janie on this," the blonde behind him said. "Of the three of us, she was by far the best student."

"Shut up!" he bellowed again. Christ. He was getting a headache. Usually, it was just this kind of shit that he liked about women—the fact that they couldn't hold a fricking thought for more than ten seconds running.

The real question was, though, why couldn't *he?* He could *always* think—his faster-than-a-speeding-bullet, think-on-his-feet mind was his number-one asset.

But from the instant he'd clapped eyes on that empty secret compartment in the other room, it seemed to have shut down on him.

"Yes, we got a little off topic," Ava agreed gently, and he turned back to look at her again. "The point is, you're supposed to be guarding the joint. Not ripping it off."

"Things change. Gimme the necklace."

"I will if you'll just put the gun down. You're making me very nervous, Tony, waving it around that way."

"That's the *point,* lady! I make you nervous, you give me what I want and I leave you to breathe another day."

"I don't think you really want to shoot us, though, do you?" the blonde asked, and he turned back once again.

"Of course I don't wanna shoot you. Doesn't mean I won't, if I have to."

But the logistics were all wrong—the damn women were spread around the entire goddamn room.

Shit. That was what had nagged at him. Even if he wanted to, he couldn't shoot them all at once. And it wasn't as if he was an ace shot even at close range.

But they didn't know that. Hell, most women knew bupkus about guns. And, banking on their ignorance, he brandished his weapon at the brunette. Thank God. The brain was back in action.

"Give me the earrings," he said to the brunette. "And you, blondie—" he turned to look at her "—I'll take those diamonds in your hair."

The pretty blonde heaved a sigh. "Oh, very well. Just…point the gun at the ceiling, okay? I don't want it accidentally going off when I'm doing my best to co-operate."

He didn't see the harm in that. "Fine." Pointing it at the ceiling, he sent her an impatient look. "Happy? Now take the damn things off."

"I am. See? They're just a little tangled."

He watched with avid eyes as she worked the gems out of her wildly curling hair and approached him cautiously. "That's far enough," he said when she was an arm's reach away.

Obediently, she stopped. "Here you go," she said softly. "As promised." She extended her hand, the diamonds in her palm glittering under the overhead light.

Mesmerized, he reached to take them.

And felt his head explode in agony.

CHAPTER TWENTY-FOUR

It's one hell of a day that goes from misery to jewels to guns to humming Disney cartoon tunes.

"OH, GOD, oh, God, did I *kill* him?" The half-full magnum Ava had used to coldcock Tony dropped from fingers gone numb. Wine slopped out of the bottle's neck in slow, sluggish glugs and soaked into the rug, but she barely noticed. When she had seen how focused the guard was on getting the hair clips from Poppy, it had seemed like a good idea to take advantage of his preoccupation. Now all she could think was, *I killed a man. Why did it seem so important that I not tell Cade I love him? I* killed *a man!*

And her breath quit penetrating deeper than the upper lobes of her lungs.

Jane rushed over, pausing only long enough to nudge the gun away from where it had fallen when Tony had collapsed, facedown, on the rug. She pushed it deeper beneath a nearby chair with the toe of her ankle boot. An instant later she was in front of Ava.

Who stared at her and wheezed, "Can't. Breathe."

"You're hyperventilating," her friend said in a voice both sympathetic and brisk. "Cup your hands over your mouth and nose and focus on your breaths." Jane rubbed gentle circles in Ava's shoulders as she spoke. "In and out, real slow. Yes, like that. I know how you feel, Av—you know I do, because I've been there. But I don't think the guard guy is dead, so just take nice, slow breaths."

"Janie's right," Poppy agreed. "Look at his back—he's breathing. You just knocked him out." Stooping, she pressed two fingers to the downed man's carotid, then looked up at Ava. "He's got a strong pulse. But we should probably tie him up before he comes to." She looked over at Beks. "Do you think you could you find something? I gotta call Jas—"

"Freeze!" a deep male voice roared, making all of them jump and Beks and Jane scream. It scared a sharp inhale out of Ava, the upside of which was that she could suddenly breathe again.

A man burst through the doorway, sweeping a gun from side to side to cover the room.

Poppy recognized him first. "Jason! Oh, God, I'm glad to see you! But, please, could you lower—" She nodded as her husband, whose gaze had taken in the unconscious, unarmed Tony, immediately holstered his gun. "Thank you," she said fervently. "I've had about all I can take of having a weapon pointed at me tonight."

"I was afraid I might find you here," Jason said, then his eyes narrowed dangerously. "He pointed a gun at you?" It only took him a second to cross over to Tony, bend down, jerk the man's hands behind his back and snap cuffs none-too-gently around his wrists. Then, rising to his feet, he hauled Poppy into his arms. "Are you okay?" he demanded, looking down at her. "And the baby?"

Watching her friend return her husband's tight hug and murmur assurances against his chest, Ava thought, *I want that.* So intent was she on the picture they made and her own intense longing, in fact, that it took her a moment to notice the man who'd entered in Jase's wake.

The man striding straight for *her*.

"Cade!" She flew to meet him, throwing herself into his arms. They wrapped around her so tightly it all but knocked the breath she had just regained back out of her.

Nothing in her life had ever felt better. Or more right.

Tucking in his chin, he looked down at her. "You all right?"

"Now that you're here, I am. I'm so sorry about last night."

"Don't worry about it." He gave her hair a rough stroke from crown to nape, then tore his gaze away to look over at his PA. "How about you, Beks?"

The younger woman nodded, her multicolored hair aquiver with the motion. "I'm okay. But I'm sure glad it's over."

"Oh, man, me, too," Ava ardently concurred and found his bluer than blue eyes locked back on hers. Her brow furrowed. "How did you manage to arrive at the same time as Jase?"

"My gut didn't like that you two were alone in this big place with a fortune in diamonds and when I debated between calling Jason or the night guy to check in on you, a burglary cop just seemed the better bet. Good thing, I'd say," he added grimly. "What happened?"

All four women burst into a cacophony of explanations until Jason said, *"Enough,"* with the cop authority he wielded so well. "Jane." He pointed a long, dark finger at the brunette. "You're usually the more concise one in the sisterhood—"

"Well, I like that!" Poppy protested, but subsided beneath the you-don't-even-want-to-mess-with-me look her husband bent on her.

He turned back to Jane. "What happened?"

She told him, concisely.

Tony started coming around, and time kicked into warp speed for Ava, whizzing by in a blur as Jason called someone in his unit to collect the erstwhile night guard. When a patrol cop showed up, he instructed her to run Phillips's prints through IAFIS.

"This might be a crime of opportunity, but let's see what turns up," he said, and as soon as the officer left, he turned to the four women to take statements.

Sometime during that, Jane called Devlin, who must have broken every speed limit between Belltown and the mansion to get there as quickly as he did.

"You can't sell this fucking place fast enough to suit me," he growled as he stalked into the room, dark red hair gleaming under the overheads, black brows gathered over the thrust of his nose. "Since Miss Agnes died, it's been nothing but dangerous for you three."

That wasn't a hundred percent true, but it had been for Jane last year and had sure as hell been tonight. So Ava had no desire to argue and noticed that neither Poppy nor Jane refuted him either.

At one point the women recalled they were still wearing the Wolcott jewelry, removed it and restored the pieces to their boxes. Jane locked them in the secret closet in Miss Agnes's bedroom. Then she and Dev took off.

Jase gathered up Poppy soon after and told Beks he'd give her a ride.

And suddenly just Ava and Cade were left.

CADE TOOK Ava's hand and led her over to Miss A's bed. Sitting on its side, he tugged her onto his lap. "I love you," he said, looking at her flushed cheeks, bright mussed hair and gorgeous eyes. "I'm not trying to pressure you into saying it back, but after a day like this, I just need to put it out there—"

She clapped a hand over his mouth, cutting him off, and he damn near howled. He wished he could force her to love him back, but he'd promised himself he'd give her the time and space to make her own decisions—and he had to stick to that. So he met her gaze and held his peace.

"When you broke my heart in high school I vowed hell would freeze over before I forgave you," she said, smooth palm still pressed to his lips. Then her lips crooked in a one-sided smile. "But that was a long time ago, Cade, and you've not only explained your reasons but have proven over and over that you've grown worlds beyond an ancient, much-regretted bet."

Removing her hand from his mouth, she swiveled in his lap, hiked her skirt up to the danger zone to straddle his thighs and leaned in to give him a soft-lipped kiss.

When she lifted her mouth from his, he looked up into lambent eyes, and his heartbeat sped up at what he saw shining in their green depths.

"When Tony was waving that gun around," she said softly, "all I could think was, 'I want Cade. Where is Cade?' I needed you."

"You did?" Jesus. Three simple words, and his heart was a fucking kettledrum.

"I needed you desperately. When I hit him with the champagne bottle, I really thought for a minute I'd killed him." Staring into his eyes, she drew in an unsteady breath. Softly exhaled it. "Believing you've done something like that, something with consequences you can't reverse no matter how much you may wish to—well, it puts things in perspective in a red-hot hurry.

"So, you are *not* pressuring me to say it back when you tell me you love me. And you're dead right that after a day like today we have to say what's in our hearts. What is in mine is the same thing in yours. I love you, Cade. I was afraid to admit it, even to myself, but I understand now that that's just dumb. We've been striking sparks off each other for what feels like forever—and that can be exciting. But so many times they were for the wrong reasons and I want more than that."

"I do, too," he agreed. "Don't get me wrong, I don't plan on giving up the sparks we generate. But you have a joy that knocks me on my butt—and I just want to roll in it, to wrap it around me like a blanket. I want the kindness that made you go get Stan Tarrof and bring him back to the mansion so he wouldn't be alone. And I want the quiet times, the day-to-day stuff that makes up a relationship. Or what I imagine makes one up, anyhow. I can't say that I've had anything close to what I envision having with you."

"Me, either. I've spent way too much time protecting my heart and damn little opening it up to anyone but my closest friends."

He grinned at her. "And may I say that I sorta dig that?"

"Oh." She gave him a look of mock outrage. "You selfish bastard. You're happy I was *alone?*" She slapped a hand to the swell of one gorgeous breast. Gave him a pathetic look. "Alone and *lonely?*"

He raised an eyebrow. "You might wanna work on those acting skills—that was a little overwrought. And, no—I'll never be happy at the idea of you unhappy for any reason. But I am pleased that you saved the real deal for me. I sure as hell saved mine for you."

"Yet I would have been much more magnanimous about it if you hadn't."

He laughed in her face. "Bullshit."

"Maybe." She grinned back at him. "I'm so happy, Cade. I can't imagine being able to sustain a feeling this great. I hope we don't screw it up."

"We won't."

"You know we're gonna fight sometimes."

"Yeah, hard not to when a reasonable guy is faced with a bullheaded, emotional woman."

"I like *that!*" she said indignantly, but her lips quirked up at the pleased-with-himself smile he couldn't contain.

He wrapped his hands around her hips. "Okay, we're both a little too bullheaded for our own good at times. But, baby, we've got a whole shipload of love and *respect* for each other. And neither of us is afraid of hard work."

She lit up. "We aren't, are we? So we just have to put the same work into us that we do into our careers. And to that end—" She drew in an audible breath. "I'll move to California with you. It might take me a while to build up a list of contacts, but give me time and I can do it."

It was as if someone had reached inside his chest, wrapped a fist around his heart and squeezed. He knew how much she loved it here, how close she was to her friends, how fierce was her pride in the career she had built with her own two hands. But she was willing to sacrifice it all…for him.

"Jesus," he breathed. "You are everything I ever wanted, even if I was too damn dumb to realize it for a while. You're sweet and special and you just rock my world." He kissed her, hot and deep.

Raising his head, he gripped hers between his hands and stared down at her. "But I can't let you move to L.A."

"Yes, you can. I want to."

"No, you don't. But it just humbles the shit out of me that you offered anyway. You've got everything we both need right here—family, friends who are even more of a family and a real home, not just a place to hang your hat like my condo. Travel is pretty much the nature of my work anyhow, so my base isn't that important. I'd love it if you'd accompany me to the occasional events I attend in Hollywood, but I'm not letting you uproot your entire life for me." He looked at her, all flushed and tousled on his lap. "Besides, look at you. Move you to Hollywood and you'd have men trailing after you with their damn tongues hanging out, every time you stepped outside the door. I'm definitely keeping you outta Tinsel Town as much as possible."

A huge smile lit up her face. "I don't think any man looks at me the way you do. And I *know* no one else makes me feel the way you do." Eyes alight, fingers splayed over her chest, she looked down at him. "I'm not sure my heart's big enough to contain everything I feel."

He kissed her again, then lifted her off his lap and onto her feet. Gave that sweet ass a light slap. "Whataya say we get out of here? Let's go to your place and get naked in front of the fireplace."

"Sounds good to me. Oh! Has it sunk in yet what the discovery of the Wolcott Suite will mean to your documentary?"

"Isn't that *sweet?*" He laughed. "It's like hitting the

daily double. Not only are we going to live the hottest love story since…I can't think who, since all the famous lovers seem to wind up either dead or alone…but I think Miss A's story has a real shot at going big."

Looping her arms around his neck, she gave him a quick smooch. "Doesn't get much better than that."

EPILOGUE

I'm an auntie!!!

October 9th

AVA'S PHONE rang as she and Cade inched forward in the switchback lanes of the security check at Sea-Tac airport. "It's Janie," she said and shot him an apologetic look. "I'll make it brief."

He felt the corner of his mouth tic up as he took her boarding pass and ID and gestured for her to answer it. He knew better than to get between his woman and her posse.

Sticking a finger in her free ear to block out the ubiquitous loud speaker announcements, she said, "Hey."

It had been an excellent several months. He'd moved into Ava's place much more seamlessly than he'd imagined, blending the few things from his own that mattered to him and giving the rest to Beks, who had accepted his offer of a permanent position and followed him to Seattle. Now—

At his side Ava stilled. "*What?* Oh, God. When?"

"What is it?" he demanded.

"Hold on," she said into the phone and lowered it. "Poppy went into labor."

"I thought she wasn't due for another three weeks."

"Baby decided it wanted to come now, apparently. Jase has taken her to Swedish."

"Tell Jane we'll be there." He reached for his own phone.

"But, your meeting—"

"Can wait. I'll— Yeah, hi, this is Cade Gallari," he said when a woman identifying herself as Sondra answered the number he'd called. "Put me through to Burt, will you?"

"I'm sorry, Mr. Gallari, but he's in a meeting and can't be disturbed. Is there anything I can help you with?"

"Yeah, when he gets out tell him I've got a family emergency and I'm sorry but I'll have to reschedule."

"Certainly. How does next Thursday at four-fifteen sound?"

"I'll have my assistant give you a call."

He hung up a moment later and found himself with an armful of warm, grateful woman.

"God, Cade, *thank* you! You are so the best man in the world. I know this meeting is important. Investors like Mr. Forde don't exactly grow on trees."

He shrugged it off. "Poppy and Jane have become important to me, too." It was truer than his casual tone suggested. In all the ways that mattered they were Ava's family and—once they accepted that he loved their "sister" like crazy and would cut off his own arm before he hurt her—they'd become his, as well.

"Good thing we just had carry-on this trip," he said. "Maybe on the way to Swedish you can check your schedule for next week and if it's clear, we'll call Beks and have her check mine and call Sondra."

"You got it. She'd probably like to know about Poppy,

anyhow. Omigawd." She turned a huge smile on him. "Do you believe this? Poppy's having a baby!"

Between Ava and Beks, they had everything rescheduled before he and Ava hit I-5. Shortly after that, they were heading up the elevator to the Swedish childbirth center.

"We're going *in* there?" Cade demanded in horror when Ava headed directly for a room. "Whatever happened to the days when people waited in a fricking waiting room?"

"Oh, honey, that is so last millennium," Jane said from inside the room as Ava opened the door.

"C'mon in, dude," Dev said. "There's a privacy screen between us and Poppy's naked bits."

"Jesus. Thank God for small favors."

"I happen to like her naked bits," Jason said from the other side of the curtain. "Breathe, baby."

The latter instruction drew attention to the sudden cessation in the rhythmic, pneumatic, "Hee! Hee! Hee! Hee!" coming from the other side.

"*You* breathe!" Poppy snarled. "But don't hold your breath about ever seeing my 'naked bits' again, because the next time you poke that big thing in my direction, I'll cut it off!"

"Ouch," Dev murmured.

"I want my girls!"

Jason came around the curtain a second later, and his swarthy skin had a definite green tinge. Jane rubbed one wide shoulder as they passed, and Ava gave it a pat and stopped a second to murmur low in his ear.

He crossed over to a rocking chair next to the window seat cushions where Dev and Cade lounged, dropped down in it and rubbed long hands over his face. "God," he muttered. "She's in such fucking pain. They call it back labor, whatever the hell that is."

It went on for another five and a half hours, with Poppy hopscotching between wanting Jason with her or Ava and Jane or her mother, who had rushed in with her father shortly after Cade and Ava's arrival. Nurses came and went, and the doctor stopped by during the early part of Cade's time there.

Then, from behind the screen, Jase suddenly exclaimed, "Holy shit!"

The nurse with him said calmly, "The head's crowning."

The doctor strode through the family part of the suite less than a minute later, and after that it was a confusion of instructions, grunts and long, heartfelt groans. Then…silence.

Broken by the wail of a baby.

"Yes!" Cade pumped his arm as everyone waiting cheered.

"What is it?" Poppy's mom demanded. "Is my grandchild a boy or a girl? Only you two, in this day and age, would decide you didn't want to know the sex."

"It's a girl," Poppy called.

"That's what we need," Dev joked. "Like we aren't already awash in estrogen around here."

Mrs. C swatted the back of Dev's head at the same time she said, "Bella Luca de Sanges" in a dreamy voice.

Jane smacked his leg.

"Shut up, Kavanagh," Jase instructed from behind the screen. "My daughter is beautiful."

Cade turned to Ava. "This is what I want," he said.

"What?" She laughed. "A baby?"

"Everything. You. Marriage. Kids."

Her laughter stilled as she looked into his eyes. "Even after this? I thought for sure it would send you running for the nearest exit."

"Hell, no, are you kidding me? This was *great*. I'd love to see my kid born. Except I'd wanna document it." He gave her a level look. "You have to promise to let me film our kids' births."

She shook her head. "Only you, Gallari. Only you could listen to all this and be inspired to propose. That is…that *is* what you're doing, right?"

"Damn straight. Contingent on the aforementioned filming—that's a deal-breaker, Spencer."

She laughed. "It must be the artist in you."

"So, will you? Marry me?" You could've heard a pin drop—even the baby had quit crying—and he looked up to see he had the attention of everyone in the room.

And behind the screen as well, it seemed. "Say yes, Ava," Poppy called from behind the wall. "And filming's actually not a bad idea. I wish I'd thought of it for Bella."

"Seriously?" Ava demanded. "According to you, Jase is never getting that 'big thing' near you again."

Her friend laughed. "Birthing talk," she said dismissively. "I guess it's true what they say—you really do forget the pain of childbirth once you clap eyes on your baby."

"So whataya say?" Cade demanded. "You want Jane's approval, too, or are you going to marry me?"

"Because you've got it if you need it," Jane said, and Mrs. C added, "Mine, too."

But Ava didn't appear to be paying attention. Her eyes were locked on his, and when she smiled at him, her entire face glowed.

Just like his heart, his soul, did when she said firmly, "Yes. Yes, you crazy man. I will definitely marry you."

"That's my *girl!*" he said with so much enthusiasm everyone laughed. But resting his forehead against Ava's, he said just for her, "Thank you, baby. You've just made me the happiest man alive—and I'm going to spend the rest of my days doing the same for you."

"Making me a happy man?"

His lips crooked up. "No, smart-ass. Making you the happiest woman."

"Well, all right." She grinned at him. "Sounds like an excellent plan to me."

* * * * *

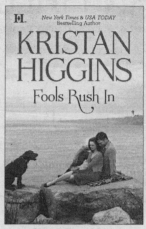

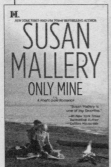
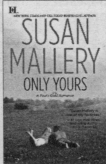
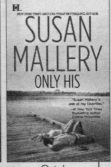

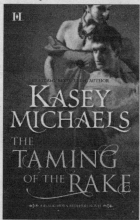

REQUEST YOUR
FREE BOOKS!

2 FREE NOVELS
FROM THE ROMANCE COLLECTION
PLUS 2 FREE GIFTS!

YES! Please send me 2 FREE novels from the Romance Collection and my 2 FREE gifts (gifts are worth about $10). After receiving them, if I don't wish to receive any more books, I can return the shipping statement marked "cancel." If I don't cancel, I will receive 4 brand-new novels every month and be billed just $5.99 per book in the U.S. or $6.49 per book in Canada. That's a saving of at least 25% off the cover price. It's quite a bargain! Shipping and handling is just 50¢ per book in the U.S. and 75¢ per book in Canada.* I understand that accepting the 2 free books and gifts places me under no obligation to buy anything. I can always return a shipment and cancel at any time. Even if I never buy another book, the two free books and gifts are mine to keep forever.

194/394 MDN FELQ

Name	(PLEASE PRINT)	
Address		Apt. #
City	State/Prov.	Zip/Postal Code

Signature (if under 18, a parent or guardian must sign)

Mail to the **Reader Service**:
IN U.S.A.: P.O. Box 1867, Buffalo, NY 14240-1867
IN CANADA: P.O. Box 609, Fort Erie, Ontario L2A 5X3

Not valid for current subscribers to the Romance Collection
or the Romance/Suspense Collection.

Want to try two free books from another line?
Call 1-800-873-8635 or visit www.ReaderService.com.

* Terms and prices subject to change without notice. Prices do not include applicable taxes. Sales tax applicable in N.Y. Canadian residents will be charged applicable taxes. Offer not valid in Quebec. This offer is limited to one order per household. All orders subject to credit approval. Credit or debit balances in a customer's account(s) may be offset by any other outstanding balance owed by or to the customer. Please allow 4 to 6 weeks for delivery. Offer available while quantities last.

Your Privacy—The Reader Service is committed to protecting your privacy. Our Privacy Policy is available online at www.ReaderService.com or upon request from the Reader Service.

We make a portion of our mailing list available to reputable third parties that offer products we believe may interest you. If you prefer that we not exchange your name with third parties, or if you wish to clarify or modify your communication preferences, please visit us at www.ReaderService.com/consumerchoice or write to us at Reader Service Preference Service, P.O. Box 9062, Buffalo, NY 14269. Include your complete name and address.